British Mystery Multipack Volume 9: The Max Carrados Mysteries

British Mystery Multipack Volume 9: The Max Carrados Mysteries

By

Ernest Bramah

Enhanced Media
2015

British Mystery Multipack Volume 9 – The Max Carrados Mysteries by Ernest Bramah.

First published as *Max Carrados* by Ernest Bramah in 1914.

First Printing: 2015

ISBN-13: 978-1519127402

ISBN-10: 1519127405

Contents

The Coin of Dionysius

It was eight o'clock at night and raining, scarcely a time when a business so limited in its clientele as that of a coin dealer could hope to attract any customer, but a light was still showing in the small shop that bore over its window the name of Baxter, and in the even smaller office at the back the proprietor himself sat reading the latest Pall Mall. His enterprise seemed to be justified, for presently the doorbell gave its announcement, and throwing down his paper Mr Baxter went forward.

As a matter of fact the dealer had been expecting someone and his manner as he passed into the shop was unmistakably suggestive of a caller of importance. But at the first glance towards his visitor the excess of deference melted out of his bearing, leaving the urbane, self-possessed shopman in the presence of the casual customer.

"Mr Baxter, I think?" said the latter. He had laid aside his dripping umbrella and was unbuttoning overcoat and coat to reach an inner pocket. "You hardly remember me, I suppose? Mr Carlyle—two years ago I took up a case for you——"

"To be sure. Mr Carlyle, the private detective——"

"Inquiry agent," corrected Mr Carlyle precisely.

"Well," smiled Mr Baxter, "for that matter I am a coin dealer and not an antiquarian or a numismatist. Is there anything in that way that I can do for you?"

"Yes," replied his visitor; "it is my turn to consult you." He had taken a small wash-leather bag from the inner pocket and now turned something carefully out upon the counter. "What can you tell me about that?"

The dealer gave the coin a moment's scrutiny.

"There is no question about this," he replied. "It is a Sicilian tetradrachm of Dionysius."

"Yes, I know that—I have it on the label out of the cabinet. I can tell you further that it's supposed to be one that Lord Seastoke gave two hundred and fifty pounds for at the Brice sale in '94."

"It seems to me that you can tell me more about it than I can tell you," remarked Mr Baxter. "What is it that you really want to know?"

"I want to know," replied Mr Carlyle, "whether it is genuine or not."

"Has any doubt been cast upon it?"

"Certain circumstances raised a suspicion—that is all."

The dealer took another look at the tetradrachm through his magnifying glass, holding it by the edge with the careful touch of an expert. Then he shook his head slowly in a confession of ignorance.

"Of course I could make a guess——"

"No, don't," interrupted Mr Carlyle hastily. "An arrest hangs on it and nothing short of certainty is any good to me."

"Is that so, Mr Carlyle?" said Mr Baxter, with increased interest. "Well, to be quite candid, the thing is out of my line. Now if it was a rare Saxon penny or a doubtful noble I'd stake my reputation on my opinion, but I do very little in the classical series."

Mr Carlyle did not attempt to conceal his disappointment as he returned the coin to the bag and replaced the bag in the inner pocket.

"I had been relying on you," he grumbled reproachfully. "Where on earth am I to go now?"

"There is always the British Museum."

"Ah, to be sure, thanks. But will anyone who can tell me be there now?"

"Now? No fear!" replied Mr Baxter. "Go round in the morning——"

"But I must know to-night," explained the visitor, reduced to despair again. "To-morrow will be too late for the purpose."

Mr Baxter did not hold out much encouragement in the circumstances.

"You can scarcely expect to find anyone at business now," he remarked. "I should have been gone these two hours myself only I happened to have an appointment with an American millionaire who fixed his own time." Something indistinguishable from a wink slid off Mr Baxter's right eye. "Offmunson he's called, and a bright young pedigree-hunter has traced his descent from Offa, King of Mercia. So he—quite naturally—wants a set of Offas as a sort of collateral proof."

"Very interesting," murmured Mr Carlyle, fidgeting with his watch. "I should love an hour's chat with you about your millionaire customers—some other time. Just now—look here, Baxter, can't you give me a line of introduction to some dealer in this sort of thing who happens to live in town? You must know dozens of experts."

"Why, bless my soul, Mr Carlyle, I don't know a man of them away from his business," said Mr Baxter, staring. "They may live in Park Lane or they may live in Petticoat Lane for all I know. Besides, there aren't so many experts as you seem to imagine. And the two best will very likely quarrel over it. You've had to do with 'expert witnesses,' I suppose?"

"I don't want a witness; there will be no need to give evidence. All I want is an absolutely authoritative pronouncement that I can act on. Is there no one who can really say whether the thing is genuine or not?"

Mr Baxter's meaning silence became cynical in its implication as he continued to look at his visitor across the counter. Then he relaxed.

"Stay a bit; there is a man—an amateur—I remember hearing wonderful things about some time ago. They say he really does know."

"There you are," exclaimed Mr Carlyle, much relieved. "There always is someone. Who is he?"

"Funny name," replied Baxter. "Something Wynn or Wynn something." He craned his neck to catch sight of an important motor car that was drawing to the kerb before his window. "Wynn Carrados! You'll excuse me now, Mr Carlyle, won't you? This looks like Mr Offmunson."

Mr Carlyle hastily scribbled the name down on his cuff.

"Wynn Carrados, right. Where does he live?"

"Haven't the remotest idea," replied Baxter, referring the arrangement of his tie to the judgment of the wall mirror. "I have never seen the man myself. Now, Mr Carlyle, I'm sorry I can't do any more for you. You won't mind, will you?"

Mr Carlyle could not pretend to misunderstand. He enjoyed the distinction of holding open the door for the transatlantic representative of the line of Offa as he went out, and then made his way through the muddy streets back to his office. There was only one way of tracing a private individual at such short notice—through the pages of the directories, and the gentleman did not flatter himself by a very high estimate of his chances.

Fortune favoured him, however. He very soon discovered a Wynn Carrados living at Richmond, and, better still, further search failed to unearth another. There was, apparently, only one householder at all events of that name in the neighbourhood of London. He jotted down the address and set out for Richmond.

The house was some distance from the station, Mr Carlyle learned. He took a taxicab and drove, dismissing the vehicle at the gate. He prided himself on his power of observation and the accuracy of the deductions which resulted from it—a detail of his business. "It's nothing more than using one's eyes and putting two and two together," he would modestly declare, when he wished to be deprecatory rather than impressive, and by the time he had reached the front door of "The Turrets" he had formed some opinion of the position and tastes of the man who lived there.

A man-servant admitted Mr Carlyle and took in his card—his private card with the bare request for an interview that would not detain Mr Carrados for ten minutes. Luck still favoured him; Mr Carrados was at home and would see him at once. The servant, the hall through which they passed, and the room into which he was shown, all contributed something to the deductions which the quietly observant gentleman was half unconsciously recording.

"Mr Carlyle," announced the servant.

The room was a library or study. The only occupant, a man of about Carlyle's own age, had been using a typewriter up to the moment of his visitor's entrance. He now turned and stood up with an expression of formal courtesy.

"It's very good of you to see me at this hour," apologized the caller.

The conventional expression of Mr Carrados's face changed a little.

"Surely my man has got your name wrong?" he exclaimed. "Isn't it Louis Calling?"

The visitor stopped short and his agreeable smile gave place to a sudden flash of anger or annoyance.

"No, sir," he replied stiffly. "My name is on the card which you have before you."

"I beg your pardon," said Mr Carrados, with perfect good-humour. "I hadn't seen it. But I used to know a Calling some years ago—at St Michael's."

"St Michael's!" Mr Carlyle's features underwent another change, no less instant and sweeping than before. "St Michael's! Wynn Carrados? Good heavens! it isn't Max Wynn—old 'Winning' Wynn?"

"A little older and a little fatter—yes," replied Carrados. "I have changed my name, you see."

"Extraordinary thing meeting like this," said his visitor, dropping into a chair and staring hard at Mr Carrados. "I have changed more than my name. How did you recognize me?"

"The voice," replied Carrados. "It took me back to that little smoke-dried attic den of yours where we——"

"My God!" exclaimed Carlyle bitterly, "don't remind me of what we were going to do in those days." He looked round the well-furnished, handsome room and recalled the other signs of wealth that he had noticed. "At all events, you seem fairly comfortable, Wynn."

"I am alternately envied and pitied," replied Carrados, with a placid tolerance of circumstance that seemed characteristic of him. "Still, as you say, I am fairly comfortable."

"Envied, I can understand. But why are you pitied?"

"Because I am blind," was the tranquil reply.

"Blind!" exclaimed Mr Carlyle, using his own eyes superlatively. "Do you mean—literally blind?"

"Literally.... I was riding along a bridle-path through a wood about a dozen years ago with a friend. He was in front. At one point a twig sprang back—you know how easily a thing like that happens. It just flicked my eye—nothing to think twice about."

"And that blinded you?"

"Yes, ultimately. It's called *amaurosis*."

"I can scarcely believe it. You seem so sure and self-reliant. Your eyes are full of expression—only a little quieter than they used to be. I believe you were typing when I came.... Aren't you having me?"

"You miss the dog and the stick?" smiled Carrados. "No; it's a fact."

"What an awful infliction for you, Max. You were always such an impulsive, reckless sort of fellow—never quiet. You must miss such a fearful lot."

"Has anyone else recognized you?" asked Carrados quietly.

"Ah, that was the voice, you said," replied Carlyle.

"Yes; but other people heard the voice as well. Only I had no blundering, self-confident eyes to be hoodwinked."

"That's a rum way of putting it," said Carlyle. "Are your ears never hoodwinked, may I ask?"

"Not now. Nor my fingers. Nor any of my other senses that have to look out for themselves."

"Well, well," murmured Mr Carlyle, cut short in his sympathetic emotions. "I'm glad you take it so well. Of course, if you find it an advantage to be blind, old man——" He stopped and reddened. "I beg your pardon," he concluded stiffly.

"Not an advantage perhaps," replied the other thoughtfully. "Still it has compensations that one might not think of. A new world to explore, new experiences, new powers awakening; strange new perceptions; life in the fourth dimension. But why do you beg my pardon, Louis?"

"I am an ex-solicitor, struck off in connexion with the falsifying of a trust account, Mr Carrados," replied Carlyle, rising.

"Sit down, Louis," said Carrados suavely. His face, even his incredibly living eyes, beamed placid good-nature. "The chair on which you will sit, the roof above you, all the comfortable surroundings to which you have so amiably alluded, are the direct result of falsifying a trust account. But do I call you 'Mr Carlyle' in consequence? Certainly not, Louis."

"I did not falsify the account," cried Carlyle hotly. He sat down, however, and added more quietly: "But why do I tell you all this? I have never spoken of it before."

"Blindness invites confidence," replied Carrados. "We are out of the running—human rivalry ceases to exist. Besides, why shouldn't you? In my case the account was falsified."

"Of course that's all bunkum, Max," commented Carlyle. "Still, I appreciate your motive."

"Practically everything I possess was left to me by an American cousin, on the condition that I took the name of Carrados. He made his fortune by an ingenious conspiracy of doctoring the crop reports and unloading favourably in consequence. And I need hardly remind you that the receiver is equally guilty with the thief."

"But twice as safe. I know something of that, Max.... Have you any idea what my business is?"

"You shall tell me," replied Carrados.

"I run a private inquiry agency. When I lost my profession I had to do something for a living. This occurred. I dropped my name, changed my appearance and opened an office. I knew the legal side down to the ground and I got a retired Scotland Yard man to organize the outside work."

"Excellent!" cried Carrados. "Do you unearth many murders?"

"No," admitted Mr Carlyle; "our business lies mostly on the conventional lines among divorce and defalcation."

"That's a pity," remarked Carrados. "Do you know, Louis, I always had a secret ambition to be a detective myself. I have even thought lately that I might still be able to do something at it if the chance came my way. That makes you smile?"

"Well, certainly, the idea——"

"Yes, the idea of a blind detective—the blind tracking the alert——"

"Of course, as you say, certain faculties are no doubt quickened," Mr Carlyle hastened to add considerately, "but, seriously, with the exception of an artist, I don't suppose there is any man who is more utterly dependent on his eyes."

Whatever opinion Carrados might have held privately, his genial exterior did not betray a shadow of dissent. For a full minute he continued to smoke as though he derived an actual visual enjoyment from the blue sprays that travelled and dispersed across the room. He had already placed before his visitor a box containing cigars of a brand which that gentleman keenly appreciated but generally regarded as unattainable, and the matter-of-fact ease and certainty with which the blind man had brought the box and put it before him had sent a questioning flicker through Carlyle's mind.

"You used to be rather fond of art yourself, Louis," he remarked presently. "Give me your opinion of my latest purchase—the bronze lion on the cabinet there." Then, as Carlyle's gaze went about the room, he added quickly: "No, not that cabinet—the one on your left."

Carlyle shot a sharp glance at his host as he got up, but Carrados's expression was merely benignly complacent. Then he strolled across to the figure.

"Very nice," he admitted. "Late Flemish, isn't it?"

"No. It is a copy of Vidal's 'Roaring lion.'"

"Vidal?"

"A French artist." The voice became indescribably flat. "He, also, had the misfortune to be blind, by the way."

"You old humbug, Max!" shrieked Carlyle, "you've been thinking that out for the last five minutes." Then the unfortunate man bit his lip and turned his back towards his host.

"Do you remember how we used to pile it up on that obtuse ass Sanders and then roast him?" asked Carrados, ignoring the half-smothered exclamation with which the other man had recalled himself.

"Yes," replied Carlyle quietly. "This is very good," he continued, addressing himself to the bronze again. "How ever did he do it?"

"With his hands."

"Naturally. But, I mean, how did he study his model?"

"Also with his hands. He called it 'seeing near.'"

"Even with a lion—handled it?"

"In such cases he required the services of a keeper, who brought the animal to bay while Vidal exercised his own particular gifts.... You don't feel inclined to put me on the track of a mystery, Louis?"

Unable to regard this request as anything but one of old Max's unquenchable pleasantries, Mr Carlyle was on the point of making a suitable reply when a sudden thought caused him to smile knowingly. Up to that point he had, indeed, completely forgotten the object of his visit. Now that he remembered the doubtful Dionysius and Mr Baxter's recommendation he immediately assumed that some mistake had been made. Either Max was not the Wynn Carrados he had been seeking or else the dealer had been misinformed; for although his host was wonderfully expert in the face of his misfortune, it was inconceivable that he could decide the genuineness of a coin without seeing it. The opportunity seemed a good one of getting even with Carrados by taking him at his word.

"Yes," he accordingly replied, with crisp deliberation, as he recrossed the room; "yes, I will, Max. Here is the clue to what seems to be a rather remarkable fraud." He put the tetradrachm into his host's hand. "What do you make of it?"

For a few seconds Carrados handled the piece with the delicate manipulation of his finger-tips while Carlyle looked on with a self-appreciative grin. Then with equal gravity the blind man weighed the coin in the balance of his hand. Finally he touched it with his tongue.

"Well?" demanded the other.

"Of course I have not much to go on, and if I was more fully in your confidence I might come to another conclusion——"

"Yes, yes," interposed Carlyle, with amused encouragement.

"Then I should advise you to arrest the parlourmaid, Nina Brun, communicate with the police authorities of Padua for particulars of the career of Helene Brunesi, and suggest to Lord Seastoke that he should return to London to see what further depredations have been made in his cabinet."

Mr Carlyle's groping hand sought and found a chair, on to which he dropped blankly. His eyes were unable to detach themselves for a single moment from the very ordinary spectacle of Mr Carrados's mildly benevolent face, while the sterilized ghost of his now forgotten amusement still lingered about his features.

"Good heavens!" he managed to articulate, "how do you know?"

"Isn't that what you wanted of me?" asked Carrados suavely.

"Don't humbug, Max," said Carlyle severely. "This is no joke." An undefined mistrust of his own powers suddenly possessed him in the presence of this mystery. "How do you come to know of Nina Brun and Lord Seastoke?"

"You are a detective, Louis," replied Carrados. "How does one know these things? By using one's eyes and putting two and two together."

Carlyle groaned and flung out an arm petulantly.

"Is it all bunkum, Max? Do you really see all the time—though that doesn't go very far towards explaining it."

"Like Vidal, I see very well—at close quarters," replied Carrados, lightly running a forefinger along the inscription on the tetradrachm. "For longer range I keep another pair of eyes. Would you like to test them?"

Mr Carlyle's assent was not very gracious; it was, in fact, faintly sulky. He was suffering the annoyance of feeling distinctly unimpressive in his own department; but he was also curious.

"The bell is just behind you, if you don't mind," said his host. "Parkinson will appear. You might take note of him while he is in."

The man who had admitted Mr Carlyle proved to be Parkinson.

"This gentleman is Mr Carlyle, Parkinson," explained Carrados the moment the man entered. "You will remember him for the future?"

Parkinson's apologetic eye swept the visitor from head to foot, but so lightly and swiftly that it conveyed to that gentleman the comparison of being very deftly dusted.

"I will endeavour to do so, sir," replied Parkinson; turning again to his master.

"I shall be at home to Mr Carlyle whenever he calls. That is all."

"Very well, sir."

"Now, Louis," remarked Mr Carrados briskly, when the door had closed again, "you have had a good opportunity of studying Parkinson. What is he like?"

"In what way?"

"I mean as a matter of description. I am a blind man—I haven't seen my servant for twelve years—what idea can you give me of him? I asked you to notice."

"I know you did, but your Parkinson is the sort of man who has very little about him to describe. He is the embodiment of the ordinary. His height is about average——"

"Five feet nine," murmured Carrados. "Slightly above the mean."

"Scarcely noticeably so. Clean-shaven. Medium brown hair. No particularly marked features. Dark eyes. Good teeth."

"False," interposed Carrados. "The teeth—not the statement."

"Possibly," admitted Mr Carlyle. "I am not a dental expert and I had no opportunity of examining Mr Parkinson's mouth in detail. But what is the drift of all this?"

"His clothes?"

"Oh, just the ordinary evening dress of a valet. There is not much room for variety in that."

"You noticed, in fact, nothing special by which Parkinson could be identified?"

"Well, he wore an unusually broad gold ring on the little finger of the left hand."

"But that is removable. And yet Parkinson has an ineradicable mole—a small one, I admit—on his chin. And you a human sleuth-hound. Oh, Louis!"

"At all events," retorted Carlyle, writhing a little under this good-humoured satire, although it was easy enough to see in it Carrados's affectionate intention—"at all events, I dare say I can give as good a description of Parkinson as he can give of me."

"That is what we are going to test. Ring the bell again."

"Seriously?"

"Quite. I am trying my eyes against yours. If I can't give you fifty out of a hundred I'll renounce my private detectorial ambition for ever."

"It isn't quite the same," objected Carlyle, but he rang the bell.

"Come in and close the door, Parkinson," said Carrados when the man appeared. "Don't look at Mr Carlyle again—in fact, you had better stand with your back towards him, he won't mind. Now describe to me his appearance as you observed it."

Parkinson tendered his respectful apologies to Mr Carlyle for the liberty he was compelled to take, by the deferential quality of his voice.

"Mr Carlyle, sir, wears patent leather boots of about size seven and very little used. There are five buttons, but on the left boot one button—the third up—is missing, leaving loose threads and not the more usual metal fastener. Mr Carlyle's trousers, sir, are of a dark material, a dark grey line of about a quarter of an inch width on a darker ground. The bottoms are turned permanently up and are, just now, a little muddy, if I may say so."

"Very muddy," interposed Mr Carlyle generously. "It is a wet night, Parkinson."

"Yes, sir; very unpleasant weather. If you will allow me, sir, I will brush you in the hall. The mud is dry now, I notice. Then, sir," continued Parkinson, reverting to the business in hand, "there are dark green cashmere hose. A curb-pattern key-chain passes into the left-hand trouser pocket."

From the visitor's nether garments the photographic-eyed Parkinson proceeded to higher ground, and with increasing wonder Mr Carlyle listened to the faithful catalogue of his possessions. His fetter-and-link albert of gold and platinum was minutely described. His spotted blue ascot, with its gentlemanly pearl scarfpin, was set forth, and the fact that the buttonhole in the left lapel of his morning coat showed signs of use was duly noted. What Parkinson saw he recorded but he made no deductions. A handkerchief carried in the cuff of the right sleeve was simply that to him and not an indication that Mr Carlyle was, indeed, left-handed.

But a more delicate part of Parkinson's undertaking remained. He approached it with a double cough.

"As regards Mr Carlyle's personal appearance; sir——"

"No, enough!" cried the gentleman concerned hastily. "I am more than satisfied. You are a keen observer, Parkinson."

"I have trained myself to suit my master's requirements, sir," replied the man. He looked towards Mr Carrados, received a nod and withdrew.

Mr Carlyle was the first to speak.

"That man of yours would be worth five pounds a week to me, Max," he remarked thoughtfully. "But, of course——"

"I don't think that he would take it," replied Carrados, in a voice of equally detached speculation. "He suits me very well. But you have the chance of using his services—indirectly."

"You still mean that—seriously?"

"I notice in you a chronic disinclination to take me seriously, Louis. It is really—to an Englishman—almost painful. Is there something inherently comic about me or the atmosphere of The Turrets?"

"No, my friend," replied Mr Carlyle, "but there is something essentially prosperous. That is what points to the improbable. Now what is it?"

"It might be merely a whim, but it is more than that," replied Carrados. "It is, well, partly vanity, partly ennui, partly"—certainly there was something more nearly tragic in his voice than comic now—"partly hope."

Mr Carlyle was too tactful to pursue the subject.

"Those are three tolerable motives," he acquiesced. "I'll do anything you want, Max, on one condition."

"Agreed. And it is?"

"That you tell me how you knew so much of this affair." He tapped the silver coin which lay on the table near them. "I am not easily flabbergasted," he added.

"You won't believe that there is nothing to explain—that it was purely second-sight?"

"No," replied Carlyle tersely; "I won't."

"You are quite right. And yet the thing is very simple."

"They always are—when you know," soliloquized the other. "That's what makes them so confoundedly difficult when you don't."

"Here is this one then. In Padua, which seems to be regaining its old reputation as the birthplace of spurious antiques, by the way, there lives an ingenious craftsman named Pietro Stelli. This simple soul, who possesses a talent not inferior to that of Cavino at his best, has for many years turned his hand to the not unprofitable occupation of forging rare Greek and Roman coins. As a collector and student of certain Greek colonials and a specialist in forgeries I have been familiar with Stelli's workmanship for years. Latterly he seems to have come under the influence of an international crook called—at the moment—Dompierre, who soon saw a way of utilizing Stelli's genius on a royal scale. Helene Brunesi, who in private life is—and really is, I believe—Madame Dompierre, readily lent her services to the enterprise."

"Quite so," nodded Mr Carlyle, as his host paused.

"You see the whole sequence, of course?"

"Not exactly—not in detail," confessed Mr Carlyle.

"Dompierre's idea was to gain access to some of the most celebrated cabinets of Europe and substitute Stelli's fabrications for the genuine coins. The princely collection of rarities that he would thus amass might be difficult to dispose of safely but I have no doubt that he had matured his plans. Helene, in the person of Nina Bran, an Anglicised French parlourmaid—a part which she fills to perfection—was to obtain wax impressions of the most valuable pieces and to make the exchange when the counterfeits reached her. In this way it was obviously hoped that the fraud would not come to light until long after the real coins had been sold, and I gather that she has already done her work successfully in several houses. Then, impressed by her excellent references and capable manner, my housekeeper engaged her, and for a few weeks she went about her duties here. It was fatal to this detail of the scheme, however, that I have the misfortune to be blind. I am told that Helene has so innocently angelic a face as to disarm suspicion, but I was incapable of being impressed and that good material was thrown away. But one morning my material fingers—which, of course, knew nothing of Helene's angelic face—discovered an unfamiliar touch about the surface of my favourite Euclideas, and, although there was doubtless nothing to be seen, my critical sense of smell reported that wax had been recently pressed against it. I began to make discreet inquiries and in the meantime my cabinets went to the local bank for safety. Helene countered by receiving a telegram from Angiers, calling her to the death-bed of her aged mother. The aged mother succumbed; duty compelled Helene to remain at the side of her stricken patriarchal father, and doubtless The Turrets was written off the syndicate's operations as a bad debt."

"Very interesting," admitted Mr Carlyle; "but at the risk of seeming obtuse"—his manner had become delicately chastened—"I must say that I fail to trace the inevitable connexion between Nina Brun and this particular forgery—assuming that it is a forgery."

"Set your mind at rest about that, Louis," replied Carrados. "It is a forgery, and it is a forgery that none but Pietro Stelli could have achieved. That is the essential connexion. Of course, there are accessories. A private detective coming urgently to see me with a notable tetradrachm in his pocket, which he announces to be the clue to a remarkable fraud—well, really, Louis, one scarcely needs to be blind to see through that."

"And Lord Seastoke? I suppose you happened to discover that Nina Brun had gone there?"

"No, I cannot claim to have discovered that, or I should certainly have warned him at once when I found out—only recently—about the gang. As a matter of fact, the last information I had of Lord Seastoke was a line in yesterday's Morning Post to the effect that he was still at Cairo. But many of these pieces——" He brushed his finger almost lovingly across the vivid chariot race that embellished the reverse of the coin, and broke off to remark: "You really ought to take up the subject, Louis. You have no idea how useful it might prove to you some day."

"I really think I must," replied Carlyle grimly. "Two hundred and fifty pounds the original of this cost, I believe."

"Cheap, too; it would make five hundred pounds in New York to-day. As I was saying, many are literally unique. This gem by Kimon is—here is his signature, you see; Peter is particularly good at lettering—and as I handled the genuine tetradrachm about two years ago, when Lord Seastoke exhibited it at a meeting of our society in Albemarle Street, there is nothing at all wonderful in my being able to fix the locale of your mystery. Indeed, I feel that I ought to apologize for it all being so simple."

"I think," remarked Mr Carlyle, critically examining the loose threads on his left boot, "that the apology on that head would be more appropriate from me."

The Knight's Cross Signal Problem

"Louis," exclaimed Mr Carrados, with the air of genial gaiety that Carlyle had found so incongruous to his conception of a blind man, "you have a mystery somewhere about you! I know it by your step."

Nearly a month had passed since the incident of the false Dionysius had led to the two men meeting. It was now December. Whatever Mr Carlyle's step might indicate to the inner eye it betokened to the casual observer the manner of a crisp, alert, self-possessed man of business. Carlyle, in truth, betrayed nothing of the pessimism and despondency that had marked him on the earlier occasion.

"You have only yourself to thank that it is a very poor one," he retorted. "If you hadn't held me to a hasty promise——"

"To give me an option on the next case that baffled you, no matter what it was——"

"Just so. The consequence is that you get a very unsatisfactory affair that has no special interest to an amateur and is only baffling because it is—well——"

"Well, baffling?"

"Exactly, Max. Your would-be jest has discovered the proverbial truth. I need hardly tell you that it is only the insoluble that is finally baffling and this is very probably insoluble. You remember the awful smash on the Central and Suburban at Knight's Cross Station a few weeks ago?"

"Yes," replied Carrados, with interest. "I read the whole ghastly details at the time."

"You read?" exclaimed his friend suspiciously.

"I still use the familiar phrases," explained Carrados, with a smile. "As a matter of fact, my secretary reads to me. I mark what I want to hear and when he comes at ten o'clock we clear off the morning papers in no time."

"And how do you know what to mark?" demanded Mr Carlyle cunningly.

Carrados's right hand, lying idly on the table, moved to a newspaper near. He ran his finger along a column heading, his eyes still turned towards his visitor.

"'The Money Market. Continued from page 2. British Railways,'" he announced.

"Extraordinary," murmured Carlyle.

"Not very," said Carrados. "If someone dipped a stick in treacle and wrote 'Rats' across a marble slab you would probably be able to distinguish what was there, blindfold."

"Probably," admitted Mr Carlyle. "At all events we will not test the experiment."

"The difference to you of treacle on a marble background is scarcely greater than that of printers' ink on newspaper to me. But anything smaller than pica I do not read with comfort, and below long primer I cannot read at all. Hence the secretary. Now the accident, Louis."

"The accident: well, you remember all about that. An ordinary Central and Suburban passenger train, non-stop at Knight's Cross, ran past the signal and crashed into a crowded electric train that was just beginning to move out. It was like sending a garden roller down a row of handlights. Two carriages of the electric train were flattened out of existence; the next two were broken up. For the first time on an English railway there was a good stand-up smash between a heavy steam-engine and a train of light cars, and it was 'bad for the coo.'"

"Twenty-seven killed, forty something injured, eight died since," commented Carrados.

"That was bad for the Co.," said Carlyle. "Well, the main fact was plain enough. The heavy train was in the wrong. But was the engine-driver responsible? He claimed, and he claimed vehemently from the first and he never varied one iota, that he had a 'clear' signal—that is to say, the green light, it being dark. The signalman concerned was equally dogged that he never pulled off the signal—that it was at 'danger' when the accident happened and that it had been for five minutes before. Obviously, they could not both be right."

"Why, Louis?" asked Mr Carrados smoothly.

"The signal must either have been up or down—red or green."

"Did you ever notice the signals on the Great Northern Railway, Louis?"

"Not particularly. Why?"

"One winterly day, about the year when you and I were concerned in being born, the engine-driver of a Scotch express received the 'clear' from a signal near a little Huntingdon station called Abbots Ripton. He went on and crashed into a goods train and into the thick of the smash a down express mowed its way. Thirteen killed and the usual tale of injured. He was positive that the signal gave him a 'clear'; the signalman was equally confident that he had never pulled it off the 'danger.' Both were right, and yet the signal was in working order. As I said, it was a winterly day; it had been snowing hard and the snow froze and accumulated on the upper edge of the signal arm until its weight bore it down. That is a fact that no fiction writer dare have invented, but to this day every signal on the Great Northern pivots from the centre of the arm instead of from the end, in memory of that snowstorm."

"That came out at the inquest, I presume?" said Mr Carlyle. "We have had the Board of Trade inquiry and the inquest here and no explanation is forthcoming. Everything was in perfect order. It rests between the word of the signalman and the word of the engine-driver—not a jot of direct evidence either way. Which is right?"

"That is what you are going to find out, Louis?" suggested Carrados.

"It is what I am being paid for finding out," admitted Mr Carlyle frankly. "But so far we are just where the inquest left it, and, between ourselves, I candidly can't see an inch in front of my face in the matter."

"Nor can I," said the blind man, with a rather wry smile. "Never mind. The engine-driver is your client, of course?"

"Yes," admitted Carlyle. "But how the deuce did you know?"

"Let us say that your sympathies are enlisted on his behalf. The jury were inclined to exonerate the signalman, weren't they? What has the company done with your man?"

"Both are suspended. Hutchins, the driver, hears that he may probably be given charge of a lavatory at one of the stations. He is a decent, bluff, short-spoken old chap, with his heart in his work. Just now you'll find him at his worst—bitter and suspicious. The thought of swabbing down a lavatory and taking pennies all day is poisoning him."

"Naturally. Well, there we have honest Hutchins: taciturn, a little touchy perhaps, grown grey in the service of the company, and manifesting quite a bulldog-like devotion to his favourite 538."

"Why, that actually was the number of his engine—how do you know it?" demanded Carlyle sharply.

"It was mentioned two or three times at the inquest, Louis," replied Carrados mildly.

"And you remembered—with no reason to?"

"You can generally trust a blind man's memory, especially if he has taken the trouble to develop it."

"Then you will remember that Hutchins did not make a very good impression at the time. He was surly and irritable under the ordeal. I want you to see the case from all sides."

"He called the signalman—Mead—a 'lying young dog,' across the room, I believe. Now, Mead, what is he like? You have seen him, of course?"

"Yes. He does not impress me favourably. He is glib, ingratiating, and distinctly 'greasy.' He has a ready answer for everything almost before the question is out of your mouth. He has thought of everything."

"And now you are going to tell me something, Louis," said Carrados encouragingly.

Mr Carlyle laughed a little to cover an involuntary movement of surprise.

"There is a suggestive line that was not touched at the inquiries," he admitted. "Hutchins has been a saving man all his life, and he has received good wages. Among his class he is regarded as wealthy. I daresay that he has five hundred pounds in the bank. He is a widower with one daughter, a very nice-mannered girl of about twenty. Mead is a young man, and he and the girl are sweethearts—have been informally engaged for some time. But old Hutchins would not hear of it; he seems to have taken a dislike to the signalman from the first and latterly he had forbidden him to come to his house or his daughter to speak to him."

"Excellent, Louis," cried Carrados in great delight. "We shall clear your man in a blaze of red and green lights yet and hang the glib, 'greasy' signalman from his own signal-post."

"It is a significant fact, seriously?"

"It is absolutely convincing."

"It may have been a slip, a mental lapse on Mead's part which he discovered the moment it was too late, and then, being too cowardly to admit his fault, and having so much at stake, he took care to make detection impossible. It may have been that, but my idea is rather that probably it was neither quite pure accident nor pure design. I can imagine Mead meanly pluming himself over the fact that the life of this man who stands in his way, and whom he must cordially dislike, lies in his power. I can imagine the idea becoming an obsession as he dwells on it. A dozen times with his hand on the lever he lets his mind explore the possibilities of a moment's defection. Then one day he pulls the signal off in sheer bravado—and hastily puts it at danger again. He may have done it once or he may have done it oftener before he was caught in a fatal moment of irresolution. The chances are about even that the engine-driver would be killed. In any case he would be disgraced, for it is easier on the face of it to believe that a man might run past a danger signal in absentmindedness, without noticing it, than that a man should pull off a signal and replace it without being conscious of his actions."

"The fireman was killed. Does your theory involve the certainty of the fireman being killed, Louis?"

"No," said Carlyle. "The fireman is a difficulty, but looking at it from Mead's point of view—whether he has been guilty of an error or a crime—it resolves itself into this: First, the fireman may be killed. Second, he may not notice the signal at all. Third, in any case he will loyally corroborate his driver and the good old jury will discount that."

Carrados smoked thoughtfully, his open, sightless eyes merely appearing to be set in a tranquil gaze across the room.

"It would not be an improbable explanation," he said presently. "Ninety-nine men out of a hundred would say: 'People do not do these things.' But you and I, who have in our different ways studied criminology, know that they sometimes do, or else there would be no curious crimes. What have you done on that line?"

To anyone who could see, Mr Carlyle's expression conveyed an answer.

"You are behind the scenes, Max. What was there for me to do? Still I must do something for my money. Well, I have had a very close inquiry made confidentially among the men. There might be a whisper of one of them knowing more than had come out—a man restrained by friendship, or enmity, or even grade jealousy. Nothing came of that. Then there was the remote chance that some private person had noticed the signal without attaching any importance to it then, one who would be able to identify it still by something associated with the time. I went over the line myself. Opposite the signal the line on one side is shut in by a high blank wall; on the other side are houses, but coming below the butt-end of a scullery the signal does not happen to be visible from any road or from any window."

"My poor Louis!" said Carrados, in friendly ridicule. "You were at the end of your tether?"

"I was," admitted Carlyle. "And now that you know the sort of job it is I don't suppose that you are keen on wasting your time over it."

"That would hardly be fair, would it?" said Carrados reasonably. "No, Louis, I will take over your honest old driver and your greasy young signalman and your fatal signal that cannot be seen from anywhere."

"But it is an important point for you to remember, Max, that although the signal cannot be seen from the box, if the mechanism had gone wrong, or anyone tampered with the arm, the automatic indicator would at once have told Mead that the green light was showing. Oh, I have gone very thoroughly into the technical points, I assure you."

"I must do so too," commented Mr Carrados gravely.

"For that matter, if there is anything you want to know, I dare say that I can tell you," suggested his visitor. "It might save your time."

"True," acquiesced Carrados. "I should like to know whether anyone belonging to the houses that bound the line there came of age or got married on the twenty-sixth of November."

Mr Carlyle looked across curiously at his host.

"I really do not know, Max," he replied, in his crisp, precise way. "What on earth has that got to do with it, may I inquire?"

"The only explanation of the Pont St Lin swing-bridge disaster of '75 was the reflection of a green bengal light on a cottage window."

Mr Carlyle smiled his indulgence privately.

"My dear chap, you mustn't let your retentive memory of obscure happenings run away with you," he remarked wisely. "In nine cases out of ten the obvious explanation is the true one. The difficulty, as here, lies in proving it. Now, you would like to see these men?"

"I expect so; in any case, I will see Hutchins first."

"Both live in Holloway. Shall I ask Hutchins to come here to see you—say to-morrow? He is doing nothing."

"No," replied Carrados. "To-morrow I must call on my brokers and my time may be filled up."

"Quite right; you mustn't neglect your own affairs for this—experiment," assented Carlyle.

"Besides, I should prefer to drop in on Hutchins at his own home. Now, Louis, enough of the honest old man for one night. I have a lovely thing by Eumenes that I want to show you. To-day is—Tuesday. Come to dinner on Sunday and pour the vials of your ridicule on my want of success."

"That's an amiable way of putting it," replied Carlyle. "All right, I will."

Two hours later Carrados was again in his study, apparently, for a wonder, sitting idle. Sometimes he smiled to himself, and once or twice he laughed a little, but for the most part his pleasant, impassive face reflected no emotion and he sat with his useless eyes tranquilly fixed on an unseen distance. It was a fantastic caprice of the man to mock his sightlessness by a parade of light, and under the soft brilliance of a dozen electric brackets the room was as bright as day. At length he stood up and rang the bell.

"I suppose Mr Greatorex isn't still here by any chance, Parkinson?" he asked, referring to his secretary.

"I think not, sir, but I will ascertain," replied the man.

"Never mind. Go to his room and bring me the last two files of The Times. Now"—when he returned—"turn to the earliest you have there. The date?"

"November the second."

"That will do. Find the Money Market; it will be in the Supplement. Now look down the columns until you come to British Railways."

"I have it, sir."

"Central and Suburban. Read the closing price and the change."

"Central and Suburban Ordinary, 66-1/2-67-1/2, fall 1/8. Preferred Ordinary, 81-81-1/2, no change. Deferred Ordinary, 27-1/2-27-3/4, fall 1/4. That is all, sir."

"Now take a paper about a week on. Read the Deferred only."

"27-27-1/4, no change."

"Another week."

"29-1/2-30, rise 5/8."

"Another."

"31-1/2-32-1/2, rise 1."

"Very good. Now on Tuesday the twenty-seventh November."

"31-7/8-32-3/4, rise 1/2."

"Yes. The next day."

"24-1/2-23-1/2, fall 9."

"Quite so, Parkinson. There had been an accident, you see."

"Yes, sir. Very unpleasant accident. Jane knows a person whose sister's young man has a cousin who had his arm torn off in it—torn off at the socket, she says, sir. It seems to bring it home to one, sir."

"That is all. Stay—in the paper you have, look down the first money column and see if there is any reference to the Central and Suburban."

"Yes, sir. 'City and Suburbans, which after their late depression on the projected extension of the motor bus service, had been steadily creeping up on the abandonment of the scheme, and as a result of their own excellent traffic returns, suffered a heavy slump through the lamentable accident of Thursday night. The Deferred in particular at one time fell eleven points as it was felt that the possible dividend, with which rumour has of late been busy, was now out of the question.'"

"Yes; that is all. Now you can take the papers back. And let it be a warning to you, Parkinson, not to invest your savings in speculative railway deferreds."

"Yes, sir. Thank you, sir, I will endeavour to remember." He lingered for a moment as he shook the file of papers level. "I may say, sir, that I have my eye on a small block of cottage property at Acton. But even cottage property scarcely seems safe from legislative depredation now, sir."

The next day Mr Carrados called on his brokers in the city. It is to be presumed that he got through his private business quicker than he expected, for after leaving Austin Friars he continued his journey to Holloway, where he found Hutchins at home and sitting morosely before his kitchen fire.

Rightly assuming that his luxuriant car would involve him in a certain amount of public attention in Klondyke Street, the blind man dismissed it some distance from the house, and walked the rest of the way, guided by the almost imperceptible touch of Parkinson's arm.

"Here is a gentleman to see you, father," explained Miss Hutchins, who had come to the door. She divined the relative positions of the two visitors at a glance.

"Then why don't you take him into the parlour?" grumbled the ex-driver. His face was a testimonial of hard work and general sobriety but at the moment one might hazard from his voice and manner that he had been drinking earlier in the day.

"I don't think that the gentleman would be impressed by the difference between our parlour and our kitchen," replied the girl quaintly, "and it is warmer here."

"What's the matter with the parlour now?" demanded her father sourly. "It was good enough for your mother and me. It used to be good enough for you."

"There is nothing the matter with it, nor with the kitchen either." She turned impassively to the two who had followed her along the narrow passage. "Will you go in, sir?"

"I don't want to see no gentleman," cried Hutchins noisily. "Unless"—his manner suddenly changed to one of pitiable anxiety—"unless you're from the Company, sir, to—to——"

"No; I have come on Mr Carlyle's behalf," replied Carrados, walking to a chair as though he moved by a kind of instinct.

Hutchins laughed his wry contempt.

"Mr Carlyle!" he reiterated; "Mr Carlyle! Fat lot of good he's been. Why don't he do something for his money?"

"He has," replied Carrados, with imperturbable good-humour; "he has sent me. Now, I want to ask you a few questions."

"A few questions!" roared the irate man. "Why, blast it, I have done nothing else but answer questions for a month. I didn't pay Mr Carlyle to ask me questions; I can get enough of that for nixes. Why don't you go and ask Mr Herbert Ananias Mead your few questions—then you might find out something."

There was a slight movement by the door and Carrados knew that the girl had quietly left the room.

"You saw that, sir?" demanded the father, diverted to a new line of bitterness. "You saw that girl—my own daughter, that I've worked for all her life?"

"No," replied Carrados.

"The girl that's just gone out—she's my daughter," explained Hutchins.

"I know, but I did not see her. I see nothing. I am blind."

"Blind!" exclaimed the old fellow, sitting up in startled wonderment. "You mean it, sir? You walk all right and you look at me as if you saw me. You're kidding surely."

"No," smiled Carrados. "It's quite right."

"Then it's a funny business, sir—you what are blind expecting to find something that those with their eyes couldn't," ruminated Hutchins sagely.

"There are things that you can't see with your eyes, Hutchins."

"Perhaps you are right, sir. Well, what is it you want to know?"

"Light a cigar first," said the blind man, holding out his case and waiting until the various sounds told him that his host was smoking contentedly. "The train you were driving at the time of the accident was the six-twenty-seven from Notcliff. It stopped everywhere until it reached Lambeth Bridge, the chief London station of your line. There it became something of an express, and leaving Lambeth Bridge at seven-eleven, should not stop again until it fetched Swanstead on Thames, eleven miles out, at seven-thirty-four. Then it stopped on and off from Swanstead to Ingerfield, the terminus of that branch, which it reached at eight-five."

Hutchins nodded, and then, remembering, said: "That's right, sir."

"That was your business all day—running between Notcliff and Ingerfield?"

"Yes, sir. Three journeys up and three down mostly."

"With the same stops on all the down journeys?"

"No. The seven-eleven is the only one that does a run from the Bridge to Swanstead. You see, it is just on the close of the evening rush, as they call it. A good many late business gentlemen living at Swanstead use the seven-eleven regular. The other journeys we stop at every station to Lambeth Bridge, and then here and there beyond."

"There are, of course, other trains doing exactly the same journey—a service, in fact?"

"Yes, sir. About six."

"And do any of those—say, during the rush—do any of those run non-stop from Lambeth to Swanstead?"

Hutchins reflected a moment. All the choler and restlessness had melted out of the man's face. He was again the excellent artisan, slow but capable and self-reliant.

"That I couldn't definitely say, sir. Very few short-distance trains pass the junction, but some of those may. A guide would show us in a minute but I haven't got one."

"Never mind. You said at the inquest that it was no uncommon thing for you to be pulled up at the 'stop' signal east of Knight's Cross Station. How often would that happen—only with the seven-eleven, mind."

"Perhaps three times a week; perhaps twice."

"The accident was on a Thursday. Have you noticed that you were pulled up oftener on a Thursday than on any other day?"

A smile crossed the driver's face at the question.

"You don't happen to live at Swanstead yourself, sir?" he asked in reply.

"No," admitted Carrados. "Why?"

"Well, sir, we were always pulled up on Thursday; practically always, you may say. It got to be quite a saying among those who used the train regular; they used to look out for it."

Carrados's sightless eyes had the one quality of concealing emotion supremely. "Oh," he commented softly, "always; and it was quite a saying, was it? And why was it always so on Thursday?"

"It had to do with the early closing, I'm told. The suburban traffic was a bit different. By rights we ought to have been set back two minutes for that day, but I suppose it wasn't thought worth while to alter us in the time-table, so we most always had to wait outside Three Deep tunnel for a west-bound electric to make good."

"You were prepared for it then?"

"Yes, sir, I was," said Hutchins, reddening at some recollection, "and very down about it was one of the jury over that. But, mayhap once in three months, I did get through even on a Thursday, and it's not for me to question whether things are right or wrong just because they are not what I may expect. The signals are my orders, sir—stop! go on! and it's for me to obey, as you would a general on the field of battle. What would happen otherwise! It was nonsense what they said about going cautious; and the man who started it was a barber who didn't know the difference between a 'distance' and a 'stop' signal down to the minute they gave their verdict. My orders, sir, given me by that signal, was 'Go right ahead and keep to your running time!'"

Carrados nodded a soothing assent. "That is all, I think," he remarked.

"All!" exclaimed Hutchins in surprise. "Why, sir, you can't have got much idea of it yet."

"Quite enough. And I know it isn't pleasant for you to be taken along the same ground over and over again."

The man moved awkwardly in his chair and pulled nervously at his grizzled beard.

"You mustn't take any notice of what I said just now, sir," he apologized. "You somehow make me feel that something may come of it; but I've been badgered about and accused and cross-examined from one to another of them these weeks till it's fairly made me bitter against everything. And now they talk of putting me in a lavatory—me that has been with the company for five and forty years and on the foot-plate thirty-two—a man suspected of running past a danger signal."

"You have had a rough time, Hutchins; you will have to exercise your patience a little longer yet," said Carrados sympathetically.

"You think something may come of it, sir? You think you will be able to clear me? Believe me, sir, if you could give me something to look forward to it might save me from——" He pulled himself up and shook his head sorrowfully. "I've been near it," he added simply.

Carrados reflected and took his resolution.

"To-day is Wednesday. I think you may hope to hear something from your general manager towards the middle of next week."

"Good God, sir! You really mean that?"

"In the interval show your good sense by behaving reasonably. Keep civilly to yourself and don't talk. Above all"—he nodded towards a quart jug that stood on the table between them, an incident that filled the simple-minded engineer with boundless wonder when he recalled it afterwards—"above all, leave that alone."

Hutchins snatched up the vessel and brought it crashing down on the hearthstone, his face shining with a set resolution.

"I've done with it, sir. It was the bitterness and despair that drove me to that. Now I can do without it."

The door was hastily opened and Miss Hutchins looked anxiously from her father to the visitors and back again.

"Oh, whatever is the matter?" she exclaimed. "I heard a great crash."

"This gentleman is going to clear me, Meg, my dear," blurted out the old man irrepressibly. "And I've done with the drink for ever."

"Hutchins! Hutchins!" said Carrados warningly.

"My daughter, sir; you wouldn't have her not know?" pleaded Hutchins, rather crest-fallen. "It won't go any further."

Carrados laughed quietly to himself as he felt Margaret Hutchins's startled and questioning eyes attempting to read his mind. He shook hands with the engine-driver without further comment, however, and walked out into the commonplace little street under Parkinson's unobtrusive guidance.

"Very nice of Miss Hutchins to go into half-mourning, Parkinson," he remarked as they went along. "Thoughtful, and yet not ostentatious."

"Yes, sir," agreed Parkinson, who had long ceased to wonder at his master's perceptions.

"The Romans, Parkinson, had a saying to the effect that gold carries no smell. That is a pity sometimes. What jewellery did Miss Hutchins wear?"

"Very little, sir. A plain gold brooch representing a merry-thought—the merry-thought of a sparrow, I should say, sir. The only other article was a smooth-backed gun-metal watch, suspended from a gun-metal bow."

"Nothing showy or expensive, eh?"

"Oh dear no, sir. Quite appropriate for a young person of her position."

"Just what I should have expected." He slackened his pace. "We are passing a hoarding, are we not?"

"Yes, sir."

"We will stand here a moment. Read me the letterpress of the poster before us."

"This 'Oxo' one, sir?"

"Yes."

"'Oxo,' sir."

Carrados was convulsed with silent laughter. Parkinson had infinitely more dignity and conceded merely a tolerant recognition of the ludicrous.

"That was a bad shot, Parkinson," remarked his master when he could speak. "We will try another."

For three minutes, with scrupulous conscientiousness on the part of the reader and every appearance of keen interest on the part of the hearer, there were set forth the particulars of a sale by auction of superfluous timber and builders' material.

"That will do," said Carrados, when the last detail had been reached. "We can be seen from the door of No. 107 still?"

"Yes, sir."

"No indication of anyone coming to us from there?"

"No, sir."

Carrados walked thoughtfully on again. In the Holloway Road they rejoined the waiting motor car. "Lambeth Bridge Station," was the order the driver received.

From the station the car was sent on home and Parkinson was instructed to take two first-class singles for Richmond, which could be reached by changing at Stafford Road. The "evening rush" had not yet commenced and they had no difficulty in finding an empty carriage when the train came in.

Parkinson was kept busy that journey describing what he saw at various points between Lambeth Bridge and Knight's Cross. For a quarter of a mile Carrados's demands on the eyes and the memory of his remarkable servant were wide and incessant. Then his questions ceased. They had passed the "stop" signal, east of Knight's Cross Station.

The following afternoon they made the return journey as far as Knight's Cross. This time, however, the surroundings failed to interest Carrados. "We are going to look at some rooms," was the information he offered on the subject, and an imperturbable "Yes, sir" had been the extent of Parkinson's comment on the unusual proceeding. After leaving the station they turned sharply along a road that ran parallel with the line, a dull thoroughfare of substantial, elderly houses that were beginning to sink into decrepitude. Here and there a corner residence displayed the brass plate of a professional occupant, but for the most part they were given up to the various branches of second-rate apartment letting.

"The third house after the one with the flagstaff," said Carrados.

Parkinson rang the bell, which was answered by a young servant, who took an early opportunity of assuring them that she was not tidy as it was rather early in the afternoon. She informed Carrados, in reply to his inquiry, that Miss Chubb was at home, and showed them into a melancholy little sitting-room to await her appearance.

"I shall be 'almost' blind here, Parkinson," remarked Carrados, walking about the room. "It saves explanation."

"Very good, sir," replied Parkinson.

Five minutes later, an interval suggesting that Miss Chubb also found it rather early in the afternoon, Carrados was arranging to take rooms for his attendant and himself for the short time that he would be in London, seeing an oculist.

"One bedroom, mine, must face north," he stipulated. "It has to do with the light."

Miss Chubb replied that she quite understood. Some gentlemen, she added, had their requirements, others their fancies. She endeavoured to suit all. The bedroom she had in view from the first did face north. She would not have known, only the last gentleman, curiously enough, had made the same request.

"A sufferer like myself?" inquired Carrados affably.

Miss Chubb did not think so. In his case she regarded it merely as a fancy. He had said that he could not sleep on any other side. She had had to turn out of her own room to accommodate him, but if one kept an apartment-house one had to be adaptable; and Mr Ghoosh was certainly very liberal in his ideas.

"Ghoosh? An Indian gentleman, I presume?" hazarded Carrados.

It appeared that Mr Ghoosh was an Indian. Miss Chubb confided that at first she had been rather perturbed at the idea of taking in "a black man," as she confessed to regarding him. She reiterated, however, that Mr Ghoosh proved to be "quite the gentleman." Five minutes of affability put Carrados in full possession of Mr Ghoosh's manner of life and movements—the dates of his arrival and departure, his solitariness and his daily habits.

"This would be the best bedroom," said Miss Chubb.

It was a fair-sized room on the first floor. The window looked out on to the roof of an outbuilding; beyond, the deep cutting of the railway line. Opposite stood the dead wall that Mr Carlyle had spoken of.

Carrados "looked" round the room with the discriminating glance that sometimes proved so embarrassing to those who knew him.

"I have to take a little daily exercise," he remarked, walking to the window and running his hand up the woodwork. "You will not mind my fixing a 'developer' here, Miss Chubb—a few small screws?"

Miss Chubb thought not. Then she was sure not. Finally she ridiculed the idea of minding with scorn.

"If there is width enough," mused Carrados, spanning the upright critically. "Do you happen to have a wooden foot-rule convenient?"

"Well, to be sure!" exclaimed Miss Chubb, opening a rapid succession of drawers until she produced the required article. "When we did out this room after Mr Ghoosh, there was this very ruler among the things that he hadn't thought worth taking. This is what you require, sir?"

"Yes," replied Carrados, accepting it, "I think this is exactly what I require." It was a common new white-wood rule, such as one might buy at any small stationer's for a penny. He carelessly took off the width of the upright, reading the figures with a touch; and then continued to run a finger-tip delicately up and down the edges of the instrument.

"Four and seven-eighths," was his unspoken conclusion.

"I hope it will do, sir."

"Admirably," replied Carrados. "But I haven't reached the end of my requirements yet, Miss Chubb."

"No, sir?" said the landlady, feeling that it would be a pleasure to oblige so agreeable a gentleman, "what else might there be?"

"Although I can see very little I like to have a light, but not any kind of light. Gas I cannot do with. Do you think that you would be able to find me an oil lamp?"

"Certainly, sir. I got out a very nice brass lamp that I have specially for Mr Ghoosh. He read a good deal of an evening and he preferred a lamp."

"That is very convenient. I suppose it is large enough to burn for a whole evening?"

"Yes, indeed. And very particular he was always to have it filled every day."

"A lamp without oil is not very useful," smiled Carrados, following her towards another room, and absentmindedly slipping the foot-rule into his pocket.

Whatever Parkinson thought of the arrangement of going into second-rate apartments in an obscure street it is to be inferred that his devotion to his master was sufficient to overcome his private emotions as a self-respecting "man." At all events, as they were approaching the station he asked, and without a trace of feeling, whether there were any orders for him with reference to the proposed migration.

"None, Parkinson," replied his master. "We must be satisfied with our present quarters."

"I beg your pardon, sir," said Parkinson, with some constraint. "I understood that you had taken the rooms for a week certain."

"I am afraid that Miss Chubb will be under the same impression. Unforeseen circumstances will prevent our going, however. Mr Greatorex must write to-morrow, enclosing a cheque, with my regrets, and adding a penny for this ruler which I seem to have brought away with me. It, at least, is something for the money."

Parkinson may be excused for not attempting to understand the course of events.

"Here is your train coming in, sir," he merely said.

"We will let it go and wait for another. Is there a signal at either end of the platform?"

"Yes, sir; at the further end."

"Let us walk towards it. Are there any of the porters or officials about here?"

"No, sir; none."

"Take this ruler. I want you to go up the steps—there are steps up the signal, by the way?"

"Yes, sir."

"I want you to measure the glass of the lamp. Do not go up any higher than is necessary, but if you have to stretch be careful not to mark on the measurement with your nail, although the impulse is a natural one. That has been done already."

Parkinson looked apprehensively around and about. Fortunately the part was a dark and unfrequented spot and everyone else was moving towards the exit at the other end of the platform. Fortunately, also, the signal was not a high one.

"As near as I can judge on the rounded surface, the glass is four and seven-eighths across," reported Parkinson.

"Thank you," replied Carrados, returning the measure to his pocket, "four and seven-eighths is quite near enough. Now we will take the next train back."

Sunday evening came, and with it Mr Carlyle to The Turrets at the appointed hour. He brought to the situation a mind poised for any eventuality and a trenchant eye. As the time went on and the impenetrable Carrados made no allusion to the case, Carlyle's manner inclined to a waggish commiseration of his host's position. Actually, he said little, but the crisp precision of his voice when the path lay open to a remark of any significance left little to be said.

It was not until they had finished dinner and returned to the library that Carrados gave the slightest hint of anything unusual being in the air. His first indication of coming events was to remove the key from the outside to the inside of the door.

"What are you doing, Max?" demanded Mr Carlyle, his curiosity overcoming the indirect attitude.

"You have been very entertaining, Louis," replied his friend, "but Parkinson should be back very soon now and it is as well to be prepared. Do you happen to carry a revolver?"

"Not when I come to dine with you, Max," replied Carlyle, with all the aplomb he could muster. "Is it usual?"

Carrados smiled affectionately at his guest's agile recovery and touched the secret spring of a drawer in an antique bureau by his side. The little hidden receptacle shot smoothly out, disclosing a pair of dull-blued pistols.

"To-night, at all events, it might be prudent," he replied, handing one to Carlyle and putting the other into his own pocket. "Our man may be here at any minute, and we do not know in what temper he will come."

"Our man!" exclaimed Carlyle, craning forward in excitement. "Max! you don't mean to say that you have got Mead to admit it?"

"No one has admitted it," said Carrados. "And it is not Mead."

"Not Mead.... Do you mean that Hutchins——?"

"Neither Mead nor Hutchins. The man who tampered with the signal—for Hutchins was right and a green light was exhibited—is a young Indian from Bengal. His name is Drishna and he lives at Swanstead."

Mr Carlyle stared at his friend between sheer surprise and blank incredulity.

"You really mean this, Carrados?" he said.

"My fatal reputation for humour!" smiled Carrados. "If I am wrong, Louis, the next hour will expose it."

"But why—why—why? The colossal villainy, the unparalleled audacity!" Mr Carlyle lost himself among incredulous superlatives and could only stare.

"Chiefly to get himself out of a disastrous speculation," replied Carrados, answering the question. "If there was another motive—or at least an incentive—which I suspect, doubtless we shall hear of it."

"All the same, Max, I don't think that you have treated me quite fairly," protested Carlyle, getting over his first surprise and passing to a sense of injury. "Here we are and I know nothing, absolutely nothing, of the whole affair."

"We both have our ideas of pleasantry, Louis," replied Carrados genially. "But I dare say you are right and perhaps there is still time to atone." In the fewest possible words he outlined the course of his investigations. "And now you know all that is to be known until Drishna arrives."

"But will he come?" questioned Carlyle doubtfully. "He may be suspicious."

"Yes, he will be suspicious."

"Then he will not come."

"On the contrary, Louis, he will come because my letter will make him suspicious. He is coming; otherwise Parkinson would have telephoned me at once and we should have had to take other measures."

"What did you say, Max?" asked Carlyle curiously.

"I wrote that I was anxious to discuss an Indo-Scythian inscription with him, and sent my car in the hope that he would be able to oblige me."

"But is he interested in Indo-Scythian inscriptions?"

"I haven't the faintest idea," admitted Carrados, and Mr Carlyle was throwing up his hands in despair when the sound of a motor car wheels softly kissing the gravel surface of the drive outside brought him to his feet.

"By gad, you are right, Max!" he exclaimed, peeping through the curtains. "There is a man inside."

"Mr Drishna," announced Parkinson, a minute later.

The visitor came into the room with leisurely self-possession that might have been real or a desperate assumption. He was a slightly built young man of about twenty-five, with black hair and eyes, a small, carefully trained moustache, and a dark olive skin. His physiognomy was not displeasing, but his expression had a harsh and supercilious tinge. In attire he erred towards the immaculately spruce.

"Mr Carrados?" he said inquiringly.

Carrados, who had risen, bowed slightly without offering his hand.

"This gentleman," he said, indicating his friend, "is Mr Carlyle, the celebrated private detective."

The Indian shot a very sharp glance at the object of this description. Then he sat down.

"You wrote me a letter, Mr Carrados," he remarked, in English that scarcely betrayed any foreign origin, "a rather curious letter, I may say. You asked me about an ancient inscription. I know nothing of antiquities; but I thought, as you had sent, that it would be more courteous if I came and explained this to you."

"That was the object of my letter," replied Carrados.

"You wished to see me?" said Drishna, unable to stand the ordeal of the silence that Carrados imposed after his remark.

"When you left Miss Chubb's house you left a ruler behind." One lay on the desk by Carrados and he took it up as he spoke.

"I don't understand what you are talking about," said Drishna guardedly. "You are making some mistake."

"The ruler was marked at four and seven-eighths inches—the measure of the glass of the signal lamp outside."

The unfortunate young man was unable to repress a start. His face lost its healthy tone. Then, with a sudden impulse, he made a step forward and snatched the object from Carrados's hand.

"If it is mine I have a right to it," he exclaimed, snapping the ruler in two and throwing it on to the back of the blazing fire. "It is nothing."

"Pardon me, I did not say that the one you have so impetuously disposed of was yours. As a matter of fact, it was mine. Yours is—elsewhere."

"Wherever it is you have no right to it if it is mine," panted Drishna, with rising excitement. "You are a thief, Mr Carrados. I will not stay any longer here."

He jumped up and turned towards the door. Carlyle made a step forward, but the precaution was unnecessary.

"One moment, Mr Drishna," interposed Carrados, in his smoothest tones. "It is a pity, after you have come so far, to leave without hearing of my investigations in the neighbourhood of Shaftesbury Avenue."

Drishna sat down again.

"As you like," he muttered. "It does not interest me."

"I wanted to obtain a lamp of a certain pattern," continued Carrados. "It seemed to me that the simplest explanation would be to say that I wanted it for a motor car. Naturally I went to Long Acre. At the first shop I said: 'Wasn't it here that a friend of mine, an Indian gentleman, recently had a lamp made with a green glass that was nearly five inches across?' No, it was not there but they could make me one. At the next shop the same; at the third, and fourth, and so on. Finally my persistence was rewarded. I found the place where the lamp had been made, and at the cost of ordering another I obtained all the details I wanted. It was news to them, the shopman informed me, that in some parts of India green was the danger colour and therefore tail lamps had to show a green light. The incident made some impression on him and he would be able to identify their customer—who paid in advance and gave no address—among a thousand of his countrymen. Do I succeed in interesting you, Mr Drishna?"

"Do you?" replied Drishna, with a languid yawn. "Do I look interested?"

"You must make allowance for my unfortunate blindness," apologized Carrados, with grim irony.

"Blindness!" exclaimed Drishna, dropping his affectation of unconcern as though electrified by the word, "do you mean—really blind—that you do not see me?"

"Alas, no," admitted Carrados.

The Indian withdrew his right hand from his coat pocket and with a tragic gesture flung a heavy revolver down on the table between them.

"I have had you covered all the time, Mr Carrados, and if I had wished to go and you or your friend had raised a hand to stop me, it would have been at the peril of your lives," he said, in a voice of melancholy triumph. "But what is the use of defying fate, and who successfully evades his destiny? A month ago I went to see one of our people who reads the future and sought to know the course of certain events. 'You need fear no human eye,' was the message given to me. Then she added: 'But when the sightless sees the unseen, make your peace with Yama.' And I thought she spoke of the Great Hereafter!"

"This amounts to an admission of your guilt," exclaimed Mr Carlyle practically.

"I bow to the decree of fate," replied Drishna. "And it is fitting to the universal irony of existence that a blind man should be the instrument. I don't imagine, Mr Carlyle," he added maliciously, "that you, with your eyes, would ever have brought that result about."

"You are a very cold-blooded young scoundrel, sir!" retorted Mr Carlyle. "Good heavens! do you realize that you are responsible for the death of scores of innocent men and women?"

"Do you realise, Mr Carlyle, that you and your Government and your soldiers are responsible for the death of thousands of innocent men and women in my country every day? If England was occupied by the Germans who quartered an army and an administration with their wives and their families and all their expensive paraphernalia on the unfortunate country until the whole nation was reduced to the verge of famine, and the appointment of every new official meant the callous death sentence on a thousand men and women to pay his salary, then if you went to Berlin and wrecked a train you would be hailed a patriot. What Boadicea did and—and Samson, so have I. If they were heroes, so am I."

"Well, upon my word!" cried the highly scandalized Carlyle, "what next! Boadicea was a—er—semi-legendary person, whom we may possibly admire at a distance. Personally, I do not profess to express an opinion. But Samson, I would remind you, is a Biblical character. Samson was mocked as an enemy. You, I do not doubt, have been entertained as a friend."

"And haven't I been mocked and despised and sneered at every day of my life here by your supercilious, superior, empty-headed men?" flashed back Drishna, his eyes leaping into malignity and his voice trembling with sudden passion. "Oh! how I hated them as I passed them in the street and recognized by a thousand petty insults their lordly English contempt for me as an inferior being—a nigger. How I longed with Caligula that a nation had a single neck that I might destroy it at one blow. I loathe you in your complacent hypocrisy, Mr Carlyle, despise and utterly abominate you from an eminence of superiority that you can never even understand."

"I think we are getting rather away from the point, Mr Drishna," interposed Carrados, with the impartiality of a judge. "Unless I am misinformed, you are not so ungallant as to include everyone you have met here in your execration?"

"Ah, no," admitted Drishna, descending into a quite ingenuous frankness. "Much as I hate your men I love your women. How is it possible that a nation should be so divided—its men so dull-witted and offensive, its women so quick, sympathetic and capable of appreciating?"

"But a little expensive, too, at times?" suggested Carrados.

Drishna sighed heavily.

"Yes; it is incredible. It is the generosity of their large nature. My allowance, though what most of you would call noble, has proved quite inadequate. I was compelled to borrow money and the interest became overwhelming. Bankruptcy was impracticable because I should have then been recalled by my people, and much as I detest England a certain reason made the thought of leaving it unbearable."

"Connected with the Arcady Theatre?"

"You know? Well, do not let us introduce the lady's name. In order to restore myself I speculated on the Stock Exchange. My credit was good through my father's position and the standing of the firm to which I am attached. I heard on reliable authority, and very early, that the Central and

Suburban, and the Deferred especially, was safe to fall heavily, through a motor bus amalgamation that was then a secret. I opened a bear account and sold largely. The shares fell, but only fractionally, and I waited. Then, unfortunately, they began to go up. Adverse forces were at work and rumours were put about. I could not stand the settlement, and in order to carry over an account I was literally compelled to deal temporarily with some securities that were not technically my own property."

"Embezzlement, sir," commented Mr Carlyle icily. "But what is embezzlement on the top of wholesale murder!"

"That is what it is called. In my case, however, it was only to be temporary. Unfortunately, the rise continued. Then, at the height of my despair, I chanced to be returning to Swanstead rather earlier than usual one evening, and the train was stopped at a certain signal to let another pass. There was conversation in the carriage and I learned certain details. One said that there would be an accident some day, and so forth. In a flash—as by an inspiration—I saw how the circumstance might be turned to account. A bad accident and the shares would certainly fall and my position would be retrieved. I think Mr Carrados has somehow learned the rest."

"Max," said Mr Carlyle, with emotion, "is there any reason why you should not send your man for a police officer and have this monster arrested on his own confession without further delay?"

"Pray do so, Mr Carrados," acquiesced Drishna. "I shall certainly be hanged, but the speech I shall prepare will ring from one end of India to the other; my memory will be venerated as that of a martyr; and the emancipation of my motherland will be hastened by my sacrifice."

"In other words," commented Carrados, "there will be disturbances at half-a-dozen disaffected places, a few unfortunate police will be clubbed to death, and possibly worse things may happen. That does not suit us, Mr Drishna."

"And how do you propose to prevent it?" asked Drishna, with cool assurance.

"It is very unpleasant being hanged on a dark winter morning; very cold, very friendless, very inhuman. The long trial, the solitude and the confinement, the thoughts of the long sleepless night before, the hangman and the pinioning and the noosing of the rope, are apt to prey on the imagination. Only a very stupid man can take hanging easily."

"What do you want me to do instead, Mr Carrados?" asked Drishna shrewdly.

Carrados's hand closed on the weapon that still lay on the table between them. Without a word he pushed it across.

"I see," commented Drishna, with a short laugh and a gleaming eye. "Shoot myself and hush it up to suit your purpose. Withhold my message to save the exposures of a trial, and keep the flame from the torch of insurrectionary freedom."

"Also," interposed Carrados mildly, "to save your worthy people a good deal of shame, and to save the lady who is nameless the unpleasant necessity of relinquishing the house and the income which you have just settled on her. She certainly would not then venerate your memory."

"What is that?"

"The transaction which you carried through was based on a felony and could not be upheld. The firm you dealt with will go to the courts, and the money, being directly traceable, will be held forfeit as no good consideration passed."

"Max!" cried Mr Carlyle hotly, "you are not going to let this scoundrel cheat the gallows after all?"

"The best use you can make of the gallows is to cheat it, Louis," replied Carrados. "Have you ever reflected what human beings will think of us a hundred years hence?"

"Oh, of course I'm not really in favour of hanging," admitted Mr Carlyle.

"Nobody really is. But we go on hanging. Mr Drishna is a dangerous animal who for the sake of pacific animals must cease to exist. Let his barbarous exploit pass into oblivion with him. The disadvantages of spreading it broadcast immeasurably outweigh the benefits."

"I have considered," announced Drishna. "I will do as you wish."

"Very well," said Carrados. "Here is some plain notepaper. You had better write a letter to someone saying that the financial difficulties in which you are involved make life unbearable."

"But there are no financial difficulties—now."

"That does not matter in the least. It will be put down to an hallucination and taken as showing the state of your mind."

"But what guarantee have we that he will not escape?" whispered Mr Carlyle.

"He cannot escape," replied Carrados tranquilly. "His identity is too clear."

"I have no intention of trying to escape," put in Drishna, as he wrote. "You hardly imagine that I have not considered this eventuality, do you?"

"All the same," murmured the ex-lawyer, "I should like to have a jury behind me. It is one thing to execute a man morally; it is another to do it almost literally."

"Is that all right?" asked Drishna, passing across the letter he had written.

Carrados smiled at this tribute to his perception.

"Quite excellent," he replied courteously. "There is a train at nine-forty. Will that suit you?"

Drishna nodded and stood up. Mr Carlyle had a very uneasy feeling that he ought to do something but could not suggest to himself what.

The next moment he heard his friend heartily thanking the visitor for the assistance he had been in the matter of the Indo-Scythian inscription, as they walked across the hall together. Then a door closed.

"I believe that there is something positively uncanny about Max at times," murmured the perturbed gentleman to himself.

"Max," said Mr Carlyle, when Parkinson had closed the door behind him, "this is Lieutenant Hollyer, whom you consented to see."

"To hear," corrected Carrados, smiling straight into the healthy and rather embarrassed face of the stranger before him. "Mr Hollyer knows of my disability?"

"Mr Carlyle told me," said the young man, "but, as a matter of fact, I had heard of you before, Mr Carrados, from one of our men. It was in connexion with the foundering of the Ivan Saratov."

Carrados wagged his head in good-humoured resignation.

"And the owners were sworn to inviolable secrecy!" he exclaimed. "Well, it is inevitable, I suppose. Not another scuttling case, Mr Hollyer?"

"No, mine is quite a private matter," replied the lieutenant. "My sister, Mrs Creake—but Mr Carlyle would tell you better than I can. He knows all about it."

"No, no; Carlyle is a professional. Let me have it in the rough, Mr Hollyer. My ears are my eyes, you know."

"Very well, sir. I can tell you what there is to tell, right enough, but I feel that when all's said and done it must sound very little to another, although it seems important enough to me."

"We have occasionally found trifles of significance ourselves," said Carrados encouragingly. "Don't let that deter you."

This was the essence of Lieutenant Hollyer's narrative:

"I have a sister, Millicent, who is married to a man called Creake. She is about twenty-eight now and he is at least fifteen years older. Neither my mother (who has since died), nor I, cared very much about Creake. We had nothing particular against him, except, perhaps, the moderate disparity of age, but none of us appeared to have anything in common. He was a dark, taciturn man, and his moody silence froze up conversation. As a result, of course, we didn't see much of each other."

"This, you must understand, was four or five years ago, Max," interposed Mr Carlyle officiously.

Carrados maintained an uncompromising silence. Mr Carlyle blew his nose and contrived to impart a hurt significance into the operation. Then Lieutenant Hollyer continued:

"Millicent married Creake after a very short engagement. It was a frightfully subdued wedding—more like a funeral to me. The man professed to have no relations and apparently he had scarcely any friends or business acquaintances. He was an agent for something or other and had an office off Holborn. I suppose he made a living out of it then, although we knew practically nothing of his private affairs, but I gather that it has been going down since, and I suspect that for the past few years they have been getting along almost entirely on Millicent's little income. You would like the particulars of that?"

"Please," assented Carrados.

"When our father died about seven years ago, he left three thousand pounds. It was invested in Canadian stock and brought in a little over a hundred a year. By his will my mother was to have the income of that for life and on her death it was to pass to Millicent, subject to the payment of a lump sum of five hundred pounds to me. But my father privately suggested to me that if I should have no particular use for the money at the time, he would propose my letting Millicent have the income of it until I did want it, as she would not be particularly well off. You see, Mr Carrados, a great deal more had been spent on my education and advancement than on her; I had my pay, and, of course, I could look out for myself better than a girl could."

"Quite so," agreed Carrados.

"Therefore I did nothing about that," continued the lieutenant. "Three years ago I was over again but I did not see much of them. They were living in lodgings. That was the only time since the marriage that I have seen them until last week. In the meanwhile our mother had died and Millicent had been receiving her income. She wrote me several letters at the time. Otherwise we did not correspond much, but about a year ago she sent me their new address—Brookbend Cottage, Mulling Common—a house that they had taken. When I got two months' leave I invited myself there as a matter of course, fully expecting to stay most of my time with them, but I made an excuse to get away after a week. The place was dismal and unendurable, the whole life and atmosphere indescribably depressing." He looked round with an instinct of caution, leaned forward earnestly, and dropped his voice. "Mr Carrados, it is my absolute conviction that Creake is only waiting for a favourable opportunity to murder Millicent."

"Go on," said Carrados quietly. "A week of the depressing surroundings of Brookbend Cottage would not alone convince you of that, Mr Hollyer."

"I am not so sure," declared Hollyer doubtfully. "There was a feeling of suspicion and—before me—polite hatred that would have gone a good way towards it. All the same there was something more definite. Millicent told me this the day after I went there. There is no doubt that a few months ago Creake deliberately planned to poison her with some weed-killer. She told me the circumstances in a rather distressed moment, but afterwards she refused to speak of it again—even weakly denied it—and, as a matter of fact, it was with the greatest difficulty that I could get her at any time to talk about her husband or his affairs. The gist of it was that she had the strongest suspicion that Creake doctored a bottle of stout which he expected she would drink for her supper when she was alone. The weed-killer, properly labelled, but also in a beer bottle, was kept with other miscellaneous liquids in the same cupboard as the beer but on a high shelf. When he found that it had miscarried he poured away the mixture, washed out the bottle and put in the dregs from another. There is no doubt in my mind that if he had come back and found Millicent dead or dying he would have contrived it to appear that she had made a mistake in the dark and drunk some of the poison before she found out."

"Yes," assented Carrados. "The open way; the safe way."

"You must understand that they live in a very small style, Mr Carrados, and Millicent is almost entirely in the man's power. The only servant they have is a woman who comes in for a few hours every day. The house is lonely and secluded. Creake is sometimes away for days and nights at a time, and Millicent, either through pride or indifference, seems to have dropped off all her old friends and to have made no others. He might poison her, bury the body in the garden, and be a thousand miles away before anyone began even to inquire about her. What am I to do, Mr Carrados?"

"He is less likely to try poison than some other means now," pondered Carrados. "That having failed, his wife will always be on her guard. He may know, or at least suspect, that others know. No.... The common-sense precaution would be for your sister to leave the man, Mr Hollyer. She will not?"

"No," admitted Hollyer, "she will not. I at once urged that." The young man struggled with some hesitation for a moment and then blurted out: "The fact is, Mr Carrados, I don't understand Millicent. She is not the girl she was. She hates Creake and treats him with a silent contempt that eats into their lives like acid, and yet she is so jealous of him that she will let nothing short of death part them. It is a horrible life they lead. I stood it for a week and I must say, much as I dislike my brother-in-law, that he has something to put up with. If only he got into a passion like a man and killed her it wouldn't be altogether incomprehensible."

"That does not concern us," said Carrados. "In a game of this kind one has to take sides and we have taken ours. It remains for us to see that our side wins. You mentioned jealousy, Mr Hollyer. Have you any idea whether Mrs Creake has real ground for it?"

"I should have told you that," replied Lieutenant Hollyer. "I happened to strike up with a newspaper man whose office is in the same block as Creake's. When I mentioned the name he grinned. 'Creake,' he said, 'oh, he's the man with the romantic typist, isn't he?' 'Well, he's my brother-in-law,' I replied. 'What about the typist?' Then the chap shut up like a knife. 'No, no,' he said, 'I didn't know he was married. I don't want to get mixed up in anything of that sort. I only said that he had a typist. Well, what of that? So have we; so has everyone.' There was nothing more to be got out of him, but the remark and the grin meant—well, about as usual, Mr Carrados."

Carrados turned to his friend.

"I suppose you know all about the typist by now, Louis?"

"We have had her under efficient observation, Max," replied Mr Carlyle, with severe dignity.

"Is she unmarried?"

"Yes; so far as ordinary repute goes, she is."

"That is all that is essential for the moment. Mr Hollyer opens up three excellent reasons why this man might wish to dispose of his wife. If we accept the suggestion of poisoning—though we have only a jealous woman's suspicion for it—we add to the wish the determination. Well, we will go forward on that. Have you got a photograph of Mr Creake?"

The lieutenant took out his pocket-book.

"Mr Carlyle asked me for one. Here is the best I could get."

Carrados rang the bell.

"This, Parkinson," he said, when the man appeared, "is a photograph of a Mr——What first name, by the way?"

"Austin," put in Hollyer, who was following everything with a boyish mixture of excitement and subdued importance.

"—of a Mr Austin Creake. I may require you to recognize him."

Parkinson glanced at the print and returned it to his master's hand.

"May I inquire if it is a recent photograph of the gentleman, sir?" he asked.

"About six years ago," said the lieutenant, taking in this new actor in the drama with frank curiosity. "But he is very little changed."

"Thank you, sir. I will endeavour to remember Mr Creake, sir."

Lieutenant Hollyer stood up as Parkinson left the room. The interview seemed to be at an end.

"Oh, there's one other matter," he remarked. "I am afraid that I did rather an unfortunate thing while I was at Brookbend. It seemed to me that as all Millicent's money would probably pass into Creake's hands sooner or later I might as well have my five hundred pounds, if only to help her with afterwards. So I broached the subject and said that I should like to have it now as I had an opportunity for investing."

"And you think?"

"It may possibly influence Creake to act sooner than he otherwise might have done. He may have got possession of the principal even and find it very awkward to replace it."

"So much the better. If your sister is going to be murdered it may as well be done next week as next year so far as I am concerned. Excuse my brutality, Mr Hollyer, but this is simply a case to me and I regard it strategically. Now Mr Carlyle's organization can look after Mrs Creake for a few weeks but it cannot look after her for ever. By increasing the immediate risk we diminish the permanent risk."

"I see," agreed Hollyer. "I'm awfully uneasy but I'm entirely in your hands."

"Then we will give Mr Creake every inducement and every opportunity to get to work. Where are you staying now?"

"Just now with some friends at St Albans."

"That is too far." The inscrutable eyes retained their tranquil depth but a new quality of quickening interest in the voice made Mr Carlyle forget the weight and burden of his ruffled dignity. "Give me a few minutes, please. The cigarettes are behind you, Mr Hollyer." The blind man walked to the window and seemed to look out over the cypress-shaded lawn. The lieutenant lit a cigarette and Mr Carlyle picked up Punch. Then Carrados turned round again.

"You are prepared to put your own arrangements aside?" he demanded of his visitor.

"Certainly."

"Very well. I want you to go down now—straight from here—to Brookbend Cottage. Tell your sister that your leave is unexpectedly cut short and that you sail to-morrow."

"The Martian?"

"No, no; the Martian doesn't sail. Look up the movements on your way there and pick out a boat that does. Say you are transferred. Add that you expect to be away only two or three months and that you really want the five hundred pounds by the time of your return. Don't stay in the house long, please."

"I understand, sir."

"St Albans is too far. Make your excuse and get away from there to-day. Put up somewhere in town, where you will be in reach of the telephone. Let Mr Carlyle and myself know where you are. Keep out of Creake's way. I don't want actually to tie you down to the house, but we may require your services. We will let you know at the first sign of anything doing and if there is nothing to be done we must release you."

"I don't mind that. Is there nothing more that I can do now?"

"Nothing. In going to Mr Carlyle you have done the best thing possible; you have put your sister into the care of the shrewdest man in London." Whereat the object of this quite unexpected eulogy found himself becoming covered with modest confusion.

"Well, Max?" remarked Mr Carlyle tentatively when they were alone.

"Well, Louis?"

"Of course it wasn't worth while rubbing it in before young Hollyer, but, as a matter of fact, every single man carries the life of any other man—only one, mind you—in his hands, do what you will."

"Provided he doesn't bungle," acquiesced Carrados.

"Quite so."

"And also that he is absolutely reckless of the consequences."

"Of course."

"Two rather large provisos. Creake is obviously susceptible to both. Have you seen him?"

"No. As I told you, I put a man on to report his habits in town. Then, two days ago, as the case seemed to promise some interest—for he certainly is deeply involved with the typist, Max, and the thing might take a sensational turn any time—I went down to Mulling Common myself. Although the house is lonely it is on the electric tram route. You know the sort of market garden rurality that about a dozen miles out of London offers—alternate bricks and cabbages. It was easy enough to get to know about Creake locally. He mixes with no one there, goes into town at irregular times but generally every day, and is reputed to be devilish hard to get money out of. Finally I made the acquaintance of an old fellow who used to do a day's gardening at Brookbend occasionally. He has a cottage and a garden of his own with a greenhouse, and the business cost me the price of a pound of tomatoes."

"Was it—a profitable investment?"

"As tomatoes, yes; as information, no. The old fellow had the fatal disadvantage from our point of view of labouring under a grievance. A few weeks ago Creake told him that he would not require him again as he was going to do his own gardening in future."

"That is something, Louis."

"If only Creake was going to poison his wife with hyoscyamine and bury her, instead of blowing her up with a dynamite cartridge and claiming that it came in among the coal."

"True, true. Still——"

"However, the chatty old soul had a simple explanation for everything that Creake did. Creake was mad. He had even seen him flying a kite in his garden where it was bound to get wrecked among the trees. 'A lad of ten would have known better,' he declared. And certainly the kite did get wrecked, for I saw it hanging over the road myself. But that a sane man should spend his time 'playing with a toy' was beyond him."

"A good many men have been flying kites of various kinds lately," said Carrados. "Is he interested in aviation?"

"I dare say. He appears to have some knowledge of scientific subjects. Now what do you want me to do, Max?"

"Will you do it?"

"Implicitly—subject to the usual reservations."

"Keep your man on Creake in town and let me have his reports after you have seen them. Lunch with me here now. 'Phone up to your office that you are detained on unpleasant business and then give the deserving Parkinson an afternoon off by looking after me while we take a motor run round Mulling Common. If we have time we might go on to Brighton, feed at the 'Ship,' and come back in the cool."

"Amiable and thrice lucky mortal," sighed Mr Carlyle, his glance wandering round the room.

But, as it happened, Brighton did not figure in that day's itinerary. It had been Carrados's intention merely to pass Brookbend Cottage on this occasion, relying on his highly developed faculties, aided by Mr Carlyle's description, to inform him of the surroundings. A hundred yards before they reached the house he had given an order to his chauffeur to drop into the lowest speed and they were leisurely drawing past when a discovery by Mr Carlyle modified their plans.

"By Jupiter!" that gentleman suddenly exclaimed, "there's a board up, Max. The place is to be let."

Carrados picked up the tube again. A couple of sentences passed and the car stopped by the roadside, a score of paces past the limit of the garden. Mr Carlyle took out his notebook and wrote down the address of a firm of house agents.

"You might raise the bonnet and have a look at the engines, Harris," said Carrados. "We want to be occupied here for a few minutes."

"This is sudden; Hollyer knew nothing of their leaving," remarked Mr Carlyle.

"Probably not for three months yet. All the same, Louis, we will go on to the agents and get a card to view, whether we use it to-day or not."

A thick hedge, in its summer dress effectively screening the house beyond from public view, lay between the garden and the road. Above the hedge showed an occasional shrub; at the corner nearest to the car a chestnut flourished. The wooden gate, once white; which they had passed, was grimed and rickety. The road itself was still the unpretentious country lane that the advent of the electric car had found it. When Carrados had taken in these details there seemed little else to notice. He was on the point of giving Harris the order to go on when his ear caught a trivial sound.

"Someone is coming out of the house, Louis," he warned his friend. "It may be Hollyer, but he ought to have gone by this time."

"I don't hear anyone," replied the other, but as he spoke a door banged noisily and Mr Carlyle slipped into another seat and ensconced himself behind a copy of The Globe.

"Creake himself," he whispered across the car, as a man appeared at the gate. "Hollyer was right; he is hardly changed. Waiting for a car, I suppose."

But a car very soon swung past them from the direction in which Mr Creake was looking and it did not interest him. For a minute or two longer he continued to look expectantly along the road. Then he walked slowly up the drive back to the house.

"We will give him five or ten minutes," decided Carrados. "Harris is behaving very naturally."

Before even the shorter period had run out they were repaid. A telegraph-boy cycled leisurely along the road, and, leaving his machine at the gate, went up to the cottage. Evidently there was no reply, for in less than a minute he was trundling past them back again. Round the bend an approaching tram clanged its bell noisily, and, quickened by the warning sound, Mr Creake again appeared, this time with a small portmanteau in his hand. With a backward glance he hurried on towards the next stopping-place, and, boarding the car as it slackened down, he was carried out of their knowledge.

"Very convenient of Mr Creake," remarked Carrados, with quiet satisfaction. "We will now get the order and go over the house in his absence. It might be useful to have a look at the wire as well."

"It might, Max," acquiesced Mr Carlyle a little dryly. "But if it is, as it probably is, in Creake's pocket, how do you propose to get it?"

"By going to the post office, Louis."

"Quite so. Have you ever tried to see a copy of a telegram addressed to someone else?"

"I don't think I have ever had occasion yet," admitted Carrados. "Have you?"

"In one or two cases I have perhaps been an accessory to the act. It is generally a matter either of extreme delicacy or considerable expenditure."

"Then for Hollyer's sake we will hope for the former here." And Mr Carlyle smiled darkly and hinted that he was content to wait for a friendly revenge.

A little later, having left the car at the beginning of the straggling High Street, the two men called at the village post office. They had already visited the house agent and obtained an order to view Brookbend Cottage, declining, with some difficulty, the clerk's persistent offer to accompany them. The reason was soon forthcoming. "As a matter of fact," explained the young man, "the present tenant is under our notice to leave."

"Unsatisfactory, eh?" said Carrados encouragingly.

"He's a corker," admitted the clerk, responding to the friendly tone. "Fifteen months and not a doit of rent have we had. That's why I should have liked——"

"We will make every allowance," replied Carrados.

The post office occupied one side of a stationer's shop. It was not without some inward trepidation that Mr Carlyle found himself committed to the adventure. Carrados, on the other hand, was the personification of bland unconcern.

"You have just sent a telegram to Brookbend Cottage," he said to the young lady behind the brasswork lattice. "We think it may have come inaccurately and should like a repeat." He took out his purse. "What is the fee?"

The request was evidently not a common one. "Oh," said the girl uncertainly, "wait a minute, please." She turned to a pile of telegram duplicates behind the desk and ran a doubtful finger along the upper sheets. "I think this is all right. You want it repeated?"

"Please." Just a tinge of questioning surprise gave point to the courteous tone.

"It will be fourpence. If there is an error the amount will be refunded."

Carrados put down a coin and received his change.

"Will it take long?" he inquired carelessly, as he pulled on his glove.

"You will most likely get it within a quarter of an hour," she replied.

"Now you've done it," commented Mr Carlyle, as they walked back to their car. "How do you propose to get that telegram, Max?"

"Ask for it," was the laconic explanation.

And, stripping the artifice of any elaboration, he simply asked for it and got it. The car, posted at a convenient bend in the road, gave him a warning note as the telegraph-boy approached. Then Carrados took up a convincing attitude with his hand on the gate while Mr Carlyle lent himself to the semblance of a departing friend. That was the inevitable impression when the boy rode up.

"Creake, Brookbend Cottage?" inquired Carrados, holding out his hand, and without a second thought the boy gave him the envelope and rode away on the assurance that there would be no reply.

"Some day, my friend," remarked Mr Carlyle, looking nervously towards the unseen house, "your ingenuity will get you into a tight corner."

"Then my ingenuity must get me out again," was the retort. "Let us have our 'view' now. The telegram can wait."

An untidy workwoman took their order and left them standing at the door. Presently a lady whom they both knew to be Mrs Creake appeared.

"You wish to see over the house?" she said, in a voice that was utterly devoid of any interest. Then, without waiting for a reply, she turned to the nearest door and threw it open.

"This is the drawing-room," she said, standing aside.

They walked into a sparsely furnished, damp-smelling room and made a pretence of looking round, while Mrs Creake remained silent and aloof.

"The dining-room," she continued, crossing the narrow hall and opening another door.

Mr Carlyle ventured a genial commonplace in the hope of inducing conversation. The result was not encouraging. Doubtless they would have gone through the house under the same frigid guidance had not Carrados been at fault in a way that Mr Carlyle had never known him fail before. In crossing the hall he stumbled over a mat and almost fell.

"Pardon my clumsiness," he said to the lady. "I am, unfortunately, quite blind. But," he added, with a smile, to turn off the mishap, "even a blind man must have a house."

The man who had eyes was surprised to see a flood of colour rush into Mrs Creake's face.

"Blind!" she exclaimed, "oh, I beg your pardon. Why did you not tell me? You might have fallen."

"I generally manage fairly well," he replied. "But, of course, in a strange house——"

She put her hand on his arm very lightly.

"You must let me guide you, just a little," she said.

The house, without being large, was full of passages and inconvenient turnings. Carrados asked an occasional question and found Mrs Creake quite amiable without effusion. Mr Carlyle followed them from room to room in the hope, though scarcely the expectation, of learning something that might be useful.

"This is the last one. It is the largest bedroom," said their guide. Only two of the upper rooms were fully furnished and Mr Carlyle at once saw, as

Carrados knew without seeing, that this was the one which the Creakes occupied.

"A very pleasant outlook," declared Mr Carlyle.

"Oh, I suppose so," admitted the lady vaguely. The room, in fact, looked over the leafy garden and the road beyond. It had a French window opening on to a small balcony, and to this, under the strange influence that always attracted him to light, Carrados walked.

"I expect that there is a certain amount of repair needed?" he said, after standing there a moment.

"I am afraid there would be," she confessed.

"I ask because there is a sheet of metal on the floor here," he continued. "Now that, in an old house, spells dry rot to the wary observer."

"My husband said that the rain, which comes in a little under the window, was rotting the boards there," she replied. "He put that down recently. I had not noticed anything myself."

It was the first time she had mentioned her husband; Mr Carlyle pricked up his ears.

"Ah, that is a less serious matter," said Carrados. "May I step out on to the balcony?"

"Oh yes, if you like to." Then, as he appeared to be fumbling at the catch, "Let me open it for you."

But the window was already open, and Carrados, facing the various points of the compass, took in the bearings.

"A sunny, sheltered corner," he remarked. "An ideal spot for a deck-chair and a book."

She shrugged her shoulders half contemptuously.

"I dare say," she replied, "but I never use it."

"Sometimes, surely," he persisted mildly. "It would be my favourite retreat. But then——"

"I was going to say that I had never even been out on it, but that would not be quite true. It has two uses for me, both equally romantic; I occasionally shake a duster from it, and when my husband returns late without his latchkey he wakes me up and I come out here and drop him mine."

Further revelation of Mr Creake's nocturnal habits was cut off, greatly to Mr Carlyle's annoyance, by a cough of unmistakable significance from the foot of the stairs. They had heard a trade cart drive up to the gate, a knock at the door, and the heavy-footed woman tramp along the hall.

"Excuse me a minute, please," said Mrs Creake.

"Louis," said Carrados, in a sharp whisper, the moment they were alone, "stand against the door."

With extreme plausibility Mr Carlyle began to admire a picture so situated that while he was there it was impossible to open the door more than a few inches. From that position he observed his confederate go through the curious procedure of kneeling down on the bedroom floor and for a full minute pressing his ear to the sheet of metal that had already engaged his attention. Then he rose to his feet, nodded, dusted his trousers, and Mr Carlyle moved to a less equivocal position.

"What a beautiful rose-tree grows up your balcony," remarked Carrados, stepping into the room as Mrs Creake returned. "I suppose you are very fond of gardening?"

"I detest it," she replied.

"But this Glorie, so carefully trained——?"

"Is it?" she replied. "I think my husband was nailing it up recently." By some strange fatality Carrados's most aimless remarks seemed to involve the absent Mr Creake. "Do you care to see the garden?"

The garden proved to be extensive and neglected. Behind the house was chiefly orchard. In front, some semblance of order had been kept up; here it was lawn and shrubbery, and the drive they had walked along. Two things interested Carrados: the soil at the foot of the balcony, which he declared on examination to be particularly suitable for roses, and the fine chestnut-tree in the corner by the road.

As they walked back to the car Mr Carlyle lamented that they had learned so little of Creake's movements.

"Perhaps the telegram will tell us something," suggested Carrados. "Read it, Louis."

Mr Carlyle cut open the envelope, glanced at the enclosure, and in spite of his disappointment could not restrain a chuckle.

"My poor Max," he explained, "you have put yourself to an amount of ingenious trouble for nothing. Creake is evidently taking a few days' holiday and prudently availed himself of the Meteorological Office forecast before going. Listen: 'Immediate prospect for London warm and settled. Further outlook cooler but fine.' Well, well; I did get a pound of tomatoes for my fourpence."

"You certainly scored there, Louis," admitted Carrados, with humorous appreciation. "I wonder," he added speculatively, "whether it is Creake's peculiar taste usually to spend his week-end holiday in London."

"Eh?" exclaimed Mr Carlyle, looking at the words again, "by gad, that's rum, Max. They go to Weston-super-Mare. Why on earth should he want to know about London?"

"I can make a guess, but before we are satisfied I must come here again. Take another look at that kite, Louis. Are there a few yards of string hanging loose from it?"

"Yes, there are."

"Rather thick string—unusually thick for the purpose?"

"Yes; but how do you know?"

As they drove home again Carrados explained, and Mr Carlyle sat aghast, saying incredulously: "Good God, Max, is it possible?"

An hour later he was satisfied that it was possible. In reply to his inquiry someone in his office telephoned him the information that "they" had left Paddington by the four-thirty for Weston.

It was more than a week after his introduction to Carrados that Lieutenant Hollyer had a summons to present himself at The Turrets again. He found Mr Carlyle already there and the two friends awaiting his arrival.

"I stayed in all day after hearing from you this morning, Mr Carrados," he said, shaking hands. "When I got your second message I was all ready to walk straight out of the house. That's how I did it in the time. I hope everything is all right?"

"Excellent," replied Carrados. "You'd better have something before we start. We probably have a long and perhaps an exciting night before us."

"And certainly a wet one," assented the lieutenant. "It was thundering over Mulling way as I came along."

"That is why you are here," said his host. "We are waiting for a certain message before we start, and in the meantime you may as well understand what we expect to happen. As you saw, there is a thunderstorm coming on. The Meteorological Office morning forecast predicted it for the whole of London if the conditions remained. That was why I kept you in readiness. Within an hour it is now inevitable that we shall experience a deluge. Here and there damage will be done to trees and buildings; here and there a person will probably be struck and killed."

"Yes."

"It is Mr Creake's intention that his wife should be among the victims."

"I don't exactly follow," said Hollyer, looking from one man to the other. "I quite admit that Creake would be immensely relieved if such a thing did happen, but the chance is surely an absurdly remote one."

"Yet unless we intervene it is precisely what a coroner's jury will decide has happened. Do you know whether your brother-in-law has any practical knowledge of electricity, Mr Hollyer?"

"I cannot say. He was so reserved, and we really knew so little of him——"

"Yet in 1896 an Austin Creake contributed an article on 'Alternating Currents' to the American Scientific World. That would argue a fairly intimate acquaintanceship."

"But do you mean that he is going to direct a flash of lightning?"

"Only into the minds of the doctor who conducts the post-mortem, and the coroner. This storm, the opportunity for which he has been waiting for weeks, is merely the cloak to his act. The weapon which he has planned to use—scarcely less powerful than lightning but much more tractable—is the high voltage current of electricity that flows along the tram wire at his gate."

"Oh!" exclaimed Lieutenant Hollyer, as the sudden revelation struck him.

"Some time between eleven o'clock to-night—about the hour when your sister goes to bed—and one-thirty in the morning—the time up to which he can rely on the current—Creake will throw a stone up at the balcony window. Most of his preparation has long been made; it only remains for him to connect up a short length to the window handle and a longer one at the other end to tap the live wire. That done, he will wake his wife in the way I have said. The moment she moves the catch of the window—and he has carefully filed its parts to ensure perfect contact—she will be electrocuted as effectually as if she sat in the executioner's chair in Sing Sing prison."

"But what are we doing here!" exclaimed Hollyer, starting to his feet, pale and horrified. "It is past ten now and anything may happen."

"Quite natural, Mr Hollyer," said Carrados reassuringly, "but you need have no anxiety. Creake is being watched, the house is being watched, and your sister is as safe as if she slept to-night in Windsor Castle. Be assured that whatever happens he will not be allowed to complete his scheme; but it is desirable to let him implicate himself to the fullest limit. Your brother-in-law, Mr Hollyer, is a man with a peculiar capacity for taking pains."

"He is a damned cold-blooded scoundrel!" exclaimed the young officer fiercely. "When I think of Millicent five years ago——"

"Well, for that matter, an enlightened nation has decided that electrocution is the most humane way of removing its superfluous citizens," suggested Carrados mildly. "He is certainly an ingenious-minded gentleman. It is his misfortune that in Mr Carlyle he was fated to be opposed by an even subtler brain——"

"No, no! Really, Max!" protested the embarrassed gentleman.

"Mr Hollyer will be able to judge for himself when I tell him that it was Mr Carlyle who first drew attention to the significance of the abandoned kite," insisted Carrados firmly. "Then, of course, its object became plain to me—as indeed to anyone. For ten minutes, perhaps, a wire must be carried from the overhead line to the chestnut-tree. Creake has everything in his favour, but it is just within possibility that the driver of an inopportune tram might notice the appendage. What of that? Why, for more than a week he has seen a derelict kite with its yards of trailing string hanging in the tree. A very calculating mind, Mr Hollyer. It would be interesting to know what line of action Mr Creake has mapped out for himself afterwards. I expect he has half-a-dozen artistic little touches up his sleeve. Possibly he would merely singe his wife's hair, burn her feet with a red-hot poker, shiver the glass of the French window, and be content with that to let well alone. You see, lightning is so varied in its effects that whatever he did or did not do would be right. He is in the impregnable position of the body showing all the symptoms of death by lightning shock and nothing else but lightning to account for it—a dilated eye, heart contracted in systole, bloodless lungs shrunk to a third the normal weight, and all the rest of it. When he has removed a few outward traces of his work Creake might quite safely 'discover' his dead wife and rush off for the nearest doctor. Or he may have decided to arrange a convincing alibi, and creep away, leaving the discovery to another. We shall never know; he will make no confession."

"I wish it was well over," admitted Hollyer. "I'm not particularly jumpy, but this gives me a touch of the creeps."

"Three more hours at the worst, Lieutenant," said Carrados cheerfully. "Ah-ha, something is coming through now."

He went to the telephone and received a message from one quarter; then made another connection and talked for a few minutes with someone else.

"Everything working smoothly," he remarked between times over his shoulder. "Your sister has gone to bed, Mr Hollyer."

Then he turned to the house telephone and distributed his orders.

"So we," he concluded, "must get up."

By the time they were ready a large closed motor car was waiting. The lieutenant thought he recognized Parkinson in the well-swathed form beside the driver, but there was no temptation to linger for a second on the steps. Already the stinging rain had lashed the drive into the semblance of a frothy estuary; all round the lightning jagged its course through the incessant tremulous glow of more distant lightning, while the thunder only ceased its muttering to turn at close quarters and crackle viciously.

"One of the few things I regret missing," remarked Carrados tranquilly; "but I hear a good deal of colour in it."

The car slushed its way down to the gate, lurched a little heavily across the dip into the road, and, steadying as it came upon the straight, began to hum contentedly along the deserted highway.

"We are not going direct?" suddenly inquired Hollyer, after they had travelled perhaps half-a-dozen miles. The night was bewildering enough but he had the sailor's gift for location.

"No; through Hunscott Green and then by a field-path to the orchard at the back," replied Carrados. "Keep a sharp look out for the man with the lantern about here, Harris," he called through the tube.

"Something flashing just ahead, sir," came the reply, and the car slowed down and stopped.

Carrados dropped the near window as a man in glistening waterproof stepped from the shelter of a lich-gate and approached.

"Inspector Beedel, sir," said the stranger, looking into the car.

"Quite right, Inspector," said Carrados. "Get in."

"I have a man with me, sir."

"We can find room for him as well."

"We are very wet."

"So shall we all be soon."

The lieutenant changed his seat and the two burly forms took places side by side. In less than five minutes the car stopped again, this time in a grassy country lane.

"Now we have to face it," announced Carrados. "The inspector will show us the way."

The car slid round and disappeared into the night, while Beedel led the party to a stile in the hedge. A couple of fields brought them to the Brookbend boundary. There a figure stood out of the black foliage, exchanged a few words with their guide and piloted them along the shadows of the orchard to the back door of the house.

"You will find a broken pane near the catch of the scullery window," said the blind man.

"Right, sir," replied the inspector. "I have it. Now who goes through?"

"Mr Hollyer will open the door for us. I'm afraid you must take off your boots and all wet things, Lieutenant. We cannot risk a single spot inside."

They waited until the back door opened, then each one divested himself in a similar manner and passed into the kitchen, where the remains of a fire still burned. The man from the orchard gathered together the discarded garments and disappeared again.

Carrados turned to the lieutenant.

"A rather delicate job for you now, Mr Hollyer. I want you to go up to your sister, wake her, and get her into another room with as little fuss as possible. Tell her as much as you think fit and let her understand that her very life depends on absolute stillness when she is alone. Don't be unduly hurried, but not a glimmer of a light, please."

Ten minutes passed by the measure of the battered old alarum on the dresser shelf before the young man returned.

"I've had rather a time of it," he reported, with a nervous laugh, "but I think it will be all right now. She is in the spare room."

"Then we will take our places. You and Parkinson come with me to the bedroom. Inspector, you have your own arrangements. Mr Carlyle will be with you."

They dispersed silently about the house. Hollyer glanced apprehensively at the door of the spare room as they passed it but within was as quiet as the grave. Their room lay at the other end of the passage.

"You may as well take your place in the bed now, Hollyer," directed Carrados when they were inside and the door closed. "Keep well down among the clothes. Creake has to get up on the balcony, you know, and he will probably peep through the window, but he dare come no farther. Then when he begins to throw up stones slip on this dressing-gown of your sister's. I'll tell you what to do after."

The next sixty minutes drew out into the longest hour that the lieutenant had ever known. Occasionally he heard a whisper pass between the two men who stood behind the window curtains, but he could see nothing. Then Carrados threw a guarded remark in his direction.

"He is in the garden now."

Something scraped slightly against the outer wall. But the night was full of wilder sounds, and in the house the furniture and the boards creaked and sprung between the yawling of the wind among the chimneys, the rattle of the thunder and the pelting of the rain. It was a time to quicken the steadiest pulse, and when the crucial moment came, when a pebble suddenly rang against the pane with a sound that the tense waiting magnified into a shivering crash, Hollyer leapt from the bed on the instant.

"Easy, easy," warned Carrados feelingly. "We will wait for another knock." He passed something across. "Here is a rubber glove. I have cut the wire but you had better put it on. Stand just for a moment at the window, move the catch so that it can blow open a little, and drop immediately. Now."

Another stone had rattled against the glass. For Hollyer to go through his part was the work merely of seconds, and with a few touches Carrados spread the dressing-gown to more effective disguise about the extended form. But an unforeseen and in the circumstances rather horrible interval followed, for Creake, in accordance with some detail of his never-revealed plan, continued to shower missile after missile against the panes until even the unimpressionable Parkinson shivered.

"The last act," whispered Carrados, a moment after the throwing had ceased. "He has gone round to the back. Keep as you are. We take cover now." He pressed behind the arras of an extemporized wardrobe, and the spirit of emptiness and desolation seemed once more to reign over the lonely house.

From half-a-dozen places of concealment ears were straining to catch the first guiding sound. He moved very stealthily, burdened, perhaps, by some strange scruple in the presence of the tragedy that he had not feared to contrive, paused for a moment at the bedroom door, then opened it very quietly, and in the fickle light read the consummation of his hopes.

"At last!" they heard the sharp whisper drawn from his relief. "At last!"

He took another step and two shadows seemed to fall upon him from behind, one on either side. With primitive instinct a cry of terror and surprise escaped him as he made a desperate movement to wrench himself free, and for a short second he almost succeeded in dragging one hand into a pocket. Then his wrists slowly came together and the handcuffs closed.

"I am Inspector Beedel," said the man on his right side. "You are charged with the attempted murder of your wife, Millicent Creake."

"You are mad," retorted the miserable creature, falling into a desperate calmness. "She has been struck by lightning."

"No, you blackguard, she hasn't," wrathfully exclaimed his brother-in-law, jumping up. "Would you like to see her?"

"I also have to warn you," continued the inspector impassively, "that anything you say may be used as evidence against you."

A startled cry from the farther end of the passage arrested their attention.

"Mr Carrados," called Hollyer, "oh, come at once."

At the open door of the other bedroom stood the lieutenant, his eyes still turned towards something in the room beyond, a little empty bottle in his hand.

"Dead!" he exclaimed tragically, with a sob, "with this beside her. Dead just when she would have been free of the brute."

The blind man passed into the room, sniffed the air, and laid a gentle hand on the pulseless heart.

"Yes," he replied. "That, Hollyer, does not always appeal to the woman, strange to say."

The Clever Mrs. Straithwaite

Mr Carlyle had arrived at The Turrets in the very best possible spirits. Everything about him, from his immaculate white spats to the choice gardenia in his buttonhole, from the brisk decision with which he took the front-door steps to the bustling importance with which he had positively brushed Parkinson aside at the door of the library, proclaimed consequence and the extremely good terms on which he stood with himself.

"Prepare yourself, Max," he exclaimed. "If I hinted at a case of exceptional delicacy that will certainly interest you by its romantic possibilities——?"

"I should have the liveliest misgivings. Ten to one it would be a jewel mystery," hazarded Carrados, as his friend paused with the point of his communication withheld, after the manner of a quizzical youngster with a promised bon-bon held behind his back. "If you made any more of it I should reluctantly be forced to the conclusion that the case involved a society scandal connected with a priceless pearl necklace."

Mr Carlyle's face fell.

"Then it is in the papers, after all?" he said, with an air of disappointment.

"What is in the papers, Louis?"

"Some hint of the fraudulent insurance of the Hon. Mrs Straithwaite's pearl necklace," replied Carlyle.

"Possibly," admitted Carrados. "But so far I have not come across it."

Mr Carlyle stared at his friend, and marching up to the table brought his hand down on it with an arresting slap.

"Then what in the name of goodness are you talking about, may I ask?" he demanded caustically. "If you know nothing of the Straithwaite affair, Max, what other pearl necklace case are you referring to?"

Carrados assumed the air of mild deprecation with which he frequently apologized for a blind man venturing to make a discovery.

"A philosopher once made the remark——"

"Had it anything to do with Mrs Straithwaite's—the Hon. Mrs Straithwaite's—pearl necklace? And let me warn you, Max, that I have read a good deal both of Mill and Spencer at odd times."

"It was neither Mill nor Spencer. He had a German name, so I will not mention it. He made the observation, which, of course, we recognize as an obvious commonplace when once it has been expressed, that in order to have an accurate knowledge of what a man will do on any occasion it is only necessary to study a single characteristic action of his."

"Utterly impracticable," declared Mr Carlyle.

"I therefore knew that when you spoke of a case of exceptional interest to me, what you really meant, Louis, was a case of exceptional interest to you."

Mr Carlyle's sudden thoughtful silence seemed to admit that possibly there might be something in the point.

"By applying, almost unconsciously, the same useful rule, I became aware that a mystery connected with a valuable pearl necklace and a beautiful young society belle would appeal the most strongly to your romantic imagination."

"Romantic! I, romantic? Thirty-five and a private inquiry agent! You are—positively feverish, Max."

"Incurably romantic—or you would have got over it by now: the worst kind."

"Max, this may prove a most important and interesting case. Will you be serious and discuss it?"

"Jewel cases are rarely either important or interesting. Pearl necklace mysteries, in nine cases out of ten, spring from the miasma of social pretence and vapid competition and only concern people who do not matter in the least. The only attractive thing about them is the name. They are so barren of originality that a criminological Linnæus could classify them with absolute nicety. I'll tell you what, we'll draw up a set of tables giving the solution to every possible pearl necklace case for the next twenty-one years."

"We will do any mortal thing you like, Max, if you will allow Parkinson to administer a bromo-seltzer and then enable me to meet the officials of the Direct Insurance without a blush."

For three minutes Carrados picked his unerring way among the furniture as he paced the room silently but with irresolution in his face. Twice his hand went to a paper-covered book lying on his desk, and twice he left it untouched.

"Have you ever been in the lion-house at feeding-time, Louis?" he demanded abruptly.

"In the very remote past, possibly," admitted Mr Carlyle guardedly.

"As the hour approaches it is impossible to interest the creatures with any other suggestion than that of raw meat. You came a day too late, Louis." He picked up the book and skimmed it adroitly into Mr Carlyle's hands. "I have already scented the gore, and tasted in imagination the joy of tearing choice morsels from other similarly obsessed animals."

"'Catalogue des monnaies grecques et romaines,'" read the gentleman. "'To be sold by auction at the Hotel Drouet, Paris, salle 8, April the 24th, 25th, etc.' H'm." He turned to the plates of photogravure illustration which gave an air to the volume. "This is an event, I suppose?"

"It is the sort of dispersal we get about once in three years," replied Carrados. "I seldom attend the little sales, but I save up and then have a week's orgy."

"And when do you go?"

"To-day. By the afternoon boat—Folkestone. I have already taken rooms at Mascot's. I'm sorry it has fallen so inopportunely, Louis."

Mr Carlyle rose to the occasion with a display of extremely gentlemanly feeling—which had the added merit of being quite genuine.

"My dear chap, your regrets only serve to remind me how much I owe to you already. Bon voyage, and the most desirable of Eu—Eu—well, perhaps it would be safer to say, of Kimons, for your collection."

"I suppose," pondered Carrados, "this insurance business might have led to other profitable connexions?"

"That is quite true," admitted his friend. "I have been trying for some time—but do not think any more of it, Max."

"What time is it?" demanded Carrados suddenly.

"Eleven-twenty-five."

"Good. Has any officious idiot had anyone arrested?"

"No, it is only——"

"Never mind. Do you know much of the case?"

"Practically nothing as yet, unfortunately. I came——"

"Excellent. Everything is on our side. Louis, I won't go this afternoon—I will put off till the night boat from Dover. That will give us nine hours."

"Nine hours?" repeated the mystified Carlyle, scarcely daring to put into thought the scandalous inference that Carrados's words conveyed.

"Nine full hours. A pearl necklace case that cannot at least be left straight after nine hours' work will require a column to itself in our chart. Now, Louis, where does this Direct Insurance live?"

Carlyle had allowed his blind friend to persuade him into—as they had seemed at the beginning—many mad enterprises. But none had ever, in the light of his own experience, seemed so foredoomed to failure as when, at eleven-thirty, Carrados ordered his luggage to be on the platform of Charing Cross Station at eight-fifty and then turned light-heartedly to the task of elucidating the mystery of Mrs Straithwaite's pearl necklace in the interval.

The head office of the Direct and Intermediate Insurance Company proved to be in Victoria Street. Thanks to Carrados's speediest car, they entered the building as the clocks of Westminster were striking twelve, but for the next twenty minutes they were consigned to the general office while Mr Carlyle fumed and displayed his watch ostentatiously. At last a clerk slid off his stool by the speaking-tube and approached them.

"Mr Carlyle?" he said. "The General Manager will see you now, but as he has another appointment in ten minutes he will be glad if you will make your business as short as possible. This way, please."

Mr Carlyle bit his lip at the pompous formality of the message but he was too experienced to waste any words about it and with a mere nod he followed, guiding his friend until they reached the Manager's room. But, though subservient to circumstance, he was far from being negligible when he wished to create an impression.

"Mr Carrados has been good enough to give us a consultation over this small affair," he said, with just the necessary touches of deference and condescension that it was impossible either to miss or to resent. "Unfortunately he can do little more as he has to leave almost at once to direct an important case in Paris."

The General Manager conveyed little, either in his person or his manner, of the brisk precision that his message seemed to promise. The name of Carrados struck him as being somewhat familiar—something a little removed from the routine of his business and a matter therefore that he could unbend over. He continued to stand comfortably before his office fire, making up by a tolerant benignity of his hard and bulbous eye for the physical deprivation that his attitude entailed on his visitors.

"Paris, egad?" he grunted. "Something in your line that France can take from us since the days of—what's-his-name—Vidocq, eh? Clever fellow, that, what? Wasn't it about him and the Purloined Letter?"

Carrados smiled discreetly.

"Capital, wasn't it?" he replied. "But there is something else that Paris can learn from London, more in your way, sir. Often when I drop in to see the principal of one of their chief houses or the head of a Government department, we fall into an entertaining discussion of this or that subject that may be on the tapis. 'Ah, monsieur,' I say, after perhaps half-an-hour's conversation, 'it is very amiable of you and sometimes I regret our insular methods, but it is not thus that great businesses are formed. At home, if I call upon one of our princes of industry—a railway director, a merchant, or the head of one of our leading insurance companies—nothing will tempt him for a moment from the stern outline of the business in hand. You are too complaisant; the merest gossip takes advantage of you.'"

"That's quite true," admitted the General Manager, occupying the revolving chair at his desk and assuming a serious and very determined expression. "Slackers, I call them. Now, Mr Carlyle, where are we in this business?"

"I have your letter of yesterday. We should naturally like all the particulars you can give us."

The Manager threw open a formidable-looking volume with an immense display of energy, sharply flattened some typewritten pages that had ventured to raise their heads, and lifted an impressive finger.

"We start here, the 27th of January. On that day Karsfeld, the Princess Street jeweller, y'know, who acted as our jewellery assessor, forwards a proposal of the Hon. Mrs Straithwaite to insure a pearl necklace against theft. Says that he has had an opportunity of examining it and passes it at five thousand pounds. That business goes through in the ordinary way; the premium is paid and the policy taken out.

"A couple of months later Karsfeld has a little unpleasantness with us and resigns. Resignation accepted. We have nothing against him, you understand. At the same time there is an impression among the directors that he has been perhaps a little too easy in his ways, a little too—let us say, expansive, in some of his valuations and too accommodating to his own clients in recommending to us business of a—well—speculative basis; business that we do not care about and which we now feel is foreign to our traditions as a firm. However"—the General Manager threw apart his stubby hands as though he would shatter any fabric of criminal intention that he might be supposed to be insidiously constructing—"that is the extent of our animadversion against Karsfeld. There are no irregularities and you may take it from me that the man is all right."

"You would propose accepting the fact that a five-thousand-pound necklace was submitted to him?" suggested Mr Carlyle.

"I should," acquiesced the Manager, with a weighty nod. "Still—this brings us to April the third—this break, so to speak, occurring in our routine, it seemed a good opportunity for us to assure ourselves on one or two points. Mr Bellitzer—you know Bellitzer, of course; know of him, I should say—was appointed vice Karsfeld and we wrote to certain of our clients, asking them—as our policies entitled us to do—as a matter of form to allow Mr Bellitzer to confirm the assessment of his predecessor. Wrapped it up in silver paper, of course; said it would certify the present value and be a guarantee that would save them some formalities in case of ensuing claim, and so on. Among others, wrote to the Hon. Mrs Straithwaite to that effect—April fourth. Here is her reply of three days later. Sorry to disappoint us, but the necklace has just been sent to her bank for custody as she is on the point of leaving town. Also scarcely sees that it is necessary in her case as the insurance was only taken so recently."

"That is dated April the seventh?" inquired Mr Carlyle, busy with pencil and pocket-book.

"April seventh," repeated the Manager, noting this conscientiousness with an approving glance and then turning to regard questioningly the indifferent attitude of his other visitor. "That put us on our guard—naturally. Wrote by return regretting the necessity and suggesting that a line to her bankers, authorizing them to show us the necklace, would meet the case and save her any personal trouble. Interval of a week. Her reply, April sixteenth. Thursday last. Circumstances have altered her plans and she has returned to London sooner than she expected. Her jewel-case has been returned from the bank, and will we send our man round—'our man,' Mr Carlyle!—on Saturday morning not later than twelve, please."

The Manager closed the record book, with a sweep of his hand cleared his desk for revelations, and leaning forward in his chair fixed Mr Carlyle with a pragmatic eye.

"On Saturday Mr Bellitzer goes to Luneburg Mansions and the Hon. Mrs Straithwaite shows him the necklace. He examines it carefully, assesses its insurable value up to five thousand, two hundred and fifty pounds, and reports us to that effect. But he reports something else, Mr Carlyle. It is not the necklace that the lady had insured."

"Not the necklace?" echoed Mr Carlyle.

"No. In spite of the number of pearls and a general similarity there are certain technical differences, well known to experts, that made the fact indisputable. The Hon. Mrs Straithwaite has been guilty of misrepresentation. Possibly she has no fraudulent intention. We are willing to pay to find out. That's your business."

Mr Carlyle made a final note and put away his book with an air of decision that could not fail to inspire confidence.

"To-morrow," he said, "we shall perhaps be able to report something."

"Hope so," vouchsafed the Manager. "'Morning."

From his position near the window, Carrados appeared to wake up to the fact that the interview was over.

"But so far," he remarked blandly, with his eyes towards the great man in the chair, "you have told us nothing of the theft."

The Manager regarded the speaker dumbly for a moment and then turned to Mr Carlyle.

"What does he mean?" he demanded pungently.

But for once Mr Carlyle's self-possession had forsaken him. He recognized that somehow Carrados had been guilty of an appalling lapse, by which his reputation for prescience was wrecked in that quarter for ever, and at the catastrophe his very ears began to exude embarrassment.

In the awkward silence Carrados himself seemed to recognize that something was amiss.

"We appear to be at cross-purposes," he observed. "I inferred that the disappearance of the necklace would be the essence of our investigation."

"Have I said a word about it disappearing?" demanded the Manager, with a contempt-laden raucity that he made no pretence of softening. "You don't seem to have grasped the simple facts about the case, Mr Carrados. Really, I hardly think——Oh, come in!"

There had been a knock at the door, then another. A clerk now entered with an open telegram.

"Mr Longworth wished you to see this at once, sir."

"We may as well go," whispered Mr Carlyle with polite depression to his colleague.

"Here, wait a minute," said the Manager, who had been biting his thumb-nail over the telegram. "No, not you"—to the lingering clerk—"you clear." Much of the embarrassment that had troubled Mr Carlyle a minute before seemed to have got into the Manager's system. "I don't understand this," he confessed awkwardly. "It's from Bellitzer. He wires: 'Have just heard alleged robbery Straithwaite pearls. Advise strictest investigation.'"

Mr Carlyle suddenly found it necessary to turn to the wall and consult a highly coloured lithographic inducement to insure. Mr Carrados alone remained to meet the Manager's constrained glance.

"Still, he tells us really nothing about the theft," he remarked sociably.

"No," admitted the Manager, experiencing some little difficulty with his breathing, "he does not."

"Well, we still hope to be able to report something to-morrow. Good-bye."

It was with an effort that Mr Carlyle straightened himself sufficiently to take leave of the Manager. Several times in the corridor he stopped to wipe his eyes.

"Max, you unholy fraud," he said, when they were outside, "you knew all the time."

"No; I told you that I knew nothing of it," replied Carrados frankly. "I am absolutely sincere."

"Then all I can say is, that I see a good many things happen that I don't believe in."

Carrados's reply was to hold out a coin to a passing newsboy and to hand the purchase to his friend who was already in the car.

"There is a slang injunction to 'keep your eyes skinned.' That being out of my power, I habitually 'keep my ears skinned.' You would be surprised to know how very little you hear, Louis, and how much you miss. In the last five minutes up there I have had three different newsboys' account of this development."

"By Jupiter, she hasn't waited long!" exclaimed Mr Carlyle, referring eagerly to the headlines. "'PEARL NECKLACE SENSATION. SOCIETY LADY'S £5000 TRINKET DISAPPEARS.' Things are moving. Where next, Max?"

"It is now a quarter to one," replied Carrados, touching the fingers of his watch. "We may as well lunch on the strength of this new turn. Parkinson will have finished packing; I can telephone him to come to us at Merrick's in case I require him. Buy all the papers, Louis, and we will collate the points."

The undoubted facts that survived a comparison were few and meagre, for in each case a conscientious journalist had touched up a few vague or doubtful details according to his own ideas of probability. All agreed that on Tuesday evening—it was now Thursday—Mrs Straithwaite had formed one of a party that had occupied a box at the new Metropolitan Opera House to witness the performance of La Pucella, and that she had been robbed of a set of pearls valued in round figures at five thousand pounds. There agreement ended. One version represented the theft as taking place at the theatre. Another asserted that at the last moment the lady had decided not to wear the necklace that evening and that its abstraction had been cleverly effected from the flat during her absence. Into a third account came an ambiguous reference to Markhams, the well-known jewellers, and a conjecture that their loss would certainly be covered by insurance.

Mr Carlyle, who had been picking out the salient points of the narratives, threw down the last paper with an impatient shrug.

"Why in heaven's name have we Markhams coming into it now?" he demanded. "What have they to lose by it, Max? What do you make of the thing?"

"There is the second genuine string—the one Bellitzer saw. That belongs to someone."

"By gad, that's true—only five days ago, too. But what does our lady stand to make by that being stolen?"

Carrados was staring into obscurity between an occasional moment of attention to his cigarette or coffee.

"By this time the lady probably stands to wish she was well out of it," he replied thoughtfully. "Once you have set this sort of stone rolling and it has got beyond you——" He shook his head.

"It has become more intricate than you expected?" suggested Carlyle, in order to afford his friend an opportunity of withdrawing.

Carrados pierced the intention and smiled affectionately.

"My dear Louis," he said, "one-fifth of the mystery is already solved."

"One-fifth? How do you arrive at that?"

"Because it is one-twenty-five and we started at eleven-thirty."

He nodded to their waiter, who was standing three tables away, and paid the bill. Then with perfect gravity he permitted Mr Carlyle to lead him by the arm into the street, where their car was waiting, Parkinson already there in attendance.

"Sure I can be of no further use?" asked Carlyle. Carrados had previously indicated that after lunch he would go on alone, but, because he was largely sceptical of the outcome, the professional man felt guiltily that he was deserting. "Say the word?"

Carrados smiled and shook his head. Then he leaned across.

"I am going to the opera house now; then, possibly, to talk to Markham a little. If I have time I must find a man who knows the Straithwaites, and after that I may look up Inspector Beedel if he is at the Yard. That is as far as I can see yet, until I call at Luneburg Mansions. Come round on the third anyway."

"Dear old chap," murmured Mr Carlyle, as the car edged its way ahead among the traffic. "Marvellous shots he makes!"

In the meanwhile, at Luneburg Mansions, Mrs Straithwaite had been passing anything but a pleasant day. She had awakened with a headache and an overnight feeling that there was some unpleasantness to be gone on with. That it did not amount to actual fear was due to the enormous self-importance and the incredible ignorance which ruled the butterfly brain of the young society beauty—for in spite of three years' experience of married life Stephanie Straithwaite was as yet on the enviable side of two and twenty.

Anticipating an early visit from a particularly obnoxious sister-in-law, she had remained in bed until after lunch in order to be able to deny herself with the more conviction. Three journalists who would have afforded her the mild excitement of being interviewed had called and been in turn put off with polite regrets by her husband. The objectionable sister-in-law postponed her visit until the afternoon and for more than an hour Stephanie "suffered agonies." When the visitor had left and the martyred hostess announced her intention of flying immediately to the consoling society of her own bridge circle, Straithwaite had advised her, with some significance, to wait for a lead. The unhappy lady cast herself bodily down upon a couch and asked whether she was to become a nun. Straithwaite merely shrugged his shoulders and remembered a club engagement. Evidently there was no need for him to become a monk: Stephanie followed him down the hall, arguing and protesting. That was how they came jointly to encounter Carrados at the door.

"I have come from the Direct Insurance in the hope of being able to see Mrs Straithwaite," he explained, when the door opened rather suddenly before he had knocked. "My name is Carrados—Max Carrados."

There was a moment of hesitation all round. Then Stephanie read difficulties in the straightening lines of her husband's face and rose joyfully to the occasion.

"Oh yes; come in, Mr Carrados," she exclaimed graciously. "We are not quite strangers, you know. You found out something for Aunt Pigs; I forget what, but she was most frantically impressed."

"Lady Poges," enlarged Straithwaite, who had stepped aside and was watching the development with slow, calculating eyes. "But, I say, you are blind, aren't you?"

Carrados's smiling admission turned the edge of Mrs Straithwaite's impulsive, "Teddy!"

"But I get along all right," he added. "I left my man down in the car and I found your door first shot, you see."

The references reminded the velvet-eyed little mercenary that the man before her had the reputation of being quite desirably rich, his queer taste merely an eccentric hobby. The consideration made her resolve to be quite her nicest possible, as she led the way to the drawing-room. Then Teddy, too, had been horrid beyond words and must be made to suffer in the readiest way that offered.

"Teddy is just going out and I was to be left in solitary bereavement if you had not appeared," she explained airily. "It wasn't very compy only to come to see me on business by the way, Mr Carrados, but if those are your only terms I must agree."

Straithwaite, however, did not seem to have the least intention of going. He had left his hat and stick in the hall and he now threw his yellow gloves down on a table and took up a negligent position on the arm of an easy-chair.

"The thing is, where do we stand?" he remarked tentatively.

"That is the attitude of the insurance company, I imagine," replied Carrados.

"I don't see that the company has any standing in the matter. We haven't reported any loss to them and we are not making any claim, so far. That ought to be enough."

"I assume that they act on general inference," explained Carrados. "A limited liability company is not subtle, Mrs Straithwaite. This one knows that you have insured a five-thousand-pound pearl necklace with it, and when it becomes a matter of common knowledge that you have had one answering to that description stolen, it jumps to the conclusion that they are one and the same."

"But they aren't—worse luck," explained the hostess. "This was a string that I let Markhams send me to see if I would keep."

"The one that Bellitzer saw last Saturday?"

"Yes," admitted Mrs Straithwaite quite simply.

Straithwaite glanced sharply at Carrados and then turned his eyes with lazy indifference to his wife.

"My dear Stephanie, what are you thinking of?" he drawled. "Of course those could not have been Markhams' pearls. Not knowing that you are much too clever to do such a foolish thing, Mr Carrados will begin to think that you have had fraudulent designs upon his company."

Whether the tone was designed to exasperate or merely fell upon a fertile soil, Stephanie threw a hateful little glance in his direction.

"I don't care," she exclaimed recklessly; "I haven't the least little objection in the world to Mr Carrados knowing exactly how it happened."

Carrados put in an instinctive word of warning, even raised an arresting hand, but the lady was much too excited, too voluble, to be denied.

"It doesn't really matter in the least, Mr Carrados, because nothing came of it," she explained. "There never were any real pearls to be insured. It would have made no difference to the company, because I did not regard this as an ordinary insurance from the first. It was to be a loan."

"A loan?" repeated Carrados.

"Yes. I shall come into heaps and heaps of money in a few years' time under Prin-Prin's will. Then I should pay back whatever had been advanced."

"But would it not have been better—simpler—to have borrowed purely on the anticipation?"

"We have," explained the lady eagerly. "We have borrowed from all sorts of people, and both Teddy and I have signed heaps and heaps of papers, until now no one will lend any more."

The thing was too tragically grotesque to be laughed at. Carrados turned his face from one to the other and by ear, and by even finer perceptions, he focussed them in his mind—the delicate, feather-headed beauty, with the heart of a cat and the irresponsibility of a kitten, eye and mouth already hardening under the stress of her frantic life, and, across the room, her debonair consort, whose lank pose and nonchalant attitude towards the situation Carrados had not yet categorized.

Straithwaite's dry voice, with its habitual drawl, broke into his reflection.

"I don't suppose for a moment that you either know or care what this means, my dear girl, but I will proceed to enlighten you. It means the extreme probability that unless you can persuade Mr Carrados to hold his tongue, you, and—without prejudice—I also, will get two years' hard. And yet, with unconscious but consummate artistry, it seems to me that you have perhaps done the trick; for, unless I am mistaken, Mr Carrados will find himself unable to take advantage of your guileless confidence, whereas he would otherwise have quite easily found out all he wanted."

"That is the most utter nonsense, Teddy," cried Stephanie, with petulant indignation. She turned to Carrados with the assurance of meeting understanding. "We know Mr Justice Enderleigh very well indeed, and if there was any bother I should not have the least difficulty in getting him to take the case privately and in explaining everything to him. But why should there be? Why indeed?" A brilliant little new idea possessed her. "Do you know any of these insurance people at all intimately, Mr Carrados?"

"The General Manager and I are on terms that almost justify us in addressing each other as 'silly ass,'" admitted Carrados.

"There you see, Teddy, you needn't have been in a funk. Mr Carrados would put everything right. Let me tell you exactly how I had arranged it. I dare say you know that insurances are only too pleased to pay for losses: it gives them an advertisement. Freddy Tantroy told me so, and his father is a director of hundreds of companies. Only, of course, it must be done quite regularly. Well, for months and months we had both been most frightfully hard up, and, unfortunately, everyone else—at least all our friends—seemed just as stony. I had been absolutely racking my poor brain for an idea when I remembered papa's wedding present. It was a string of pearls that he sent me from Vienna, only a month before he died; not real, of course, because poor papa was always quite utterly on the verge himself, but very good imitation and in perfect taste. Otherwise I am sure papa would rather have sent a silver penwiper, for although he had to live abroad because of what people said, his taste was simply exquisite and he was most romantic in his ideas. What do you say, Teddy?"

"Nothing, dear; it was only my throat ticking."

"I wore the pearls often and millions of people had seen them. Of course our own people knew about them, but others took it for granted that they were genuine for me to be wearing them. Teddy will tell you that I was almost babbling in delirium, things were becoming so ghastly, when an idea occurred. Tweety—she's a cousin of Teddy's, but quite an aged person—has a whole coffer full of jewels that she never wears and I knew that there was a necklace very like mine among them. She was going almost immediately to Africa for some shooting, so I literally flew into the wilds of

Surrey and begged her on my knees to lend me her pearls for the Lycester House dance. When I got back with them I stamped on the clasp and took it at once to Karsfeld in Princess Street. I told him they were only paste but I thought they were rather good and I wanted them by the next day. And of course he looked at them, and then looked again, and then asked me if I was certain they were imitation, and I said, Well, we had never thought twice about it, because poor papa was always rather chronic, only certainly he did occasionally have fabulous streaks at the tables, and finally, like a great owl, Karsfeld said:

"'I am happy to be able to congratulate you, madam. They are undoubtedly Bombay pearls of very fine orient. They are certainly worth five thousand pounds.'"

From this point Mrs Straithwaite's narrative ran its slangy, obvious course. The insurance effected—on the strict understanding of the lady with herself that it was merely a novel form of loan, and after satisfying her mind on Freddy Tantroy's authority that the Direct and Intermediate could stand a temporary loss of five thousand pounds—the genuine pearls were returned to the cousin in the wilds of Surrey and Stephanie continued to wear the counterfeit. A decent interval was allowed to intervene and the plot was on the point of maturity when the company's request for a scrutiny fell like a thunderbolt. With many touching appeals to Mr Carrados to picture her frantic distraction, with appropriate little gestures of agony and despair, Stephanie described her absolute prostration, her subsequent wild scramble through the jewel stocks of London to find a substitute. The danger over, it became increasingly necessary to act without delay, not only to anticipate possible further curiosity on the part of the insurance, but in order to secure the means with which to meet an impending obligation held over them by an inflexibly obdurate Hebrew.

The evening of the previous Tuesday was to be the time; the opera house, during the performance of La Pucella, the place. Straithwaite, who was not interested in that precise form of drama, would not be expected to be present, but with a false moustache and a few other touches which his experience as an amateur placed within his easy reach, he was to occupy a stall, an end stall somewhere beneath his wife's box. At an agreed signal Stephanie would jerk open the catch of the necklace, and as she leaned forward the ornament would trickle off her neck and disappear into the arena beneath. Straithwaite, the only one prepared for anything happening, would have no difficulty in securing it. He would look up quickly as if to identify the box, and with the jewels in his hand walk deliberately out into the passage. Before anyone had quite realized what was happening he would have left the house.

Carrados turned his face from the woman to the man.

"This scheme commended itself to you, Mr Straithwaite?"

"Well, you see, Stephanie is so awfully clever that I took it for granted that the thing would go all right."

"And three days before, Bellitzer had already reported misrepresentation and that two necklaces had been used!"

"Yes," admitted Straithwaite, with an air of reluctant candour, "I had a suspicion that Stephanie's native ingenuity rather fizzled there. You know, Stephanie dear, there is a difference, it seems, between Bombay and Californian pearls."

"The wretch!" exclaimed the girl, grinding her little teeth vengefully. "And we gave him champagne!"

"But nothing came of it; so it doesn't matter?" prompted Straithwaite.

"Except that now Markhams' pearls have gone and they are hinting at all manner of diabolical things," she wrathfully reminded him.

"True," he confessed. "That is by way of a sequel, Mr Carrados. I will endeavour to explain that part of the incident, for even yet Stephanie seems unable to do me justice."

He detached himself from the arm of the chair and lounged across the room to another chair, where he took up exactly the same position.

"On the fatal evening I duly made my way to the theatre—a little late, so as to take my seat unobserved. After I had got the general hang I glanced up occasionally until I caught Stephanie's eye, by which I knew that she was there all right and concluded that everything was going along quite jollily. According to arrangement, I was to cross the theatre immediately the first curtain fell and standing opposite Stephanie's box twist my watch chain until it was certain that she had seen me. Then Stephanie was to fan herself three times with her programme. Both, you will see, perfectly innocent operations, and yet conveying to each other the intimation that all was well. Stephanie's idea, of course. After that, I would return to my seat and Stephanie would do her part at the first opportunity in Act II.

"However, we never reached that. Towards the end of the first act something white and noiseless slipped down and fell at my feet. For the moment I thought they were the pearls gone wrong. Then I saw that it was a glove—a lady's glove. Intuition whispered that it was Stephanie's before I touched it. I picked it up and quietly got out. Down among the fingers was a scrap of paper—the corner torn off a programme. On it were pencilled words to this effect:

"*'Something quite unexpected. Can do nothing to-night. Go back at once and wait. May return early. Frightfully worried.—S.'*"

"You kept the paper, of course?"

"Yes. It is in my desk in the next room. Do you care to see it?"

"Please."

Straithwaite left the room and Stephanie flung herself into a charming attitude of entreaty.

"Mr Carrados, you will get them back for us, won't you? It would not really matter, only I seem to have signed something and now Markhams threaten to bring an action against us for culpable negligence in leaving them in an empty flat."

"You see," explained Straithwaite, coming back in time to catch the drift of his wife's words, "except to a personal friend like yourself, it is quite impossible to submit these clues. The first one alone would raise embarrassing inquiries; the other is beyond explanation. Consequently I have been obliged to concoct an imaginary burglary in our absence and to drop the necklace case among the rhododendrons in the garden at the back, for the police to find."

"Deeper and deeper," commented Carrados.

"Why, yes. Stephanie and I are finding that out, aren't we, dear? However, here is the first note; also the glove. Of course I returned immediately. It was Stephanie's strategy and I was under her orders. In something less than half-an-hour I heard a motor car stop outside. Then the bell here rang.

"I think I have said that I was alone. I went to the door and found a man who might have been anything standing there. He merely said: 'Mr Straithwaite?' and on my nodding handed me a letter. I tore it open in the hall and read it. Then I went into my room and read it again. This is it:

"'Dear T.,—Absolutely ghastly. We simply must put off to-night. Will explain that later. Now what do you think? Bellitzer is here in the stalls and young K. D. has asked him to join us at supper at the Savoy. It appears that the creature is Something and I suppose the D.'s want to borrow off him. I can't get out of it and I am literally quaking. Don't you see, he will spot something? Send me the M. string at once and I will change somehow before supper. I am scribbling this in the dark. I have got the Willoughby's man to take it. Don't, don't fail.—S.'"

"It is ridiculous, preposterous," snapped Stephanie. "I never wrote a word of it—or the other. There was I, sitting the whole evening. And Teddy—oh, it is maddening!"

"I took it into my room and looked at it closely," continued the unruffled Straithwaite. "Even if I had any reason to doubt, the internal evidence was convincing, but how could I doubt? It read like a continuation of the previous message. The writing was reasonably like Stephanie's under the circumstances, the envelope had obviously been obtained from the box-office of the theatre and the paper itself was a sheet of the programme. A corner was torn off; I put against it the previous scrap and they exactly fitted." The gentleman shrugged his shoulders, stretched his legs with deliberation and walked across the room to look out of the window. "I made them up into a neat little parcel and handed it over," he concluded.

Carrados put down the two pieces of paper which he had been minutely examining with his finger-tips and still holding the glove addressed his small audience collectively.

"The first and most obvious point is that whoever carried out the scheme had more than a vague knowledge of your affairs, not only in general but also relating to this—well, loan, Mrs Straithwaite."

"Just what I have insisted," agreed Straithwaite. "You hear that, Stephanie?"

"But who is there?" pleaded Stephanie, with weary intonation. "Absolutely no one in the wide world. Not a soul."

"So one is liable to think offhand. Let us go further, however, merely accounting for those who are in a position to have information. There are the officials of the insurance company who suspect something; there is Bellitzer, who perhaps knows a little more. There is the lady in Surrey from whom the pearls were borrowed, a Mr Tantroy who seems to have been consulted, and, finally, your own servants. All these people have friends, or underlings, or observers. Suppose Mr Bellitzer's confidential clerk happens to be the sweetheart of your maid?"

"They would still know very little."

"The arc of a circle may be very little, but, given that, it is possible to construct the entire figure. Now your servants, Mrs Straithwaite? We are accusing no one, of course."

"There is the cook, Mullins. She displayed alarming influenza on Tuesday morning, and although it was most frightfully inconvenient I packed her off home without a moment's delay. I have a horror of the influ. Then Fraser, the parlourmaid. She does my hair—I haven't really got a maid, you know."

"Peter," prompted Straithwaite.

"Oh yes, Beta. She's a daily girl and helps in the kitchen. I have no doubt she is capable of any villainy."

"And all were out on Tuesday evening?"

"Yes. Mullins gone home. Beta left early as there was no dinner, and I told Fraser to take the evening after she had dressed me so that Teddy could make up and get out without being seen."

Carrados turned to his other witness.

"The papers and the glove have been with you ever since?"

"Yes, in my desk."

"Locked?"

"Yes."

"And this glove, Mrs Straithwaite? There is no doubt that it is yours?"

"I suppose not," she replied. "I never thought. I know that when I came to leave the theatre one had vanished and Teddy had it here."

"That was the first time you missed it?"

"Yes."

"But it might have gone earlier in the evening—mislaid or lost or stolen?"

"I remember taking them off in the box. I sat in the corner farthest from the stage—the front row, of course—and I placed them on the support."

"Where anyone in the next box could abstract one without much difficulty at a favourable moment."

"That is quite likely. But we didn't see anyone in the next box."

"I have half an idea that I caught sight of someone hanging back," volunteered Straithwaite.

"Thank you," said Carrados, turning towards him almost gratefully. "That is most important—that you think you saw someone hanging back. Now the other glove, Mrs Straithwaite; what became of that?"

"An odd glove is not very much good, is it?" said Stephanie. "Certainly I wore it coming back. I think I threw it down somewhere in here. Probably it is still about. We are in a frantic muddle and nothing is being done."

The second glove was found on the floor in a corner. Carrados received it and laid it with the other.

"You use a very faint and characteristic scent, I notice, Mrs Straithwaite," he observed.

"Yes; it is rather sweet, isn't it? I don't know the name because it is in Russian. A friend in the Embassy sent me some bottles from Petersburg."

"But on Tuesday you supplemented it with something stronger," he continued, raising the gloves delicately one after the other to his face.

"Oh, eucalyptus; rather," she admitted. "I simply drenched my handkerchief with it."

"You have other gloves of the same pattern?"

"Have I? Now let me think! Did you give them to me, Teddy?"

"No," replied Straithwaite from the other end of the room. He had lounged across to the window and his attitude detached him from the discussion. "Didn't Whitstable?" he added shortly.

"Of course. Then there are three pairs, Mr Carrados, because I never let Bimbi lose more than that to me at once, poor boy."

"I think you are rather tiring yourself out, Stephanie," warned her husband.

Carrados's attention seemed to leap to the voice; then he turned courteously to his hostess.

"I appreciate that you have had a trying time lately, Mrs Straithwaite," he said. "Every moment I have been hoping to let you out of the witness-box——"

"Perhaps to-morrow——" began Straithwaite, recrossing the room.

"Impossible; I leave town to-night," replied Carrados firmly. "You have three pairs of these gloves, Mrs Straithwaite. Here is one. The other two——?"

"One pair I have not worn yet. The other—good gracious, I haven't been out since Tuesday! I suppose it is in my glove-box."

"I must see it, please."

Straithwaite opened his mouth, but as his wife obediently rose to her feet to comply he turned sharply away with the word unspoken.

"These are they," she said, returning.

"Mr Carrados and I will finish our investigation in my room," interposed Straithwaite, with quiet assertiveness. "I should advise you to lie down for half-an-hour, Stephanie, if you don't want to be a nervous wreck to-morrow."

"You must allow the culprit to endorse that good advice, Mrs Straithwaite," added Carrados. He had been examining the second pair of gloves as they spoke and he now handed them back again. "They are undoubtedly of the same set," he admitted, with extinguished interest, "and so our clue runs out."

"I hope you don't mind," apologized Straithwaite, as he led his guest to his own smoking-room. "Stephanie," he confided, becoming more cordial as two doors separated them from the lady, "is a creature of nerves and indiscretions. She forgets. To-night she will not sleep. To-morrow she will suffer." Carrados divined the grin. "So shall I!"

"On the contrary, pray accept my regrets," said the visitor. "Besides," he continued, "there is nothing more for me to do here, I suppose...."

"It is a mystery," admitted Straithwaite, with polite agreement. "Will you try a cigarette?"

"Thanks. Can you see if my car is below?" They exchanged cigarettes and stood at the window lighting them.

"There is one point, by the way, that may have some significance." Carrados had begun to recross the room and stopped to pick up the two fictitious messages. "You will have noticed that this is the outside sheet of a programme. It is not the most suitable for the purpose; the first inner sheet is more convenient to write on, but there the date appears. You see the inference? The programme was obtained before——"

"Perhaps. Well——?" for Carrados had broken off abruptly and was listening.

"You hear someone coming up the steps?"

"It is the general stairway."

"Mr Straithwaite, I don't know how far this has gone in other quarters. We may only have a few seconds before we are interrupted."

"What do you mean?"

"I mean that the man who is now on the stairs is a policeman or has worn the uniform. If he stops at your door——"

The heavy tread ceased. Then came the authoritative knock.

"Wait," muttered Carrados, laying his hand impressively on Straithwaite's tremulous arm. "I may recognize the voice."

They heard the servant pass along the hall and the door unlatched; then caught the jumble of a gruff inquiry.

"Inspector Beedel of Scotland Yard!" The servant repassed their door on her way to the drawing-room. "It is no good disguising the fact from you, Mr Straithwaite, that you may no longer be at liberty. But I am. Is there anything you wish done?"

There was no time for deliberation. Straithwaite was indeed between the unenviable alternatives of the familiar proverb, but, to do him justice, his voice had lost scarcely a ripple of its usual sang-froid.

"Thanks," he replied, taking a small stamped and addressed parcel from his pocket, "you might drop this into some obscure pillar-box, if you will."

"The Markham necklace?"

"Exactly. I was going out to post it when you came."

"I am sure you were."

"And if you could spare five minutes later—if I am here——"

Carrados slid his cigarette-case under some papers on the desk.

"I will call for that," he assented. "Let us say about half-past eight."

"I am still at large, you see, Mr Carrados; though after reflecting on the studied formality of the inspector's business here, I imagine that you will scarcely be surprised."

"I have made it a habit," admitted Carrados, "never to be surprised."

"However, I still want to cut a rather different figure in your eyes. You regard me, Mr Carrados, either as a detected rogue or a repentant ass?"

"Another excellent rule is never to form deductions from uncertainties."

Straithwaite made a gesture of mild impatience.

"You only give me ten minutes. If I am to put my case before you, Mr Carrados, we cannot fence with phrases.... To-day you have had an exceptional opportunity of penetrating into our mode of life. You will, I do not doubt, have summed up our perpetual indebtedness and the easy credit that our connexion procures; Stephanie's social ambitions and expensive popularity; her utterly extravagant incapacity to see any other possible existence; and my tacit acquiescence. You will, I know, have correctly gauged her irresponsible, neurotic temperament, and judged the result of it in conflict with my own. What possibly has escaped you, for in society one has to disguise these things, is that I still love my wife.

"When you dare not trust the soundness of your reins you do not try to pull up a bolting horse. For three years I have endeavoured to guide Stephanie round awkward comers with as little visible restraint as possible. When we differ over any project upon which she has set her heart Stephanie has one strong argument."

"That you no longer love her?"

"Well, perhaps; but more forcibly expressed. She rushes to the top of the building—there are six floors, Mr Carrados, and we are on the second—and climbing on to the banister she announces her intention of throwing herself down into the basement. In the meanwhile I have followed her and drag her back again. One day I shall stay where I am and let her do as she intends."

"I hope not," said Carrados gravely.

"Oh, don't be concerned. She will then climb back herself. But it will mark an epoch. It was by that threat that she obtained my acquiescence to this scheme—that and the certainty that she would otherwise go on without me. But I had no intention of allowing her to land herself—to say nothing of us both—behind the bars of a prison if I could help it. And, above all, I wished to cure her of her fatuous delusion that she is clever, in the hope that she may then give up being foolish.

"To fail her on the occasion was merely to postpone the attempt. I conceived the idea of seeming to cooperate and at the same time involving us in what appeared to be a clever counter-fraud. The thought of the real loss will perhaps have a good effect; the publicity will certainly prevent her from daring a second 'theft.' A sordid story, Mr Carrados," he concluded. "Do not forget your cigarette-case in reality."

The paternal shake of Carrados's head over the recital was neutralized by his benevolent smile.

"Yes, yes," he said. "I think we can classify you, Mr Straithwaite. One point—the glove?"

"That was an afterthought. I had arranged the whole story and the first note was to be brought to me by an attendant. Then, on my way, in my overcoat pocket I discovered a pair of Stephanie's gloves which she had asked me to carry the day before. The suggestion flashed—how much more convincing if I could arrange for her to seem to drop the writing in that way. As she said, the next box was empty; I merely took possession of it for a few minutes and quietly drew across one of her gloves. And that reminds me—of course there was nothing in it, but your interest in them made me rather nervous."

Carrados laughed outright. Then he stood up and held out his hand.

"Good-night, Mr Straithwaite," he said, with real friendliness. "Let me give you the quaker's advice: Don't attempt another conspiracy—but if you do, don't produce a 'pair' of gloves of which one is still suggestive of scent, and the other identifiable with eucalyptus!"

"Oh——!" said Straithwaite.

"Quite so. But at all hazard suppress a second pair that has the same peculiarity. Think over what it must mean. Good-bye."

Twelve minutes later Mr Carlyle was called to the telephone.

"It is eight-fifty-five and I am at Charing Cross," said a voice he knew. "If you want local colour contrive an excuse to be with Markham when the first post arrives to-morrow." A few more words followed, and an affectionate valediction.

"One moment, my dear Max, one moment. Do I understand you to say that you will post me on the report of the case from Dover?"

"No, Louis," replied Carrados, with cryptic discrimination. "I only said that I will post you on a report of the case from Dover."

The Last Exploit of Harry the Actor

The one insignificant fact upon which turned the following incident in the joint experiences of Mr Carlyle and Max Carrados was merely this: that having called upon his friend just at the moment when the private detective was on the point of leaving his office to go to the safe deposit in Lucas Street, Piccadilly, the blind amateur accompanied him, and for ten minutes amused himself by sitting quite quietly among the palms in the centre of the circular hall while Mr Carlyle was occupied with his deed-box in one of the little compartments provided for the purpose.

The Lucas Street depository was then (it has since been converted into a picture palace) generally accepted as being one of the strongest places in London. The front of the building was constructed to represent a gigantic safe door, and under the colloquial designation of "The Safe" the place had passed into a synonym for all that was secure and impregnable. Half of the marketable securities in the west of London were popularly reported to have seen the inside of its coffers at one time or another, together with the same generous proportion of family jewels. However exaggerated an estimate this might be, the substratum of truth was solid and auriferous enough to dazzle the imagination. When ordinary safes were being carried bodily away with impunity or ingeniously fused open by the scientifically equipped cracksman, nervous bond-holders turned with relief to the attractions of an establishment whose modest claim was summed up in its telegraphic address: "Impregnable." To it went also the jewel-case between the lady's social engagements, and when in due course "the family" journeyed north—or south, east or west—whenever, in short, the London house was closed, its capacious storerooms received the plate-chest as an established custom. Not a few traders also—jewellers, financiers, dealers in pictures, antiques and costly bijouterie, for instance—constantly used its facilities for any stock that they did not requite immediately to hand.

There was only one entrance to the place, an exaggerated keyhole, to carry out the similitude of the safe-door alluded to. The ground floor was occupied by the ordinary offices of the company; all the strong-rooms and safes lay in the steel-cased basement. This was reached both by a lift and by a flight of steps. In either case the visitor found before him a grille of massive proportions. Behind its bars stood a formidable commissionaire who never left his post, his sole duty being to open and close the grille to arriving and departing clients. Beyond this, a short passage led into the round central hall where Carrados was waiting. From this part, other passages radiated off to the vaults and strong-rooms, each one barred from the hall by a grille scarcely less ponderous than the first one. The doors of the various private rooms put at the disposal of the company's clients, and that of the manager's office, filled the wall-space between the radiating passages. Everything was very quiet, everything looked very bright, and everything seemed hopelessly impregnable.

"But I wonder?" ran Carrados's dubious reflection; as he reached this point.

"Sorry to have kept you so long, my dear Max," broke in Mr Carlyle's crisp voice. He had emerged from his compartment and was crossing the hall, deed-box in hand. "Another minute and I will be with you."

Carrados smiled and nodded and resumed his former expression, which was merely that of an uninterested gentleman waiting patiently for another. It is something of an attainment to watch closely without betraying undue curiosity, but others of the senses—hearing and smelling, for instance—can be keenly engaged while the observer possibly has the appearance of falling asleep.

"Now," announced Mr Carlyle, returning briskly to his friend's chair, and drawing on his grey suede gloves.

"You are in no particular hurry?"

"No," admitted the professional man, with the slowness of mild surprise. "Not at all. What do you propose?"

"It is very pleasant here," replied Carrados tranquilly. "Very cool and restful with this armoured steel between us and the dust and scurry of the hot July afternoon above. I propose remaining here for a few minutes longer."

"Certainly," agreed Mr Carlyle, taking the nearest chair and eyeing Carrados as though he had a shrewd suspicion of something more than met the ear. "I believe some very interesting people rent safes here. We may encounter a bishop, or a winning jockey, or even a musical comedy actress. Unfortunately it seems to be rather a slack time."

"Two men came down while you were in your cubicle," remarked Carrados casually. "The first took the lift. I imagine that he was a middle-aged, rather portly man. He carried a stick, wore a silk hat, and used spectacles for close sight. The other came by the stairway. I infer that he arrived at the top immediately after the lift had gone. He ran down the steps, so that the two were admitted at the same time, but the second man, though the more active of the pair, hung back for a moment in the passage and the portly one was the first to go to his safe."

Mr Carlyle's knowing look expressed: "Go on, my friend; you are coming to something." But he merely contributed an encouraging "Yes?"

"When you emerged just now our second man quietly opened the door of his pen a fraction. Doubtless he looked out. Then he closed it as quietly again. You were not his man, Louis."

"I am grateful," said Mr Carlyle expressively. "What next, Louis?"

"That is all; they are still closeted."

Both were silent for a moment. Mr Carlyle's feeling was one of unconfessed perplexity. So far the incident was utterly trivial in his eyes; but he knew that the trifles which appeared significant to Max had a way of standing out like signposts when the time came to look back over an episode. Carrados's sightless faculties seemed indeed to keep him just a move ahead as the game progressed.

"Is there really anything in it, Max?" he asked at length.

"Who can say?" replied Carrados. "At least we may wait to see them go. Those tin deed-boxes now. There is one to each safe, I think?"

"Yes, so I imagine. The practice is to carry the box to your private lair and there unlock it and do your business. Then you lock it up again and take it back to your safe."

"Steady! our first man," whispered Carrados hurriedly. "Here, look at this with me." He opened a paper—a prospectus—which he pulled from his pocket, and they affected to study its contents together.

"You were about right, my friend," muttered Mr Carlyle, pointing to a paragraph of assumed interest. "Hat, stick and spectacles. He is a clean-shaven, pink-faced old boy. I believe—yes, I know the man by sight. He is a bookmaker in a large way, I am told."

"Here comes the other," whispered Carrados.

The bookmaker passed across the hall, joined on his way by the manager whose duty it was to counterlock the safe, and disappeared along one of the passages. The second man sauntered up and down, waiting his turn. Mr Carlyle reported his movements in an undertone and described him. He was a younger man than the other, of medium height, and passably well dressed in a quiet lounge suit, green Alpine hat and brown shoes. By the time the detective had reached his wavy chestnut hair, large and rather ragged moustache, and sandy, freckled complexion, the first man had completed his business and was leaving the place.

"It isn't an exchange lay, at all events," said Mr Carlyle. "His inner case is only half the size of the other and couldn't possibly be substituted."

"Come up now," said Carrados, rising. "There is nothing more to be learned down here."

They requisitioned the lift and on the steps outside the gigantic keyhole stood for a few minutes discussing an investment as a couple of trustees or a lawyer and a client who were parting there might do. Fifty yards away, a very large silk hat with a very curly brim marked the progress of the bookmaker towards Piccadilly.

The lift in the hall behind them swirled up again and the gate clashed. The second man walked leisurely out and sauntered away without a backward glance.

"He has gone in the opposite direction," exclaimed Mr Carlyle, rather blankly. "It isn't the 'lame goat' nor the 'follow-me-on,' nor even the homely but efficacious sand-bag."

"What colour were his eyes?" asked Carrados.

"Upon my word, I never noticed," admitted the other.

"Parkinson would have noticed," was the severe comment.

"I am not Parkinson," retorted Mr Carlyle, with asperity, "and, strictly as one dear friend to another, Max, permit me to add, that while cherishing an unbounded admiration for your remarkable gifts, I have the strongest suspicion that the whole incident is a ridiculous mare's nest, bred in the fantastic imagination of an enthusiastic criminologist."

Mr Carrados received this outburst with the utmost benignity. "Come and have a coffee, Louis," he suggested. "Mehmed's is only a street away."

Mehmed proved to be a cosmopolitan gentleman from Mocha whose shop resembled a house from the outside and an Oriental divan when one was within. A turbaned Arab placed cigarettes and cups of coffee spiced with saffron before the customers, gave salaam and withdrew.

"You know, my dear chap," continued Mr Carlyle, sipping his black coffee and wondering privately whether it was really very good or very bad, "speaking quite seriously, the one fishy detail—our ginger friend's watching for the other to leave—may be open to a dozen very innocent explanations."

"So innocent that to-morrow I intend taking a safe myself."

"You think that everything is all right?"

"On the contrary, I am convinced that something is very wrong."

"Then why——?"

"I shall keep nothing there, but it will give me the entrée. I should advise you, Louis, in the first place to empty your safe with all possible speed, and in the second to leave your business card on the manager."

Mr Carlyle pushed his cup away, convinced now that the coffee was really very bad.

"But, my dear Max, the place—'The Safe'—is impregnable!"

"When I was in the States, three years ago, the head porter at one hotel took pains to impress on me that the building was absolutely fireproof. I at once had my things taken off to another hotel. Two weeks later the first place was burnt out. It was fireproof, I believe, but of course the furniture and the fittings were not and the walls gave way."

"Very ingenious," admitted Mr Carlyle, "but why did you really go? You know you can't humbug me with your superhuman sixth sense, my friend."

Carrados smiled pleasantly, thereby encouraging the watchful attendant to draw near and replenish their tiny cups.

"Perhaps," replied the blind man, "because so many careless people were satisfied that it was fireproof."

"Ah-ha, there you are—the greater the confidence the greater the risk. But only if your self-confidence results in carelessness. Now do you know how this place is secured, Max?"

"I am told that they lock the door at night," replied Carrados, with bland malice.

"And hide the key under the mat to be ready for the first arrival in the morning," crowed Mr Carlyle, in the same playful spirit. "Dear old chap! Well, let me tell you——"

"That force is out of the question. Quite so," admitted his friend.

"That simplifies the argument. Let us consider fraud. There again the precautions are so rigid that many people pronounce the forms a nuisance. I confess that I do not. I regard them as a means of protecting my own property and I cheerfully sign my name and give my password, which the manager compares with his record-book before he releases the first lock of my safe. The signature is burned before my eyes in a sort of crucible there, the password is of my own choosing and is written only in a book that no one but the manager ever sees, and my key is the sole one in existence."

"No duplicate or master-key?"

"Neither. If a key is lost it takes a skilful mechanic half-a-day to cut his way in. Then you must remember that clients of a safe-deposit are not multitudinous. All are known more or less by sight to the officials there, and a stranger would receive close attention. Now, Max, by what combination of circumstances is a rogue to know my password, to be able to forge my signature, to possess himself of my key, and to resemble me personally? And, finally, how is he possibly to determine beforehand whether there is anything in my safe to repay so elaborate a plant?" Mr Carlyle concluded in triumph and was so carried away by the strength of his position that he drank off the contents of his second cup before he realized what he was doing.

"At the hotel I just spoke of," replied Carrados, "there was an attendant whose one duty in case of alarm was to secure three iron doors. On the night of the fire he had a bad attack of toothache and slipped away for just a quarter of an hour to have the thing out. There was a most up-to-date system of automatic fire alarm; it had been tested only the day before and the electrician, finding some part not absolutely to his satisfaction, had taken it away and not had time to replace it. The night watchman, it turned out, had received leave to present himself a couple of hours later on that particular night, and the hotel fireman, whose duties he took over, had missed being notified. Lastly, there was a big riverside blaze at the same time and all the engines were down at the other end of the city."

Mr Carlyle committed himself to a dubious monosyllable. Carrados leaned forward a little.

"All these circumstances formed a coincidence of pure chance. Is it not conceivable, Louis, that an even more remarkable series might be brought about by design?"

"Our tawny friend?"

"Possibly. Only he was not really tawny." Mr Carlyle's easy attitude suddenly stiffened into rigid attention. "He wore a false moustache."

"He wore a false moustache!" repeated the amazed gentleman. "And you cannot see! No, really, Max, this is beyond the limit!"

"If only you would not trust your dear, blundering old eyes so implicitly you would get nearer that limit yourself," retorted Carrados. "The man carried a five-yard aura of spirit gum, emphasized by a warm, perspiring skin. That inevitably suggested one thing. I looked for further evidence of making-up and found it—these preparations all smell. The hair you described was characteristically that of a wig—worn long to hide the joining and made wavy to minimize the length. All these things are trifles. As yet we have not gone beyond the initial stage of suspicion. I will tell you another trifle. When this man retired to a compartment with his deed-box, he never even opened it. Possibly it contains a brick and a newspaper. He is only watching."

"Watching the bookmaker."

"True, but it may go far wider than that. Everything points to a plot of careful elaboration. Still, if you are satisfied——"

"I am quite satisfied," replied Mr Carlyle gallantly. "I regard 'The Safe' almost as a national institution, and as such I have an implicit faith in its precautions against every kind of force or fraud." So far Mr Carlyle's attitude had been suggestive of a rock, but at this point he took out his watch, hummed a little to pass the time, consulted his watch again, and continued: "I am afraid that there were one or two papers which I overlooked. It would perhaps save me coming again to-morrow if I went back now——"

"Quite so," acquiesced Carrados, with perfect gravity. "I will wait for you."

For twenty minutes he sat there, drinking an occasional tiny cup of boiled coffee and to all appearance placidly enjoying the quaint atmosphere which Mr Mehmed had contrived to transplant from the shore of the Persian Gulf.

At the end of that period Carlyle returned, politely effusive about the time he had kept his friend waiting but otherwise bland and unassailable. Anyone with eyes might have noticed that he carried a parcel of about the same size and dimensions as the deed-box that fitted his safe.

The next day Carrados presented himself at the safe-deposit as an intending renter. The manager showed him over the vaults and strong-rooms, explaining the various precautions taken to render the guile or force of man impotent: the strength of the chilled-steel walls, the casing of electricity-resisting concrete, the stupendous isolation of the whole inner fabric on metal pillars so that the watchman, while inside the building, could walk above, below, and all round the outer walls of what was really—although it bore no actual relationship to the advertising device of the front—a monstrous safe; and, finally, the arrangement which would enable the basement to be flooded with steam within three minutes of an alarm. These details were public property. "The Safe" was a showplace and its directors held that no harm could come of displaying a strong hand.

Accompanied by the observant eyes of Parkinson, Carrados gave an adventurous but not a hopeful attention to these particulars. Submitting the problem of the tawny man to his own ingenuity, he was constantly putting before himself the question: How shall I set about robbing this place? and he had already dismissed force as impracticable. Nor, when it came to the consideration of fraud, did the simple but effective safeguards which Mr Carlyle had specified seem to offer any loophole.

"As I am blind I may as well sign in the book," he suggested, when the manager passed to him a gummed slip for the purpose. The precaution against one acquiring particulars of another client might well be deemed superfluous in his case.

But the manager did not fall into the trap.

"It is our invariable rule in all cases, sir," he replied courteously. "What word will you take?" Parkinson, it may be said, had been left in the hall.

"Suppose I happen to forget it? How do we proceed?"

"In that case I am afraid that I might have to trouble you to establish your identity," the manager explained. "It rarely happens."

"Then we will say 'Conspiracy.'"

The word was written down and the book closed.

"Here is your key, sir. If you will allow me—your key-ring——"

A week went by and Carrados was no nearer the absolute solution of the problem he had set himself. He had, indeed, evolved several ways by which the contents of the safes might be reached, some simple and desperate, hanging on the razor-edge of chance to fall this way or that; others more elaborate, safer on the whole, but more liable to break down at some point of their ingenious intricacy. And setting aside complicity on the part of the manager—a condition that Carrados had satisfied himself did not exist—they all depended on a relaxation of the forms by which security was assured. Carrados continued to have several occasions to visit the safe during the week, and he "watched" with a quiet persistence that was deadly in its scope. But from beginning to end there was no indication of slackness in the business-like methods of the place; nor during any of his visits did the "tawny man" appear in that or any other disguise. Another week passed; Mr Carlyle was becoming inexpressibly waggish, and Carrados himself, although he did not abate a jot of his conviction, was compelled to bend to the realities of the situation. The manager, with the obstinacy of a conscientious man who had become obsessed with the pervading note of security, excused himself from discussing abstract methods of fraud. Carrados was not in a position to formulate a detailed charge; he withdrew from active investigation, content to await his time.

It came, to be precise, on a certain Friday morning, seventeen days after his first visit to "The Safe." Returning late on the Thursday night, he was informed that a man giving the name of Draycott had called to see him. Apparently the matter had been of some importance to the visitor for he had returned three hours later on the chance of finding Mr Carrados in. Disappointed in this, he had left a note. Carrados cut open the envelope and ran a finger along the following words:—

"Dear Sir,—I have to-day consulted Mr Louis Carlyle, who thinks that you would like to see me. I will call again in the morning, say at nine o'clock. If this is too soon or otherwise inconvenient I entreat you to leave a message fixing as early an hour as possible. to leave a message fixing as early an hour as possible.

Yours faithfully,
Herbert Draycott."

"P.S.—I should add that I am the renter of a safe at the Lucas Street depository. H. D."

A description of Mr Draycott made it clear that he was not the West-End bookmaker. The caller, the servant explained, was a thin, wiry, keen-faced man. Carrados felt agreeably interested in this development, which seemed to justify his suspicion of a plot.

At five minutes to nine the next morning Mr Draycott again presented himself.

"Very good of you to see me so soon, sir," he apologized, on Carrados at once receiving him. "I don't know much of English ways—I'm an Australian—and I was afraid it might be too early."

"You could have made it a couple of hours earlier as far as I am concerned," replied Carrados. "Or you either for that matter, I imagine," he added, "for I don't think that you slept much last night."

"I didn't sleep at all last night," corrected Mr Draycott. "But it's strange that you should have seen that. I understood from Mr Carlyle that you—excuse me if I am mistaken, sir—but I understood that you were blind."

Carrados laughed his admission lightly.

"Oh yes," he said. "But never mind that. What is the trouble?"

"I'm afraid it means more than just trouble for me, Mr Carrados." The man had steady, half-closed eyes, with the suggestion of depth which one notices in the eyes of those whose business it is to look out over great expanses of land or water; they were turned towards Carrados's face with quiet resignation in their frankness now. "I'm afraid it spells disaster. I am a working engineer from the Mount Magdalena district of Coolgardie. I don't want to take up your time with outside details so I will only say that about two years ago I had an opportunity of acquiring a share in a very promising claim—gold, you understand, both reef and alluvial. As the work went on I put more and more into the undertaking—you couldn't call it a venture by that time. The results were good, better than we had dared to expect, but from one cause and another the expenses were terrible. We saw that it was a bigger thing than we had bargained for and we admitted that we must get outside help."

So far Mr Draycott's narrative had proceeded smoothly enough under the influence of the quiet despair that had come over the man. But at this point a sudden recollection of his position swept him into a frenzy of bitterness.

"Oh, what the blazes is the good of going over all this again!" he broke out. "What can you or anyone else do anyhow? I've been robbed, rooked, cleared out of everything I possess," and tormented by recollections and by the impotence of his rage the unfortunate engineer beat the oak table with the back of his hand until his knuckles bled.

Carrados waited until the fury had passed.

"Continue, if you please, Mr Draycott," he said. "Just what you thought it best to tell me is just what I want to know."

"I'm sorry, sir," apologized the man, colouring under his tanned skin. "I ought to be able to control myself better. But this business has shaken me. Three times last night I looked down the barrel of my revolver, and three times I threw it away.... Well, we arranged that I should come to London to interest some financiers in the property. We might have done it locally or in Perth, to be sure, but then, don't you see, they would have wanted to get control. Six weeks ago I landed here. I brought with me specimens of the quartz and good samples of extracted gold, dust and nuggets, the clearing up of several weeks' working, about two hundred and forty ounces in all. That includes the Magdalena Lodestar, our lucky nugget, a lump weighing just under seven pounds of pure gold.

"I had seen an advertisement of this Lucas Street safe-deposit and it seemed just the thing I wanted. Besides the gold, I had all the papers to do with the claims—plans, reports, receipts, licences and so on. Then when I cashed my letter of credit I had about one hundred and fifty pounds in notes. Of course I could have left everything at a bank but it was more convenient to have it, as it were, in my own safe, to get at any time, and to have a private room that I could take any gentlemen to. I hadn't a suspicion that anything could be wrong. Negotiations hung on in several quarters—it's a bad time to do business here, I find. Then, yesterday, I wanted something. I went to Lucas Street, as I had done half-a-dozen times before, opened my safe, and had the inner case carried to a room.... Mr Carrados, it was empty!"

"Quite empty?"

"No." He laughed bitterly. "At the bottom was a sheet of wrapper paper. I recognized it as a piece I had left there in case I wanted to make up a parcel. But for that I should have been convinced that I had somehow opened the wrong safe. That was my first idea."

"It cannot be done."

"So I understand, sir. And, then, there was the paper with my name written on it in the empty tin. I was dazed; it seemed impossible. I think I stood there without moving for minutes—it was more like hours. Then I closed the tin box again, took it back, locked up the safe and came out."

"Without notifying anything wrong?"

"Yes, Mr Carrados." The steady blue eyes regarded him with pained thoughtfulness. "You see, I reckoned it out in that time that it must be someone about the place who had done it."

"You were wrong," said Carrados.

"So Mr Carlyle seemed to think. I only knew that the key had never been out of my possession and I had told no one of the password. Well, it did come over me rather like cold water down the neck, that there was I alone in the strongest dungeon in London and not a living soul knew where I was."

"Possibly a sort of up-to-date Sweeney Todd's?"

"I'd heard of such things in London," admitted Draycott. "Anyway, I got out. It was a mistake; I see it now. Who is to believe me as it is—it sounds a sort of unlikely tale. And how do they come to pick on me? to know what I had? I don't drink, or open my mouth, or hell round. It beats me."

"They didn't pick on you—you picked on them," replied Carrados. "Never mind how; you'll be believed all right. But as for getting anything back——" The unfinished sentence confirmed Mr Draycott in his gloomiest anticipations.

"I have the numbers of the notes," he suggested, with an attempt at hopefulness. "They can be stopped, I take it?"

"Stopped? Yes," admitted Carrados. "And what does that amount to? The banks and the police stations will be notified and every little public-house between here and Land's End will change one for the scribbling of 'John Jones' across the back. No, Mr Draycott, it's awkward, I dare say, but you must make up your mind to wait until you can get fresh supplies from home. Where are you staying?"

Draycott hesitated.

"I have been at the Abbotsford, in Bloomsbury, up to now," he said, with some embarrassment. "The fact is, Mr Carrados, I think I ought to have told you how I was placed before consulting you, because I—I see no prospect of being able to pay my way. Knowing that I had plenty in the safe, I had run it rather close. I went chiefly yesterday to get some notes. I have a week's hotel bill in my pocket, and"—he glanced down at his trousers—"I've ordered one or two other things unfortunately."

"That will be a matter of time, doubtless," suggested the other encouragingly.

Instead of replying Draycott suddenly dropped his arms on to the table and buried his face between them. A minute passed in silence.

"It's no good, Mr Carrados," he said, when he was able to speak; "I can't meet it. Say what you like, I simply can't tell those chaps that I've lost everything we had and ask them to send me more. They couldn't do it if I did. Understand, sir. The mine is a valuable one; we have the greatest faith in it, but it has gone beyond our depth. The three of us have put everything we own into it. While I am here they are doing labourers' work for a wage, just to keep going ... waiting, oh, my God! waiting for good news from me!"

Carrados walked round the table to his desk and wrote. Then, without a word, he held out a paper to his visitor.

"What's this?" demanded Draycott, in bewilderment. "It's—it's a cheque for a hundred pounds."

"It will carry you on," explained Carrados imperturbably. "A man like you isn't going to throw up the sponge for this set-back. Cable to your partners that you require copies of all the papers at once. They'll manage it, never fear. The gold ... must go. Write fully by the next mail. Tell them everything and add that in spite of all you feel that you are nearer success than ever."

Mr Draycott folded the cheque with thoughtful deliberation and put it carefully away in his pocket-book.

"I don't know whether you've guessed as much, sir," he said in a queer voice, "but I think that you've saved a man's life to-day. It's not the money, it's the encouragement ... and faith. If you could see you'd know better than I can say how I feel about it."

Carrados laughed quietly. It always amused him to have people explain how much more he would learn if he had eyes.

"Then we'll go on to Lucas Street and give the manager the shock of his life," was all he said. "Come, Mr Draycott, I have already rung up the car."

But, as it happened, another instrument had been destined to apply that stimulating experience to the manager. As they stepped out of the car opposite "The Safe" a taxicab drew up and Mr Carlyle's alert and cheery voice hailed them.

"A moment, Max," he called, turning to settle with his driver, a transaction that he invested with an air of dignified urbanity which almost made up for any small pecuniary disappointment that may have accompanied it. "This is indeed fortunate. Let us compare notes for a moment. I have just received an almost imploring message from the manager to come at once. I assumed that it was the affair of our colonial friend here, but he went on to mention Professor Holmfast Bulge. Can it really be possible that he also has made a similar discovery?"

"What did the manager say?" asked Carrados.

"He was practically incoherent, but I really think it must be so. What have you done?"

"Nothing," replied Carrados. He turned his back on "The Safe" and appeared to be regarding the other side of the street. "There is a tobacconist's shop directly opposite?"

"There is."

"What do they sell on the first floor?"

"Possibly they sell 'Rubbo.' I hazard the suggestion from the legend 'Rub in Rubbo for Everything' which embellishes each window."

"The windows are frosted?"

"They are, to half-way up, mysterious man."

Carrados walked back to his motor car.

"While we are away, Parkinson, go across and buy a tin, bottle, box or packet of 'Rubbo.'"

"What is 'Rubbo,' Max?" chirped Mr Carlyle with insatiable curiosity.

"So far we do not know. When Parkinson gets some, Louis, you shall be the one to try it."

They descended into the basement and were passed in by the grille-keeper, whose manner betrayed a discreet consciousness of something in the air. It was unnecessary to speculate why. In the distance, muffled by the armoured passages, an authoritative voice boomed like a sonorous bell heard under water.

"What, however, are the facts?" it was demanding, with the causticity of baffled helplessness. "I am assured that there is no other key in existence; yet my safe has been unlocked. I am given to understand that without the password it would be impossible for an unauthorized person to tamper with my property. My password, deliberately chosen, is 'anthropophaginian,' sir. Is it one that is familiarly on the lips of the criminal classes? But my safe is empty! What is the explanation? Who are the guilty persons? What is being done? Where are the police?"

"If you consider that the proper course to adopt is to stand on the doorstep and beckon in the first constable who happens to pass, permit me to say, sir, that I differ from you," retorted the distracted manager. "You may rely on everything possible being done to clear up the mystery. As I told you, I have already telephoned for a capable private detective and for one of my directors."

"But that is not enough," insisted the professor angrily. "Will one mere private detective restore my #6000 Japanese 4-1/2 per cent. bearer bonds? Is the return of my irreplaceable notes on 'Polyphyletic Bridal Customs among the mid-Pleistocene Cave Men' to depend on a solitary director? I demand that the police shall be called in—as many as are available. Let Scotland Yard be set in motion. A searching inquiry must be made. I have only been a user of your precious establishment for six months, and this is the result."

"There you hold the key of the mystery, Professor Bulge," interposed Carrados quietly.

"Who is this, sir?" demanded the exasperated professor at large.

"Permit me," explained Mr Carlyle, with bland assurance. "I am Louis Carlyle, of Bampton Street. This gentleman is Mr Max Carrados, the eminent amateur specialist in crime."

"I shall be thankful for any assistance towards elucidating this appalling business," condescended the professor sonorously. "Let me put you in possession of the facts——"

"Perhaps if we went into your room," suggested Carrados to the manager, "we should be less liable to interruption."

"Quite so; quite so," boomed the professor, accepting the proposal on everyone else's behalf. "The facts, sir, are these: I am the unfortunate possessor of a safe here, in which, a few months ago, I deposited—among less important matter—sixty bearer bonds of the Japanese Imperial Loan—the bulk of my small fortune—and the manuscript of an important projected work on 'Polyphyletic Bridal Customs among the mid-Pleistocene Cave Men.' To-day I came to detach the coupons which fall due on the fifteenth, to pay them into my bank a week in advance, in accordance with my custom. What do I find? I find the safe locked and apparently intact, as when I last saw it a month ago. But it is far from being intact, sir. It has been opened; ransacked, cleared out. Not a single bond; not a scrap of paper remains."

It was obvious that the manager's temperature had been rising during the latter part of this speech and now he boiled over.

"Pardon my flatly contradicting you, Professor Bulge. You have again referred to your visit here a month ago as your last. You will bear witness of that, gentlemen. When I inform you that the professor had access to his safe as recently as on Monday last you will recognize the importance that the statement may assume."

The professor glared across the room like an infuriated animal, a comparison heightened by his notoriously hircine appearance.

"How dare you contradict me, sir!" he cried, slapping the table sharply with his open hand. "I was not here on Monday."

The manager shrugged his shoulders coldly.

"You forget that the attendants also saw you," he remarked. "Cannot we trust our own eyes?"

"A common assumption, yet not always a strictly reliable one," insinuated Carrados softly.

"I cannot be mistaken."

"Then can you tell me, without looking, what colour Professor Bulge's eyes are?"

There was a curious and expectant silence for a minute. The professor turned his back on the manager and the manager passed from thoughtfulness to embarrassment.

"I really do not know, Mr Carrados," he declared loftily at last. "I do not refer to mere trifles like that."

"Then you can be mistaken," replied Carrados mildly yet with decision.

"But the ample hair, the venerable flowing beard, the prominent nose and heavy eyebrows——"

"These are just the striking points that are most easily counterfeited. They 'take the eye.' If you would ensure yourself against deception, learn rather to observe the eye itself, and particularly the spots on it, the shape of the fingernails, the set of the ears. These things cannot be simulated."

"You seriously suggest that the man was not Professor Bulge—that he was an impostor?"

"The conclusion is inevitable. Where were you on Monday, Professor?"

"I was on a short lecturing tour in the Midlands. On Saturday I was in Nottingham. On Monday in Birmingham. I did not return to London until yesterday."

Carrados turned to the manager again and indicated Draycott, who so far had remained in the background.

"And this gentleman? Did he by any chance come here on Monday?"

"He did not, Mr Carrados. But I gave him access to his safe on Tuesday afternoon and again yesterday."

Draycott shook his head sadly.

"Yesterday I found it empty," he said. "And all Tuesday afternoon I was at Brighton, trying to see a gentleman on business."

The manager sat down very suddenly.

"Good God, another!" he exclaimed faintly.

"I am afraid the list is only beginning," said Carrados. "We must go through your renters' book."

The manager roused himself to protest.

"That cannot be done. No one but myself or my deputy ever sees the book. It would be—unprecedented."

"The circumstances are unprecedented," replied Carrados.

"If any difficulties are placed in the way of these gentlemen's investigations, I shall make it my duty to bring the facts before the Home Secretary," announced the professor; speaking up to the ceiling with the voice of a brazen trumpet.

Carrados raised a deprecating hand.

"May I make a suggestion?" he remarked. "Now; I am blind. If, therefore——?"

"Very well," acquiesced the manager. "But I must request the others to withdraw."

For five minutes Carrados followed the list of safe-renters as the manager read them to him. Sometimes he stopped the catalogue to reflect a moment; now and then he brushed a finger-tip over a written signature and compared it with another. Occasionally a password interested him. But when the list came to an end he continued to look into space without any sign of enlightenment.

"So much is perfectly clear and yet so much is incredible," he mused. "You insist that you alone have been in charge for the last six months?"

"I have not been away a day this year."

"Meals?"

"I have my lunch sent in."

"And this room could not be entered without your knowledge while you were about the place?"

"It is impossible. The door is fitted with a powerful spring and a feather-touch self-acting lock. It cannot be left unlocked unless you deliberately prop it open."

"And, with your knowledge, no one has had an opportunity of having access to this book?"

"No," was the reply.

Carrados stood up and began to put on his gloves.

"Then I must decline to pursue my investigation any further," he said icily.

"Why?" stammered the manager.

"Because I have positive reason for believing that you are deceiving me."

"Pray sit down, Mr Carrados. It is quite true that when you put the last question to me a circumstance rushed into my mind which—so far as the strict letter was concerned—might seem to demand 'Yes' instead of 'No.' But not in the spirit of your inquiry. It would be absurd to attach any importance to the incident I refer to."

"That would be for me to judge."

"You shall do so, Mr Carrados. I live at Windermere Mansions with my sister. A few months ago she got to know a married couple who had recently come to the opposite flat. The husband was a middle-aged, scholarly man who spent most of his time in the British Museum. His wife's tastes were different; she was much younger, brighter, gayer; a mere girl in fact, one of the most charming and unaffected I have ever met. My sister Amelia does not readily——"

"Stop!" exclaimed Carrados. "A studious middle-aged man and a charming young wife! Be as brief as possible. If there is any chance it may turn on a matter of minutes at the ports. She came here, of course?"

"Accompanied by her husband," replied the manager stiffly. "Mrs Scott had travelled and she had a hobby of taking photographs wherever she went. When my position accidentally came out one evening she was carried away by the novel idea of adding views of a safe-deposit to her collection—as enthusiastic as a child. There was no reason why she should not; the place has often been taken for advertising purposes."

"She came, and brought her camera—under your very nose!"

"I do not know what you mean by 'under my very nose.' She came with her husband one evening just about our closing time. She brought her camera, of course—quite a small affair."

"And contrived to be in here alone?"

"I take exception to the word 'contrived.' It—it happened. I sent out for some tea, and in the course——"

"How long was she alone in here?"

"Two or three minutes at the most. When I returned she was seated at my desk. That was what I referred to. The little rogue had put on my glasses and had got hold of a big book. We were great chums, and she delighted to mock me. I confess that I was startled—merely instinctively—to see that she had taken up this book, but the next moment I saw that she had it upside down."

"Clever! She couldn't get it away in time. And the camera, with half-a-dozen of its specially sensitized films already snapped over the last few pages, by her side!"

"That child!"

"Yes. She is twenty-seven and has kicked hats off tall men's heads in every capital from Petersburg to Buenos Aires! Get through to Scotland Yard and ask if Inspector Beedel can come up."

The manager breathed heavily through his nose.

"To call in the police and publish everything would ruin this establishment—confidence would be gone. I cannot do it without further authority."

"Then the professor certainly will."

"Before you came I rang up the only director who is at present in town and gave him the facts as they then stood. Possibly he has arrived by this. If you will accompany me to the boardroom we will see."

They went up to the floor above, Mr Carlyle joining them on the way.

"Excuse me a moment," said the manager.

Parkinson, who had been having an improving conversation with the hall porter on the subject of land values, approached.

"I am sorry, sir," he reported, "but I was unable to procure any 'Rubbo.' The place appears to be shut up."

"That is a pity; Mr Carlyle had set his heart on it."

"Will you come this way, please?" said the manager, reappearing.

In the boardroom they found a white-haired old gentleman who had obeyed the manager's behest from a sense of duty, and then remained in a distant corner of the empty room in the hope that he might be overlooked. He was amiably helpless and appeared to be deeply aware of it.

"This is a very sad business, gentlemen," he said, in a whispering, confiding voice. "I am informed that you recommend calling in the Scotland Yard authorities. That would be a disastrous course for an institution that depends on the implicit confidence of the public."

"It is the only course," replied Carrados.

"The name of Mr Carrados is well known to us in connexion with a delicate case. Could you not carry this one through?"

"It is impossible. A wide inquiry must be made. Every port will have to be watched. The police alone can do that." He threw a little significance into the next sentence. "I alone can put the police in the right way of doing it."

"And you will do that, Mr Carrados?"

Carrados smiled engagingly. He knew exactly what constituted the great attraction of his services.

"My position is this," he explained. "So far my work has been entirely amateur. In that capacity I have averted one or two crimes, remedied an occasional injustice, and now and then been of service to my professional friend, Louis Carlyle. But there is no reason at all why I should serve a commercial firm in an ordinary affair of business for nothing. For any information I should require a fee, a quite nominal fee of, say, one hundred pounds."

The director looked as though his faith in human nature had received a rude blow.

"A hundred pounds would be a very large initial fee for a small firm like this, Mr Carrados," he remarked in a pained voice.

"And that, of course, would be independent of Mr Carlyle's professional charges," added Carrados.

"Is that sum contingent on any specific performance?" inquired the manager.

"I do not mind making it conditional on my procuring for you, for the police to act on, a photograph and a description of the thief."

The two officials conferred apart for a moment. Then the manager returned.

"We will agree, Mr Carrados, on the understanding that these things are to be in our hands within two days. Failing that——"

"No, no!" cried Mr Carlyle indignantly, but Carrados good-humouredly put him aside.

"I will accept the condition in the same sporting spirit that inspires it. Within forty-eight hours or no pay. The cheque, of course, to be given immediately the goods are delivered?"

"You may rely on that."

Carrados took out his pocket-book, produced an envelope bearing an American stamp, and from it extracted an unmounted print.

"Here is the photograph," he announced. "The man is called Ulysses K. Groom, but he is better known as 'Harry the Actor.' You will find the description written on the back."

Five minutes later, when they were alone, Mr Carlyle expressed his opinion of the transaction.

"You are an unmitigated humbug, Max," he said, "though an amiable one, I admit. But purely for your own private amusement you spring these things on people."

"On the contrary," replied Carrados, "people spring these things on me."

"Now this photograph. Why have I heard nothing of it before?"

Carrados took out his watch and touched the fingers.

"It is now three minutes to eleven. I received the photograph at twenty past eight."

"Even then, an hour ago you assured me that you had done nothing."

"Nor had I—so far as result went. Until the keystone of the edifice was wrung from the manager in his room, I was as far away from demonstrable certainty as ever."

"So am I—as yet," hinted Mr Carlyle.

"I am coming to that, Louis. I turn over the whole thing to you. The man has got two clear days' start and the chances are nine to one against catching him. We know everything, and the case has no further interest for me. But it is your business. Here is your material.

"On that one occasion when the 'tawny' man crossed our path, I took from the first a rather more serious view of his scope and intention than you did. That same day I sent a cipher cable to Pierson of the New York service. I asked for news of any man of such and such a description—merely negative—who was known to have left the States; an educated man, expert in the use of disguises, audacious in his operations, and a specialist in 'dry' work among banks and strong-rooms."

"Why the States, Max?"

"That was a sighting shot on my part. I argued that he must be an English-speaking man. The smart and inventive turn of the modern Yank has made him a specialist in ingenious devices, straight or crooked. Unpickable locks and invincible lock-pickers, burglar-proof safes and safe-specializing burglars, come equally from the States. So I tried a very simple test. As we talked that day and the man walked past us, I dropped the words 'New York'—or, rather, 'Noo Y'rk'—in his hearing."

"I know you did. He neither turned nor stopped."

"He was that much on his guard; but into his step there came—though your poor old eyes could not see it, Louis—the 'psychological pause,' an absolute arrest of perhaps a fifth of a second; just as it would have done with you if the word 'London' had fallen on your ear in a distant land. However, the whys and the wherefores don't matter. Here is the essential story.

"Eighteen months ago 'Harry the Actor' successfully looted the office safe of M'Kenkie, J. F. Higgs & Co.; of Cleveland, Ohio. He had just married a smart but very facile third-rate vaudeville actress—English by origin—and wanted money for the honeymoon. He got about five hundred pounds, and with that they came to Europe and stayed in London for some months. That period is marked by the Congreave Square post office burglary, you may remember. While studying such of the British institutions as most appealed to him, the 'Actor's' attention became fixed on this safe-deposit. Possibly the implied challenge contained in its telegraphic address grew on him until it became a point of professional honour with him to despoil it; at all events he was presumedly attracted by an undertaking that promised not only glory but very solid profit. The first part of the plot was, to the most skilful criminal 'impersonator' in the States, mere skittles. Spreading over those months he appeared at 'The Safe' in twelve different characters and rented twelve safes of different sizes. At the same time he made a thorough study of the methods of the place. As soon as possible he got the keys back again into legitimate use, having made duplicates for his own private ends, of course. Five he seems to have returned during his first stay; one was received later, with profuse apologies, by registered post; one was returned through a leading Berlin bank. Six months ago he made a flying visit here, purely to work off two more. One he kept from first to last, and the remaining couple he got in at the beginning of his second long residence here, three or four months ago.

"This brings us to the serious part of the cool enterprise. He had funds from the Atlantic and South-Central Mail-car coup when he arrived here last

April. He appears to have set up three establishments; a home, in the guise of an elderly scholar with a young wife, which, of course, was next door to our friend the manager; an observation point, over which he plastered the inscription 'Rub in Rubbo for Everything' as a reason for being; and, somewhere else, a dressing-room with essential conditions of two doors into different streets.

"About six weeks ago he entered the last stage. Mrs Harry, with quite ridiculous ease, got photographs of the necessary page or two of the record-book. I don't doubt that for weeks before then everyone who entered the place had been observed, but the photographs linked them up with the actual men into whose hands the 'Actor's' old keys had passed—gave their names and addresses, the numbers of their safes, their passwords and signatures. The rest was easy."

"Yes, by Jupiter; mere play for a man like that," agreed Mr Carlyle, with professional admiration. "He could contrive a dozen different occasions for studying the voice and manner and appearance of his victims. How much has he cleared?"

"We can only speculate as yet. I have put my hand on seven doubtful callers on Monday and Tuesday last. Two others he had ignored for some reason; the remaining two safes had not been allotted. There is one point that raises an interesting speculation."

"What is that, Max?"

"The 'Actor' has one associate, a man known as 'Billy the Fondant,' but beyond that—with the exception of his wife, of course—he does not usually trust anyone. It is plain, however, that at least seven men must latterly have been kept under close observation. It has occurred to me——"

"Yes, Max?"

"I have wondered whether Harry has enlisted the innocent services of one or other of our clever private inquiry offices."

"Scarcely," smiled the professional. "It would hardly pass muster."

"Oh, I don't know. Mrs Harry, in the character of a jealous wife or a suspicious sweetheart, might reasonably——"

Mr Carlyle's smile suddenly faded.

"By Jupiter!" he exclaimed. "I remember——"

"Yes, Louis?" prompted Carrados, with laughter in his voice.

"I remember that I must telephone to a client before Beedel comes," concluded Mr Carlyle, rising in some haste.

At the door he almost ran into the subdued director, who was wringing his hands in helpless protest at a new stroke of calamity.

"Mr Carrados," wailed the poor old gentleman in a tremulous bleat, "Mr Carrados, there is another now—Sir Benjamin Gump. He insists on seeing me. You will not—you will not desert us?"

"I should have to stay a week," replied Carrados briskly, "and I'm just off now. There will be a procession. Mr Carlyle will support you, I am sure."

He nodded "Good-morning" straight into the eyes of each and found his way out with the astonishing certainty of movement that made so many forget his infirmity. Possibly he was not desirous of encountering Draycott's embarrassed gratitude again, for in less than a minute they heard the swirl of his departing car.

"Never mind, my dear sir," Mr Carlyle assured his client, with impenetrable complacency. "Never mind. I will remain instead. Perhaps I had better make myself known to Sir Benjamin at once."

The director turned on him the pleading, trustful look of a cornered dormouse.

"He is in the basement," he whispered. "I shall be in the boardroom—if necessary."

Mr Carlyle had no difficulty in discovering the centre of interest in the basement. Sir Benjamin was expansive and reserved, bewildered and decisive, long-winded and short-tempered, each in turn and more or less all at once. He had already demanded the attention of the manager, Professor Bulge, Draycott and two underlings to his case and they were now involved in a babel of inutile reiteration. The inquiry agent was at once drawn into a circle of interrogation that he did his best to satisfy impressively while himself learning the new facts.

The latest development was sufficiently astonishing. Less than an hour before Sir Benjamin had received a parcel by district messenger. It contained a jewel-case which ought at that moment to have been securely reposing in one of the deposit safes. Hastily snatching it open, the recipient's incredible forebodings were realized. It was empty—empty of jewels, that is to say, for, as if to add a sting to the blow, a neatly inscribed card had been placed inside, and on it the agitated baronet read the appropriate but at the moment rather gratuitous maxim: "Lay not up for yourselves treasures upon earth——"

The card was passed round and all eyes demanded the expert's pronouncement.

"'—where moth and rust doth corrupt and where thieves break through and steal.' H'm," read Mr Carlyle with weight. "This is a most important clue, Sir Benjamin——"

"Hey, what? What's that?" exclaimed a voice from the other side of the hall. "Why, damme if I don't believe you've got another! Look at that, gentlemen; look at that. What's on, I say? Here now, come; give me my safe. I want to know where I am."

It was the bookmaker who strode tempestuously in among them, flourishing before their faces a replica of the card that was in Mr Carlyle's hand.

"Well, upon my soul this is most extraordinary," exclaimed that gentleman, comparing the two. "You have just received this, Mr—Mr Berge, isn't it?"

"That's right, Berge—'Iceberg' on the course. Thank the Lord Harry, I can take my losses coolly enough, but this—this is a facer. Put into my hand half-an-hour ago inside an envelope that ought to be here and as safe as in the Bank of England. What's the game, I say? Here, Johnny, hurry and let me into my safe."

Discipline and method had for the moment gone by the board. There was no suggestion of the boasted safeguards of the establishment. The manager added his voice to that of the client, and when the attendant did not at once appear he called again.

"John, come and give Mr Berge access to his safe at once."

"All right, sir," pleaded the harassed key-attendant; hurrying up with the burden of his own distraction. "There's a silly fathead got in what thinks this is a left-luggage office, so far as I can make out—a foreigner."

"Never mind that now," replied the manager severely. "Mr Berge's safe: No. 01724."

The attendant and Mr Berge went off together down one of the brilliant colonnaded vistas. One or two of the others who had caught the words glanced across and became aware of a strange figure that was drifting indecisively towards them. He was obviously an elderly German tourist of pronounced type—long-haired, spectacled, outrageously garbed and involved in the mental abstraction of his philosophical race. One hand was occupied with the manipulation of a pipe, as markedly Teutonic as its owner; the other grasped a carpet-bag that would have ensured an opening laugh to any low comedian.

Quite impervious to the preoccupation of the group, the German made his way up to them and picked out the manager.

"This was a safety deposit, nicht wahr?"

"Quite so," acquiesced the manager loftily, "but just now——"

"Your fellow was dense of gomprehension." The eyes behind the clumsy glasses wrinkled to a ponderous humour. "He forgot his own business. Now this goot bag——"

Brought into fuller prominence, the carpet-bag revealed further details of its overburdened proportions. At one end a flannel shirt cuff protruded in limp dejection; at the other an ancient collar, with the grotesque attachment known as a "dickey," asserted its presence. No wonder the manager frowned his annoyance. "The Safe" was in low enough repute among its patrons at that moment without any burlesque interlude to its tragic hour.

"Yes, yes," he whispered, attempting to lead the would-be depositor away, "but you are under a mistake. This is not——"

"It was a safety deposit? Goot. Mine bag—I would deposit him in safety till the time of mine train. Ja?"

"Nein, nein!" almost hissed the agonized official. "Go away, sir, go away! It isn't a cloakroom. John, let this gentleman out."

The attendant and Mr Berge were returning from their quest. The inner box had been opened and there was no need to ask the result. The bookmaker was shaking his head like a baffled bull.

"Gone, no effects," he shouted across the hall. "Lifted from 'The Safe,' by crumb!"

To those who knew nothing of the method and operation of the fraud it seemed as if the financial security of the Capital was tottering. An amazed silence fell, and in it they heard the great grille door of the basement clang on the inopportune foreigner's departure. But, as if it was impossible to stand still on that morning of dire happenings, he was immediately succeeded by a dapper, keen-faced man in severe clerical attire who had been let in as the intruder passed out.

"Canon Petersham!" exclaimed the professor, going forward to greet him.

"My dear Professor Bulge!" reciprocated the canon. "You here! A most disquieting thing has happened to me. I must have my safe at once." He divided his attention between the manager and the professor as he monopolized them both. "A most disquieting and—and outrageous circumstance. My safe, please—yes, yes, Rev. Henry Noakes Petersham. I have just received by hand a box, a small box of no value but one that I thought, yes, I am convinced that it was the one, a box that was used to contain certain valuables of family interest which should at this moment be in my safe here. No. 7436? Very likely, very likely. Yes, here is my key. But not content with the disconcerting effect of that, professor, the box contained—and I protest that it's a most unseemly thing to quote any text from the Bible in this way to a clergyman of my position—well, here it is. 'Lay not up for yourselves treasures upon earth——' Why, I have a dozen sermons of my own in my desk now on that very verse. I'm particularly partial to the very needful lesson that it teaches. And to apply it to me! It's monstrous!"

"No. 7436, John," ordered the manager, with weary resignation.

The attendant again led the way towards another armour-plated aisle. Smartly turning a corner, he stumbled over something, bit a profane exclamation in two, and looked back.

"It's that bloomin' foreigner's old bag again," he explained across the place in aggrieved apology. "He left it here after all."

"Take it upstairs and throw it out when you've finished," said the manager shortly.

"Here, wait a minute," pondered John, in absent-minded familiarity. "Wait a minute. This is a funny go. There's a label on that wasn't here before. 'Why not look inside?'"

"'Why not look inside?'" repeated someone.

"That's what it says."

There was another puzzled silence. All were arrested by some intangible suggestion of a deeper mystery than they had yet touched. One by one they began to cross the hall with the conscious air of men who were not curious but thought that they might as well see.

"Why, curse my crumpet," suddenly exploded Mr Berge, "if that ain't the same writing as these texts!"

"By gad, but I believe you are right," assented Mr Carlyle. "Well, why not look inside?"

The attendant, from his stooping posture, took the verdict of the ring of faces and in a trice tugged open the two buckles. The central fastening was not locked, and yielded to a touch. The flannel shirt, the weird collar and a few other garments in the nature of a "top-dressing" were flung out and John's hand plunged deeper....

Harry the Actor had lived up to his dramatic instinct. Nothing was wrapped up; nay, the rich booty had been deliberately opened out and displayed, as it were, so that the overturning of the bag, when John the keybearer in an access of riotous extravagance lifted it up and strewed its contents broadcast on the floor, was like the looting of a smuggler's den, or the realization of a speculator's dream, or the bursting of an Aladdin's cave, or something incredibly lavish and bizarre. Bank-notes fluttered down and lay about in all directions, relays of sovereigns rolled away like so much dross, bonds and scrip for thousands and tens of thousands clogged the downpouring stream of jewellery and unset gems. A yellow stone the size of a four-pound weight and twice as heavy dropped plump upon the canon's toes and sent him hopping and grimacing to the wall. A ruby-hilted kris cut across the manager's wrist as he strove to arrest the splendid rout. Still the miraculous cornucopia deluged the ground, with its pattering, ringing, bumping, crinkling, rolling, fluttering produce until, like the final tableau of some spectacular ballet, it ended with a golden rain that masked the details of the heap beneath a glittering veil of yellow sand.

"My dust!" gasped Draycott.

"My fivers, by golly!" ejaculated the bookmaker, initiating a plunge among the spoil.

"My Japanese bonds, coupons and all, and—yes, even the manuscript of my work on 'Polyphyletic Bridal Customs among the mid-Pleistocene Cave Men.' Hah!" Something approaching a cachinnation of delight closed the professor's contribution to the pandemonium, and eyewitnesses afterwards declared that for a moment the dignified scientist stood on one foot in the opening movement of a can-can.

"My wife's diamonds, thank heaven!" cried Sir Benjamin, with the air of a schoolboy who was very well out of a swishing.

"But what does it mean?" demanded the bewildered canon. "Here are my family heirlooms—a few decent pearls, my grandfather's collection of camei and other trifles—but who——?"

"Perhaps this offers some explanation," suggested Mr Carlyle, unpinning an envelope that had been secured to the lining of the bag. "It is addressed 'To Seven Rich Sinners.' Shall I read it for you?"

For some reason the response was not unanimous, but it was sufficient. Mr Carlyle cut open the envelope.

"My dear Friends,—Aren't you glad? Aren't you happy at this moment? Ah yes; but not with the true joy of regeneration that alone can bring lightness to the afflicted soul. Pause while there is yet time. Cast off the burden of your sinful lusts, for what shall it profit a man if he shall gain the whole world and lose his own soul? (Mark, chap. viii., v. 36.)

"Oh, my friends, you have had an all-fired narrow squeak. Up till the Friday in last week I held your wealth in the hollow of my ungodly hand and rejoiced in my nefarious cunning, but on that day as I with my guilty female accomplice stood listening with worldly amusement to the testimony of a converted brother at a meeting of the Salvation Army on Clapham Common, the gospel light suddenly shone into our rebellious souls and then and there we found salvation. Hallelujah!

"What we have done to complete the unrighteous scheme upon which we had laboured for months has only been for your own good, dear friends that you are, though as yet divided from us by your carnal lusts. Let this be a lesson to you. Sell all you have and give it to the poor—through the organization of the Salvation Army by preference—and thereby lay up for yourselves treasures where neither moth nor rust doth corrupt and where thieves do not break through and steal. (Matthew, chap, vi., v. 20.)

"Yours in good works,

"Private Henry, the Salvationist.

"P.S. (in haste).—I may as well inform you that no crib is really uncrackable, though the Cyrus J. Coy Co.'s Safe Deposit on West 24th Street, N.Y., comes nearest the kernel. And even that I could work to the bare rock if I took hold of the job with both hands—that is to say I could have done in my sinful days. As for you, I should recommend you to change your T. A. to 'Peanut.'

"U. K. G."

"There sounds a streak of the old Adam in that postscript, Mr Carlyle," whispered Inspector Beedel, who had just arrived in time to hear the letter read.

"I will see Miss George now," assented Carrados. Parkinson retired and Greatorex looked round from his chair. The morning "clearing-up" was still in progress.

"Shall I go?" he inquired.

"Not unless the lady desires it. I don't know her at all."

The secretary was not unobservant and he had profited from his association with Mr Carrados. Without more ado, he began to get his papers quietly together.

The door opened and a girl of about twenty came eagerly yet half timorously into the room. Her eyes for a moment swept Carrados with an anxious scrutiny. Then, with a slight shade of disappointment, she noticed that they were not alone.

"I have come direct from Oakshire to see you, Mr Carrados," she announced, in a quick, nervous voice that was evidently the outcome of a desperate resolution to be brave and explicit. "The matter is a dreadfully important one to me and I should very much prefer to tell it to you alone."

There was no need for Carrados to turn towards his secretary; that discriminating young gentleman was already on his way. Miss George flashed him a shy look of thanks and filled in the moment with a timid survey of the room.

"Is it something that you think I can help you with?"

"I had hoped so. I had heard in a roundabout way of your wonderful power—ought I to tell you how—does it matter?"

"Not in the least if it has nothing to do with the case," replied Carrados.

"When this dreadful thing happened I instinctively thought of you. I felt sure that I ought to come and get you to help me at once. But I—I have very little money, Mr Carrados, only a few pounds, and I am not so childish as not to know that very clever men require large fees. Then when I got here my heart sank, for I saw at once from your house and position that what seemed little even to me would be ridiculous to you—that if you did help me it would be purely out of kindness of heart and generosity."

"Suppose you tell me what the circumstances are," suggested Carrados cautiously. Then, to afford an opening, he added: "You have recently gone into mourning, I see."

"See!" exclaimed the girl almost sharply. "Then you are not blind?"

"Oh yes," he replied; "only I use the familiar expression, partly from custom, partly because it sounds unnecessarily pedantic to say, 'I deduce from certain observations.'"

"I beg your pardon. I suppose I was startled not so much by the expression as by your knowledge. I ought to have been prepared. But I am already wasting your time and I came so determined to be business-like. I got a copy of the local paper on the way, because I thought that the account in it would be clearer to you than I could tell it. Shall I read it?"

"Please; if that was your intention."

"It is The Stinbridge Herald," explained the girl, taking a closely folded newspaper from the handbag which she carried. "Stinbridge is our nearest town—about six miles from Tilling Shaw, where we live. This is the account:

"'MYSTERIOUS TRAGEDY AT TILLING

"'Well-known Agriculturalist Attempts Murder and Commits Suicide

"'The districts of Great Tilling, Tilling Shaw and the immediate neighbourhood were thrown into a state of unusual excitement on Thursday last by the report of a tragedy in their midst such as has rarely marked the annals of our law-abiding country-side.

"'A Herald representative was early on the scene, and his inquiries elucidated the fact that it was only too true that in this case rumour had not exaggerated the circumstances, rather the reverse indeed.

"'On the afternoon of the day in question, Mr Frank Whitmarsh, of High Barn, presented himself at Barony, the residence of his uncle, Mr William Whitmarsh, with the intention of seeing him in reference to a dispute that was pending between them. This is understood to be connected with an alleged trespass in pursuit of game, each relative claiming exclusive sporting rights over a piece of water known as Hunstan Mere.

"'On this occasion the elder gentleman was not at home and Mr Frank Whitmarsh, after waiting for some time, departed, leaving a message to the effect that he would return, and, according to one report, "have it out with Uncle William," later in the evening.

"'This resolution he unfortunately kept. Returning about eight-forty-five p.m. he found his uncle in and for some time the two men remained together in the dining-room. What actually passed between them has not yet transpired, but it is said that for half-an-hour there had been nothing to indicate to the other occupants of the house that anything unusual was in progress when suddenly two shots rang out in rapid succession. Mrs Lawrence, the housekeeper at Barony, and a servant were the soonest on the spot, and, conquering the natural terror that for a moment held them outside the now silent room, they summoned up courage to throw open the door and to enter. The first thing that met their eyes was the body of Mr Frank Whitmarsh lying on the floor almost at their feet. In their distressed state it was immediately assumed by the horrified women that he was dead, or at least seriously wounded, but a closer examination revealed the fact that the gentleman had experienced an almost miraculous escape. At the time of the tragedy he was wearing a large old-fashioned silver watch; and in this the bullet intended for his heart was found, literally embedded deep in the works. The second shot had, however, effected its purpose, for at the other side of the room, still seated at the table, was Mr William Whitmarsh, already quite dead, with a terrible wound in his head and the weapon, a large-bore revolver of obsolete pattern, lying at his feet.

"'Mr Frank Whitmarsh subsequently explained that the shock of the attack, and the dreadful appearance presented by his uncle when, immediately afterwards, he turned his hand against himself, must have caused him to faint.

"'Readers of The Herald will join in our expression of sympathy for all members of the Whitmarsh family, and in our congratulations to Mr Frank Whitmarsh on his providential escape.

"'The inquest is fixed for Monday and it is anticipated that the funeral will take place on the following day.'"

"That is all," concluded Miss George.

"All that is in the paper," amended Carrados.

"It is the same everywhere—'attempted murder and suicide'—that is what everyone accepts as a matter of course," went on the girl quickly. "How do they know that my father tried to kill Frank, or that he killed himself? How can they know, Mr Carrados?"

"Your father, Miss George?"

"Yes. My name is Madeline Whitmarsh. At home everyone looks at me as if I was an object of mingled pity and reproach. I thought that they might know the name here, so I gave the first that came into my head. I think it is a street I was directed along. Besides, I don't want it to be known that I came to see you in any case."

"Why?"

Much of the girl's conscious nervousness had stiffened into an attitude of unconscious hardness. Grief takes many forms, and whatever she had been before, the tragic episode had left Miss Whitmarsh a little hurt and cynical.

"You are a man living in a town and can do as you like. I am a girl living in the country and have therefore to do largely as my neighbours like. For me to set up my opinion against popular feeling would constitute no small offence; to question its justice would be held to be adding outrageous insult to enormous injury."

"So far I am unable to go beyond the newspaper account. On the face of it, your father—with what provocation of course I do not know—did attempt this Mr Frank Whitmarsh's life and then take his own. You imply another version. What reason have you?"

"That is the terrible part of it," exclaimed the girl, with rising distress. "It was that which made me so afraid of coming to you, although I felt that I must, for I dreaded that when you asked me for proofs and I could give you none you would refuse to help me. We were not even in time to hear him speak, and yet I know, know with absolute conviction, that my father would not have done this. There are things that you cannot explain, Mr Carrados, and—well, there is an end of it."

Her voice sank to an absent-minded whisper.

"Everyone will condemn him now that he cannot defend himself, and yet he could not even have had the revolver that was found at his feet."

"What is that?" demanded Carrados sharply. "Do you mean that?"

"Mean what?" she asked, with the blankness of one who has lost the thread of her own thoughts.

"What you said about the revolver—that your father could not have had it?"

"The revolver?" she repeated half wearily; "oh yes. It was a heavy, old-fashioned affair. It had been lying in a drawer of his desk for more than ten years because once a dog came into the orchard in broad daylight light and worried half-a-dozen lambs before anyone could do anything."

"Yes, but why could he not have it on Thursday?"

"I noticed that it was gone. After Frank had left in the afternoon I went into the room where he had been waiting, to finish dusting. The paper says the dining-room, but it was really papa's business-room and no one else used it. Then when I was dusting the desk I saw that the revolver was no longer there."

"You had occasion to open the drawer?"

"It is really a very old bureau and none of the drawers fit closely. Dust lies on the ledges and you always have to open them a little to dust properly. They were never kept locked."

"Possibly your father had taken the revolver with him."

"No. I had seen it there after he had gone. He rode to Stinbridge immediately after lunch and did not return until nearly eight. After he left I went to dust his room. It was then that I saw it. I was doing the desk when Frank knocked and interrupted me. That is how I came to be there twice."

"But you said that you had no proof, Miss Whitmarsh," Carrados reminded her, with deep seriousness. "Do you not recognize the importance—the deadly importance—that this one shred of evidence may assume?"

"Does it?" she replied simply. "I am afraid that I am rather dull just now. All yesterday I was absolutely dazed; I could not do the most ordinary things. I found myself looking at the clock for minutes together, yet absolutely incapable of grasping what time it was. In the same way I know that it struck me as being funny about the revolver but I always had to give it up. It was as though everything was there but things would not fit in."

"You are sure, absolutely sure, that you saw the revolver there after your father had left, and missed it before he returned?"

"Oh yes," said the girl quickly; "I remember realizing how curious it was at the time. Besides there is something else. I so often had things to ask papa about when he was out of the house that I got into the way of making little notes to remind me later. This morning I found on my dressing-table one that I had written on Thursday afternoon."

"About this weapon?"

"Yes; to ask him what could have become of it."

Carrados made a further inquiry, and this was Madeline Whitmarsh's account of affairs existing between the two branches of the family:

Until the time of William Whitmarsh, father of the William Whitmarsh just deceased, the properties of Barony and High Barn had formed one estate, descending from a William senior to a William junior down a moderately long line of yeomen Whitmarshes. Through the influence of his second wife this William senior divided the property, leaving Barony with its four hundred acres of good land to William junior, and High Barn, with which went three hundred acres of poor land, to his other son, father of the Frank implicated in the recent tragedy. But though divided, the two farms still had one common link. Beneath their growing corn and varied pasturage lay, it was generally admitted, a seam of coal at a depth and of a thickness that would render its working a paying venture. Even in William the Divider's time, when the idea was new, money in plenty would have been forthcoming, but he would have none of it, and when he died his will contained a provision restraining either son from mining or exploiting his land for mineral without the consent and co-operation of the other.

This restriction became a legacy of hate. The brothers were only half-brothers and William having suffered unforgettably at the hands of his step-mother had old scores to pay off. Quite comfortably prosperous on his own rich farm, and quite satisfied with the excellent shooting and the congenial life, he had not the slightest desire to increase his wealth. He had the old dour, peasant-like instinct to cling to the house and the land of his forefathers. From this position no argument moved him.

In the meanwhile, on the other side of the new boundary fence, Frank senior was growing poorer year by year. To his periodical entreaties that William would agree to shafts being sunk on High Barn he received an emphatic "Never in my time!" The poor man argued, besought, threatened and swore; the prosperous one shook his head and grinned. Carrados did not need to hear the local saying: "Half brothers: whole haters; like the Whitmarshes," to read the situation.

"Of course I do not really understand the business part of it," said Madeline, "and many people blamed poor papa, especially when Uncle Frank drank himself to death. But I know that it was not mere obstinacy. He loved the undisturbed, peaceful land just as it was, and his father had wished it to remain the same. Collieries would bring swarms of strange men into the neighbourhood, poachers and trespassers, he said. The smoke and dust would ruin the land for miles round and drive away the game, and in the end, if the work did not turn out profitable, we should all be much worse off than before."

"Does the restriction lapse now; will Mr Frank junior be able to mine?"

"It will now lie with Frank and my brother William, just as it did before with their fathers. I should expect Willie to be quite favourable. He is more—modern."

"You have not spoken of your brother."

"I have two. Bob, the younger, is in Mexico," she explained; "and Willie in Canada with an engineering firm. They did not get on very well with papa and they went away."

It did not require preternatural observation to deduce that the late William Whitmarsh had been "a little difficult."

"When Uncle Frank died, less than six months ago, Frank came back to High Barn from South Africa. He had been away about two years."

"Possibly he did not get on well with his father?"

Madeline smiled sadly.

"I am afraid that no two Whitmarsh men ever did get on well together," she admitted.

"Your father and young Frank, for instance?"

"Their lands adjoin; there were always quarrels and disputes," she replied. "Then Frank had his father's grievance over again."

"He wished to mine?"

"Yes. He told me that he had had experience of coal in Natal."

"There was no absolute ostracism between you then? You were to some extent friends?"

"Scarcely." She appeared to reflect. "Acquaintances.... We met occasionally, of course, at people's houses."

"You did not visit High Barn?"

"Oh no."

"But there was no particular reason why you should not?"

"Why do you ask me that?" she demanded quickly, and in a tone that was quite incompatible with the simple inquiry. Then, recognizing the fact, she added, with shamefaced penitence: "I beg your pardon, Mr Carrados. I am afraid that my nerves have gone to pieces since Thursday. The most ordinary things affect me inexplicably."

"That is a common experience in such circumstances," said Carrados reassuringly. "Where were you at the time of the tragedy?"

"I was in my bedroom, which is rather high up, changing. I had driven down to the village, to give an order, and had just returned. Mrs Lawrence told me that she had been afraid there might be quarrelling, but no one would ever have dreamed of this, and then came a loud shot and then, after a few seconds, another not so loud, and we rushed to the door—she and Mary first—and everything was absolutely still."

"A loud shot and then another not so loud?"

"Yes; I noticed that even at the time. I happened to speak to Mrs Lawrence of it afterwards and then she also remembered that it had been like that."

Afterwards Carrados often recalled with grim pleasantry that the two absolutely vital points in the fabric of circumstantial evidence that was to exonerate her father and fasten the guilt upon another had dropped from the girl's lips utterly by chance. But at the moment the facts themselves monopolized his attention.

"You are not disappointed that I can tell you so little?" she asked timidly.

"Scarcely," he replied. "A suicide who could not have had the weapon he dies by, a victim who is miraculously preserved by an opportune watch, and two shots from the same pistol that differ materially in volume, all taken together do not admit of disappointment."

"I am very stupid," she said. "I do not seem able to follow things. But you will come and clear my father's name?"

"I will come," he replied. "Beyond that who shall prophesy?"

It had been arranged between them that the girl should return at once, while Carrados would travel down to Great Tilling late that same afternoon and put up at the local fishing inn. In the evening he would call at Barony, where Madeline would accept him as a distant connexion of the family. The arrangement was only for the benefit of the domestics and any casual visitor who might be present, for there was no possibility of a near relation being in attendance. Nor was there any appreciable danger of either his name or person being recognized in those parts, a consideration that seemed to have some weight with the girl, for, more than once, she entreated him not to disclose to anyone his real business there until he had arrived at a definite conclusion.

It was nine o'clock, but still just light enough to distinguish the prominent features of the landscape, when Carrados, accompanied by Parkinson, reached Barony. The house, as described by the man-servant, was a substantial grey stone building, very plain, very square, very exposed to the four winds. It had not even a porch to break the flat surface, and here and there in the line of its three solid storeys a window had been built up by some frugal, tax-evading Whitmarsh of a hundred years ago.

"Sombre enough," commented Carrados, "but the connexion between environment and crime is not yet capable of analysis. We get murders in brand-new suburban villas and the virtues, light-heartedness and good-fellowship, in moated granges. What should you say about it, eh, Parkinson?"

"I should say it was damp, sir," observed Parkinson, with his wisest air.

Madeline Whitmarsh herself opened the door. She took them down the long flagged hall to the dining-room, a cheerful enough apartment whatever its exterior might forebode.

"I am glad you have come now, Mr Carrados," she said hurriedly, when the door was closed. "Sergeant Brewster is here from Stinbridge police station to make some arrangements for the inquest. It is to be held at the schools here on Monday. He says that he must take the revolver with him to produce. Do you want to see it before he goes?"

"I should like to," replied Carrados.

"Will you come into papa's room then? He is there."

The sergeant was at the table, making notes in his pocket-book, when they entered. An old-fashioned revolver lay before him.

"This gentleman has come a long way on hearing about poor papa," said the girl. "He would like to see the revolver before you take it, Mr Brewster."

"Good-evening, sir," said Brewster. "It's a bad business that brings us here."

Carrados "looked" round the room and returned the policeman's greeting. Madeline hesitated for a moment, and then, picking up the weapon, put it into the blind man's hand.

"A bit out of date, sir," remarked Brewster, with a nod. "But in good order yet, I find."

"An early French make, I should say; one of Lefaucheux's probably," said Carrados. "You have removed the cartridges?"

"Why, yes," admitted the sergeant, producing a matchbox from his pocket. "They're pin-fire, you see, and I'm not too fond of carrying a thing like that loaded in my pocket as I'm riding a young horse."

"Quite so," agreed Carrados, fingering the cartridges. "I wonder if you happened to mark the order of these in the chambers?"

"That was scarcely necessary, sir. Two, together, had been fired; the other four had not."

"I once knew a case—possibly I read of it—where a pack of cards lay on the floor. It was a murder case and the guilt or innocence of an accused man depended on the relative positions of the fifty-first and fifty-second cards."

"I think you must have read of that, sir," replied Brewster, endeavouring to implicate first Miss Whitmarsh and then Parkinson in his meaning smile. "However, this is straightforward enough."

"Then, of course, you have not thought it worth while to look for anything else?"

"I have noted all the facts that have any bearing on the case. Were you referring to any particular point, sir?"

"I was only wondering," suggested Carrados, with apologetic mildness, "whether you, or anyone, had happened to find a wad lying about anywhere."

The sergeant stroked his well-kept moustache to hide the smile that insisted, however, on escaping through his eyes.

"Scarcely, sir," he replied, with fine irony. "Bulleted revolver cartridges contain no wad. You are thinking of a shot-gun, sir."

"Oh," said Carrados, bending over the spent cartridge he was examining, "that settles it, of course."

"I think so, sir," assented the sergeant, courteously but with a quiet enjoyment of the situation. "Well, miss, I'll be getting back now. I think I have everything I want."

"You will excuse me a few minutes?" said Miss Whitmarsh, and the two callers were left alone.

"Parkinson," said Carrados softly, as the door closed, "look round on the floor. There is no wad lying within sight?"

"No, sir."

"Then take the lamp and look behind things. But if you find one don't disturb it."

For a minute strange and gigantic shadows chased one another across the ceiling as Parkinson moved the table-lamp to and fro behind the furniture. The man to whom blazing sunlight and the deepest shade were as one sat with his eyes fixed tranquilly on the unseen wall before him.

"There is a little pellet of paper here behind the couch, sir," announced Parkinson.

"Then put the lamp back."

Together they drew the cumbrous old piece of furniture from the wall and Carrados went behind. On hands and knees, with his face almost to the floor, he appeared to be studying even the dust that lay there. Then with a light, unerring touch he carefully picked up the thing that Parkinson had found. Very gently he unrolled it, using his long, delicate fingers so skilfully that even at the end the particles of dust still clung here and there to the surface of the paper.

"What do you make of it, Parkinson?"

Parkinson submitted it to the judgment of a single sense.

"A cigarette-paper to all appearance, sir. I can't say it's a kind that I've had experience of. It doesn't seem to have any distinct watermark but there is a half-inch of glossy paper along one edge."

"Amber-tipped. Yes?"

"Another edge is a little uneven; it appears to have been cut."

"This edge opposite the mouthpiece. Yes, yes."

"Patches are blackened, and little holes—like pinpricks—burned through. In places it is scorched brown."

"Anything else?"

"I hope there is nothing I have failed to observe, sir," said Parkinson, after a pause.

Carrados's reply was a strangely irrelevant question.

"What is the ceiling made of?" he demanded.

"Oak boards, sir, with a heavy cross-beam."

"Are there any plaster figures about the room?"

"No, sir."

"Or anything at all that is whitewashed?"

"Nothing, sir."

Carrados raised the scrap of tissue paper to his nose again, and for the second time he touched it with his tongue.

"Very interesting, Parkinson," he remarked, and Parkinson's responsive "Yes, sir" was a model of discreet acquiescence.

"I am sorry that I had to leave you," said Miss Whitmarsh, returning, "but Mrs Lawrence is out and my father made a practice of offering everyone refreshment."

"Don't mention it," said Carrados. "We have not been idle. I came from London to pick up a scrap of paper, lying on the floor of this room. Well, here it is." He rolled the tissue into a pellet again and held it before her eyes.

"The wad!" she exclaimed eagerly. "Oh, that proves that I was right?"

"Scarcely 'proves,' Miss Whitmarsh."

"But it shows that one of the shots was a blank charge, as you suggested this morning might have been the case."

"Hardly even that."

"What then?" she demanded, with her large dark eyes fixed in a curious fascination on his inscrutable face.

"That behind the couch we have found this scrap of powder-singed paper."

There was a moment's silence. The girl turned away her head.

"I am afraid that I am a little disappointed," she murmured.

"Perhaps better now than later. I wished to warn you that we must prove every inch of ground. Does your cousin Frank smoke cigarettes?"

"I cannot say, Mr Carrados. You see ... I knew so little of him."

"Quite so; there was just the chance. And your father?"

"He never did. He despised them."

"That is all I need ask you now. What time to-morrow shall I find you in, Miss Whitmarsh? It is Sunday, you remember."

"At any time. The curiosity I inspire doesn't tempt me to encounter my friends, I can assure you," she replied, her face hardening at the recollection. "But ... Mr Carrados——"

"Yes?"

"The inquest is on Monday afternoon.... I had a sort of desperate faith that you would be able to vindicate papa."

"By the time of the inquest, you mean?"

"Yes. Otherwise——"

"The verdict of a coroner's jury means nothing, Miss Whitmarsh. It is the merest formality."

"It means a very great deal to me. It haunts and oppresses me. If they say—if it goes out—that papa is guilty of the attempt of murder, and of suicide, I shall never raise my head again."

Carrados had no desire to prolong a futile discussion.

"Good-night," he said, holding out his hand.

"Good-night, Mr Carrados." She detained him a moment, her voice vibrant with quiet feeling. "I already owe you more than I can ever hope to express. Your wonderful kindness——"

"A strange case," moralized Carrados, as they walked out of the quadrangular yard into the silent lane. "Instructive, but I more than half wish I'd never heard of it."

"The young lady seems grateful, sir," Parkinson ventured to suggest.

"The young lady is the case, Parkinson," replied his master rather grimly.

A few score yards farther on a swing gate gave access to a field-path, cutting off the corner that the high road made with the narrow lane. This was their way, but instead of following the brown line of trodden earth Carrados turned to the left and indicated the line of buildings that formed the back of one side of the quadrangle they had passed through.

"We will investigate here," he said. "Can you see a way in?"

Most of the buildings opened on to the yard, but at one end of the range Parkinson discovered a door, secured only by a wooden latch. The place beyond was impenetrably dark, but the sweet, dusty smell of hay, and, from beyond, the occasional click of a horse's shoe on stone and the rattle of a head-stall chain through the manger ring told them that they were in the chaff-pen at the back of the stable.

Carrados stretched out his hand and touched the wall with a single finger.

"We need go no farther," he remarked, and as they resumed their way across the field he took out a handkerchief to wipe the taste of whitewash off his tongue.

Madeline had spoken of the gradual decay of High Barn, but Carrados was hardly prepared for the poverty-stricken desolation which Parkinson described as they approached the homestead on the following afternoon. He had purposely selected a way that took them across many of young Whitmarsh's ill-stocked fields, fields in which sedge and charlock wrote an indictment of neglected drains and half-hearted tillage. On the land, the gates and hedges had been broken and unkempt; the buildings, as they passed through the farmyard, were empty and showed here and there a skeletonry of bare rafters to the sky.

"Starved," commented the blind man, as he read the signs. "The thirsty owner and the hungry land: they couldn't both be fed."

Although it was afternoon the bolts and locks of the front door had to be unfastened in answer to their knock. When at last the door was opened a shrivelled little old woman, rather wicked-looking in a comic way, and rather begrimed, stood there.

"Mr Frank Whitmarsh?" she replied to Carrados's polite inquiry; "oh yes, he lives here. Frank," she called down the passage, "you're wanted."

"What is it, mother?" responded a man's full, strong voice rather lazily.

"Come and see!" and the old creature ogled Carrados with her beady eyes as though the situation constituted an excellent joke between them.

There was the sound of a chair being moved and at the end of the passage a tall man appeared in his shirt sleeves.

"I am a stranger to you," explained Carrados, "but I am staying at the Bridge Inn and I heard of your wonderful escape on Thursday. I was so interested that I have taken the liberty of coming across to congratulate you on it."

"Oh, come in, come in," said Whitmarsh. "Yes ... it was a sort of miracle, wasn't it?"

He led the way back into the room he had come from, half kitchen, half parlour. It at least had the virtue of an air of rude comfort, and some of the pewter and china that ornamented its mantelpiece and dresser would have rejoiced a collector's heart.

"You find us a bit rough," apologized the young man, with something of contempt towards his surroundings. "We weren't expecting visitors."

"And I was hesitating to come because I thought that you would be surrounded by your friends."

This very ordinary remark seemed to afford Mrs Whitmarsh unbounded entertainment and for quite a number of seconds she was convulsed with silent amusement at the idea.

"Shut up, mother," said her dutiful son. "Don't take any notice of her," he remarked to his visitors, "she often goes on like that. The fact is," he added, "we Whitmarshes aren't popular in these parts. Of course that doesn't trouble me; I've seen too much of things. And, taken as a boiling, the Whitmarshes deserve it."

"Ah, wait till you touch the coal, my boy, then you'll see," put in the old lady, with malicious triumph.

"I reckon we'll show them then, eh, mother?" he responded bumptiously. "Perhaps you've heard of that, Mr——?"

"Carrados—Wynn Carrados. This is my man, Parkinson. I have to be attended because my sight has failed me. Yes, I had heard something about coal. Providence seems to be on your side just now, Mr Whitmarsh. May I offer you a cigarette?"

"Thanks, I don't mind for once in a way."

"They're Turkish; quite innocuous, I believe."

"Oh, it isn't that. I can smoke cutty with any man, I reckon, but the paper affects my lips. I make my own and use a sort of paper with an end that doesn't stick."

"The paper is certainly a drawback sometimes," agreed Carrados. "I've found that. Might I try one of yours?"

They exchanged cigarettes and Whitmarsh returned to the subject of the tragedy.

"This has made a bit of a stir, I can tell you," he remarked, with complacency.

"I am sure it would. Well, it was the chief topic of conversation when I was in London."

"Is that a fact?" Avowedly indifferent to the opinion of his neighbours, even Whitmarsh was not proof against the pronouncement of the metropolis. "What do they say about it up there?"

"I should be inclined to think that the interest centres round the explanation you will give at the inquest of the cause of the quarrel."

"There! What did I tell you?" exclaimed Mrs Whitmarsh.

"Be quiet, mother. That's easily answered, Mr Carrados. There was a bit of duck shooting that lay between our two places. But perhaps you saw that in the papers?"

"Yes," admitted Carrados, "I saw that. Frankly, the reason seemed inadequate to so deadly a climax."

"What did I say?" demanded the irrepressible dame. "They won't believe it."

The young man cast a wrathful look in his mother's direction and turned again to the visitor.

"That's because you don't know Uncle William. Any reason was good enough for him to quarrel over. Here, let me give you an instance. When I went in on Thursday he was smoking a pipe. Well, after a bit I took out a cigarette and lit it. I'm damned if he didn't turn round and start on me for that. How does that strike you for one of your own family, Mr Carrados?"

"Unreasonable, I am bound to admit. I am afraid that I should have been inclined to argue the point. What did you do, Mr Whitmarsh?"

"I hadn't gone there to quarrel," replied the young man, half sulky at the recollection. "It was his house. I threw it into the fireplace."

"Very obliging," said Carrados. "But, if I may say so, it isn't so much a matter of speculation why he should shoot you as why he should shoot himself."

"The gentleman seems friendly. Better ask his advice, Frank," put in the old woman in a penetrating whisper.

"Stow it, mother!" said Whitmarsh sharply. "Are you crazy? Her idea of a coroner's inquest," he explained to Carrados, with easy contempt, "is that I am being tried for murder. As a matter of fact, Uncle William was a very passionate man, and, like many of that kind, he frequently went beyond himself. I don't doubt that he was sure he'd killed me, for he was a good shot and the force of the blow sent me backwards. He was a very proud man too, in a way—wouldn't stand correction or any kind of authority, and when he realized what he'd done and saw in a flash that he would be tried and hanged for it, suicide seemed the easiest way out of his difficulties, I suppose."

"Yes; that sounds reasonable enough," admitted Carrados.

"Then you don't think there will be any trouble, sir?" insinuated Mrs Whitmarsh anxiously.

Frank had already professed his indifference to local opinion, but Carrados was conscious that both of them hung rather breathlessly on to his reply.

"Why, no," he declared weightily. "I should see no reason for anticipating any. Unless," he added thoughtfully, "some clever lawyer was instructed to insist that there must be more in the dispute than appears on the surface."

"Oh, them lawyers, them lawyers!" moaned the old lady in a panic. "They can make you say anything."

"They can't make me say anything." A cunning look came into his complacent face. "And, besides, who's going to engage a lawyer?"

"The family of the deceased gentleman might wish to do so."

"Both of the sons are abroad and could not be back in time."

"But is there not a daughter here? I understood so."

Whitmarsh gave a short, unpleasant laugh and turned to look at his mother.

"Madeline won't. You may bet your bottom tikkie it's the last thing she would want."

The little old creature gazed admiringly at her big showy son and responded with an appreciative grimace that made her look more humorously rat-like than ever.

"He! he! Missie won't," she tittered. "That would never do. He! he!" Wink succeeded nod and meaning smile until she relapsed into a state of quietness; and Parkinson, who had been fascinated by her contortions, was unable to decide whether she was still laughing or had gone to sleep.

Carrados stayed a few more minutes and before they left he asked to see the watch.

"A unique memento, Mr Whitmarsh," he remarked, examining it. "I should think this would become a family heirloom."

"It's no good for anything else," said Whitmarsh practically. "A famous time-keeper it was, too."

"The fingers are both gone."

"Yes; the glass was broken, of course, and they must have caught in the cloth of my pocket and ripped off."

"They naturally would; it was ten minutes past nine when the shot was fired."

The young man thought and then nodded.

"About that," he agreed.

"Nearer than 'about,' if your watch was correct. Very interesting, Mr Whitmarsh. I am glad to have seen the watch that saved your life."

Instead of returning to the inn Carrados directed Parkinson to take the road to Barony. Madeline was at home, and from the sound of voices it appeared that she had other visitors, but she came out to Carrados at once, and at his request took him into the empty dining-room while Parkinson stayed in the hall.

"Yes?" she said eagerly.

"I have come to tell you that I must throw up my brief," he said. "There is nothing more to be done and I return to town to-night."

"Oh!" she stammered helplessly. "I thought—I thought——"

"Your cousin did not abstract the revolver when he was here on Thursday, Miss Whitmarsh. He did not at his leisure fire a bullet into his own watch to make it appear, later in the day, as if he had been attacked. He did not reload the cartridge with a blank charge. He did not deliberately shoot your father and then fire off the blank cartridge. He was attacked and the newspaper version is substantially correct. The whole fabric so delicately suggested by inference and innuendo falls to pieces."

"Then you desert me, Mr Carrados?" she said, in a low, bitter voice.

"I have seen the watch—the watch that saved Whitmarsh's life," he continued, unmoved. "It would save it again if necessary. It indicates ten minutes past nine—the time to a minute at which it is agreed the shot was fired. By what prescience was he to know at what exact minute his opportunity would occur?"

"When I saw the watch on Thursday night the fingers were not there."

"They are not, but the shaft remains. It is of an old-fashioned pattern and it will only take the fingers in one position. That position indicates ten minutes past nine."

"Surely it would have been an easy matter to have altered that afterwards?"

"In this case fate has been curiously systematic, Miss Whitmarsh. The bullet that shattered the works has so locked the action that it will not move a fraction this way or that."

"There is something more than this—something that I do not understand," she persisted. "I think I have a right to know."

"Since you insist, there is. There is the wad of the blank cartridge that you fired in the outbuilding."

"Oh!" she exclaimed, in the moment of startled undefence, "how do you—how can you——"

"You must leave the conjurer his few tricks for effect. Of course you naturally would fire it where the precious pellet could not get lost—the paper you steamed off the cigarette that Whitmarsh threw into the empty fire-grate; and of course the place must be some distance from the house or even that slight report might occasion remark."

"Yes," she confessed, in a sudden abandonment to weary indifference, "it has been useless. I was a fool to set my cleverness against yours. Now, I suppose, Mr Carrados, you will have to hand me over to justice?

"Well; why don't you say something?" she demanded impatiently, as he offered no comment.

"People frequently put me in this embarrassing position," he explained diffidently, "and throw the responsibility on me. Now a number of years ago a large and stately building was set up in London and it was beautifully called 'The Royal Palace of Justice.' That was its official name and that was what it was to be; but very soon people got into the way of calling it the Law Courts, and to-day, if you asked a Londoner to direct you to the Palace of Justice he would undoubtedly set you down as a religious maniac. You see my difficulty?"

"It is very strange," she said, intent upon her own reflections, "but I do not feel a bit ashamed to you of what I have done. I do not even feel afraid to tell you all about it, although of some of that I must certainly be ashamed. Why is it?"

"Because I am blind?"

"Oh no," she replied very positively.

Carrados smiled at her decision but he did not seek to explain that when he could no longer see the faces of men the power was gradually given to him of looking into their hearts, to which some in their turn—strong, free spirits—instinctively responded.

"There is such a thing as friendship at first sight," he suggested.

"Why, yes; like quite old friends," she agreed. "It is a pity that I had no very trusty friend, since my mother died when I was quite little. Even my father has been—it is queer to think of it now—well, almost a stranger to me really."

She looked at Carrados's serene and kindly face and smiled.

"It is a great relief to be able to talk like this, without the necessity for lying," she remarked. "Did you know that I was engaged?"

"No; you had not told me that."

"Oh no, but you might have heard of it. He is a clergyman whom I met last summer. But, of course, that is all over now."

"You have broken it off?"

"Circumstances have broken it off. The daughter of a man who had the misfortune to be murdered might just possibly be tolerated as a vicar's wife, but the daughter of a murderer and suicide—it is unthinkable! You see, the requirements for the office are largely social, Mr Carrados."

"Possibly your vicar may have other views."

"Oh, he isn't a vicar yet, but he is rather well-connected, so it is quite assured. And he would be dreadfully torn if the choice lay with him. As it is, he will perhaps rather soon get over my absence. But, you see, if we married he could never get over my presence; it would always stand in the way of his preferment. I worked very hard to make it possible, but it could not be."

"You were even prepared to send an innocent man to the gallows?"

"I think so, at one time," she admitted frankly. "But I scarcely thought it would come to that. There are so many well-meaning people who always get up petitions.... No, as I stand here looking at myself over there, I feel that I couldn't quite have hanged Frank, no matter how much he deserved it.... You are very shocked, Mr Carrados?"

"Well," admitted Carrados, with pleasant impartiality, "I have seen the young man, but the penalty, even with a reprieve, still seems to me a little severe."

"Yet how do you know, even now, that he is, as you say, an innocent man?"

"I don't," was the prompt admission. "I only know, in this astonishing case, that so far as my investigation goes, he did not murder your father by the act of his hand."

"Not according to your Law Courts?" she suggested. "But in the great Palace of Justice?... Well, you shall judge."

She left his side, crossed the room, and stood by the square, ugly window, looking out, but as blind as Carrados to the details of the somnolent landscape.

"I met Frank for the first time after I was at all grown-up about three years ago, when I returned from boarding-school. I had not seen him since I was a child, and I thought him very tall and manly. It seemed a frightfully romantic thing in the circumstances to meet him secretly—of course my thoughts flew to Romeo and Juliet. We put impassioned letters for one another in a hollow tree that stood on the boundary hedge. But presently I found out—gradually and incredulously at first and then one night with a sudden terrible certainty—that my ideas of romance were not his.... I had what is called, I believe, a narrow escape. I was glad when he went abroad, for it was only my self-conceit that had suffered. I was never in love with him: only in love with the idea of being in love with him.

"A few months ago Frank came back to High Barn. I tried never to meet him anywhere, but one day he overtook me in the lanes. He said that he had thought a lot about me while he was away, and would I marry him. I told him that it was impossible in any case, and, besides, I was engaged. He coolly replied that he knew. I was dumbfounded and asked him what he meant.

"Then he took out a packet of my letters that he had kept somewhere all the time. He insisted on reading parts of them up and telling me what this and that meant and what everyone would say it proved. I was horrified at the construction that seemed capable of being put on my foolish but innocent gush. I called him a coward and a blackguard and a mean cur and a sneaking cad and everything I could think of in one long breath, until I found myself faint and sick with excitement and the nameless growing terror of it.

"He only laughed and told me to think it over, and then walked on, throwing the letters up into the air and catching them.

"It isn't worth while going into all the times he met and threatened me. I was to marry him or he would expose me. He would never allow me to marry anyone else. And then finally he turned round and said that he didn't really want to marry me at all; he only wanted to force father's consent to start mining and this had seemed the easiest way."

"That is what is called blackmail, Miss Whitmarsh; a word you don't seem to have applied to him. The punishment ranges up to penal servitude for life in extreme cases."

"Yes, that is what it really was. He came on Thursday with the letters in his pocket. That was his last threat when he could not move me. I can guess what happened. He read the letters and proposed a bargain. And my father, who was a very passionate man, and very proud in certain ways, shot him as he thought, and then, in shame and in the madness of despair, took his own life.... Now, Mr Carrados, you were to be my judge."

"I think," said the blind man, with a great pity in his voice, "that it will be sufficient for you to come up for Judgment when called upon."

Three weeks later a registered letter bearing the Liverpool postmark was delivered at The Turrets. After he had read it Carrados put it away in a special drawer of his desk, and once or twice in after years, when his work seemed rather barren, he took it out and read it. This is what it contained:

"Dear Mr Carrados,—Some time after you had left me that Sunday afternoon, a man came in the dark to the door and asked for me. I did not see his face for he kept in the shade, but his figure was not very unlike that of your servant Parkinson. A packet was put into my hands and he was gone without a word. From this I imagine that perhaps you did not leave quite as soon as you had intended.

"Thank you very much indeed for the letters. I was glad to have the miserable things, to drop them into the fire, and to see them pass utterly out of my own and everybody else's life. I wonder who else in the world would have done so much for a forlorn creature who just flashed across a few days of his busy life? and then I wonder who else could.

"But there is something else for which I thank you now far, far more, and that is for saving me from the blindness of my own passionate folly. When I look back on the abyss of meanness, treachery and guilt into which I would have wilfully cast myself, and been condemned to live in all my life, I can scarcely trust myself to write.

"I will not say that I do not suffer now. I think I shall for many years to come, but all the bitterness and I think all the hardness have been drawn out.

"You will see that I am writing from Liverpool. I have taken a second-class passage to Canada and we sail to-night. Willie, who returned to Barony last week, has lent me all the money I shall need until I find work. Do not be apprehensive. It is not with the vague uncertainty of an indifferent typist or a downtrodden governess that I go, but as an efficient domestic servant—a capable cook, housemaid or 'general,' as need be. It sounds rather incredible at first, does it not, but such things happen, and I shall get on very well.

"Good-bye, Mr Carrados; I shall remember you very often and very gratefully.

"Madeline Whitmarsh.

"P.S.—Yes, there is friendship at first sight."

The Comedy at Fountain Cottage

Carrados had rung up Mr Carlyle soon after the inquiry agent had reached his office in Bampton Street on a certain morning in April. Mr Carlyle's face at once assumed its most amiable expression as he recognized his friend's voice.

"Yes, Max," he replied, in answer to the call, "I am here and at the top of form, thanks. Glad to know that you are back from Trescoe. Is there—anything?"

"I have a couple of men coming in this evening whom you might like to meet," explained Carrados. "Manoel the Zambesia explorer is one and the other an East-End slum doctor who has seen a few things. Do you care to come round to dinner?"

"Delighted," warbled Mr Carlyle, without a moment's consideration. "Charmed. Your usual hour, Max?" Then the smiling complacence of his face suddenly changed and the wire conveyed an exclamation of annoyance. "I am really very sorry, Max, but I have just remembered that I have an engagement. I fear that I must deny myself after all."

"Is it important?"

"No," admitted Mr Carlyle. "Strictly speaking, it is not in the least important; this is why I feel compelled to keep it. It is only to dine with my niece. They have just got into an absurd doll's house of a villa at Groat's Heath and I had promised to go there this evening."

"Are they particular to a day?"

There was a moment's hesitation before Mr Carlyle replied.

"I am afraid so, now it is fixed," he said. "To you, Max, it will be ridiculous or incomprehensible that a third to dinner—and he only a middle-aged uncle—should make a straw of difference. But I know that in their bijou way it will be a little domestic event to Elsie—an added anxiety in giving the butcher an order, an extra course for dinner, perhaps; a careful drilling of the one diminutive maid-servant, and she is such a charming little woman—eh? Who, Max? No! No! I did not say the maid-servant; if I did it is the fault of this telephone. Elsie is such a delightful little creature that, upon my soul, it would be too bad to fail her now."

"Of course it would, you old humbug," agreed Carrados, with sympathetic laughter in his voice. "Well, come to-morrow instead. I shall be alone."

"Oh, besides, there is a special reason for going, which for the moment I forgot," explained Mr Carlyle, after accepting the invitation. "Elsie wishes for my advice with regard to her next-door neighbour. He is an elderly man of retiring disposition and he makes a practice of throwing kidneys over into her garden."

"Kittens! Throwing kittens?"

"No, no, Max. Kidneys. Stewed k-i-d-n-e-y-s. It is a little difficult to explain plausibly over a badly vibrating telephone, I admit, but that is what Elsie's letter assured me, and she adds that she is in despair."

"At all events it makes the lady quite independent of the butcher, Louis!"

"I have no further particulars, Max. It may be a solitary diurnal offering, or the sky may at times appear to rain kidneys. If it is a mania the symptoms may even have become more pronounced and the man is possibly showering beef-steaks across by this time. I will make full inquiry and let you know."

"Do," assented Carrados, in the same light-hearted spirit. "Mrs Nickleby's neighbourly admirer expressed his feelings by throwing cucumbers, you remember, but this man puts him completely in the shade."

It had not got beyond the proportions of a jest to either of them when they rang off—one of those whimsical occurrences in real life that sound so fantastic in outline. Carrados did not give the matter another thought until the next evening when his friend's arrival revived the subject.

"And the gentleman next door?" he inquired among his greetings. "Did the customary offering arrive while you were there?"

"No," admitted Mr Carlyle, beaming pleasantly upon all the familiar appointments of the room, "it did not, Max. In fact, so diffident has the mysterious philanthropist become, that no one at Fountain Cottage has been able to catch sight of him lately, although I am told that Scamp—Elsie's terrier—betrays a very self-conscious guilt and suspiciously muddy paws every morning."

"Fountain Cottage?"

"That is the name of the toy villa."

"Yes, but Fountain something, Groat's Heath—Fountain Court: wasn't that where Metrobe——?"

"Yes, yes, to be sure, Max. Metrobe the traveller, the writer and scientist——"

"Scientist!"

"Well, he took up spiritualism or something, didn't he? At any rate, he lived at Fountain Court, an old red-brick house in a large neglected garden there, until his death a couple of years ago. Then, as Groat's Heath had suddenly become a popular suburb with a tube railway, a land company acquired the estate, the house was razed to the ground and in a twinkling a colony of Noah's ark villas took its place. There is Metrobe Road here, and Court Crescent there, and Mansion Drive and what not, and Elsie's little place perpetuates another landmark."

"I have Metrobe's last book there," said Carrados, nodding towards a point on his shelves. "In fact he sent me a copy. 'The Flame beyond the Dome' it is called—the queerest farrago of balderdash and metaphysics imaginable. But what about the neighbour, Louis? Did you settle what we might almost term 'his hash'?"

"Oh, he is mad, of course. I advised her to make as little fuss about it as possible, seeing that the man lives next door and might become objectionable, but I framed a note for her to send which will probably have a good effect."

"Is he mad, Louis?"

"Well, I don't say that he is strictly a lunatic, but there is obviously a screw loose somewhere. He may carry indiscriminate benevolence towards Yorkshire terriers to irrational lengths. Or he may be a food specialist with a grievance. In effect he is mad on at least that one point. How else are we to account for the circumstances?"

"I was wondering," replied Carrados thoughtfully.

"You suggest that he really may have a sane object?"

"I suggest it—for the sake of argument. If he has a sane object, what is it?"

"That I leave to you, Max," retorted Mr Carlyle conclusively. "If he has a sane object, pray what is it?"

"For the sake of the argument I will tell you that in half-a-dozen words, Louis," replied Carrados, with good-humoured tolerance. "If he is not mad in the sense which you have defined, the answer stares us in the face. His object is precisely that which he is achieving."

Mr Carlyle looked inquiringly into the placid, unemotional face of his blind friend, as if to read there whether, incredible as it might seem, Max should be taking the thing seriously after all.

"And what is that?" he asked cautiously.

"In the first place he has produced the impression that he is eccentric or irresponsible. That is sometimes useful in itself. Then what else has he done?"

"What else, Max?" replied Mr Carlyle, with some indignation. "Well, whatever he wishes to achieve by it I can tell you one thing else that he has done. He has so demoralized Scamp with his confounded kidneys that Elsie's neatly arranged flower-beds—and she took Fountain Cottage principally on account of an unusually large garden—are hopelessly devastated. If she keeps the dog up, the garden is invaded night and day by an army of peregrinating feline marauders that scent the booty from afar. He has gained the everlasting annoyance of an otherwise charming neighbour, Max. Can you tell me what he has achieved by that?"

"The everlasting esteem of Scamp probably. Is he a good watch-dog, Louis?"

"Good heavens, Max!" exclaimed Mr Carlyle, coming to his feet as though he had the intention of setting out for Groat's Heath then and there, "is it possible that he is planning a burglary?"

"Do they keep much of value about the house?"

"No," admitted Mr Carlyle, sitting down again with considerable relief. "No, they don't. Bellmark is not particularly well endowed with worldly goods—in fact, between ourselves, Max, Elsie could have done very much better from a strictly social point of view, but he is a thoroughly good fellow and idolizes her. They have no silver worth speaking of, and for the rest—well, just the ordinary petty cash of a frugal young couple."

"Then he probably is not planning a burglary. I confess that the idea did not appeal to me. If it is only that, why should he go to the trouble of preparing this particular succulent dish to throw over his neighbour's ground when cold liver would do quite as well?"

"If it is not only that, why should he go to the trouble, Max?"

"Because by that bait he produces the greatest disturbance of your niece's garden."

"And, if sane, why should he wish to do that?"

"Because in those conditions he can the more easily obliterate his own traces if he trespasses there at nights."

"Well, upon my word, that's drawing a bow at a venture, Max. If it isn't burglary, what motive could the man have for any such nocturnal perambulation?"

An expression of suave mischief came into Carrados's usually imperturbable face.

"Many imaginable motives surely, Louis. You are a man of the world. Why not to meet a charming little woman——"

"No, by gad!" exclaimed the scandalized uncle warmly; "I decline to consider the remotest possibility of that explanation. Elsie——"

"Certainly not," interposed Carrados, smothering his quiet laughter. "The maid-servant, of course."

Mr Carlyle reined in his indignation and recovered himself with his usual adroitness.

"But, you know, that is an atrocious libel, Max," he added. "I never said such a thing. However, is it probable?"

"No," admitted Carrados. "I don't think that in the circumstances it is at all probable."

"Then where are we, Max?"

"A little further than we were at the beginning. Very little.... Are you willing to give me a roving commission to investigate?"

"Of course, Max, of course," assented Mr Carlyle heartily. "I—well, as far as I was concerned, I regarded the matter as settled."

Carrados turned to his desk and the ghost of a smile might possibly have lurked about his face. He produced some stationery and indicated it to his visitor.

"You don't mind giving me a line of introduction to your niece?"

"Pleasure," murmured Carlyle, taking up a pen. "What shall I say?"

Carrados took the inquiry in its most literal sense and for reply he dictated the following letter:—

"'My dear Elsie,'—

"If that is the way you usually address her," he parenthesized.

"Quite so," acquiesced Mr Carlyle, writing.

"'The bearer of this is Mr Carrados, of whom I have spoken to you.'

"You have spoken of me to her, I trust, Louis?" he put in.

"I believe that I have casually referred to you," admitted the writer.

"I felt sure you would have done. It makes the rest easier.

"'He is not in the least mad although he frequently does things which to the uninitiated appear more or less eccentric at the moment. I think that you would be quite safe in complying with any suggestion he may make.

"'Your affectionate uncle,

"'Louis Carlyle.'"

He accepted the envelope and put it away in a pocket-book that always seemed extraordinarily thin for the amount of papers it contained.

"I may call there to-morrow," he added.

Neither again referred to the subject during the evening, but when Parkinson came to the library a couple of hours after midnight to know whether he would be required again, he found his master rather deeply immersed in a book and a gap on the shelf where "The Flame beyond the Dome" had formerly stood.

It is not impossible that Mr Carlyle supplemented his brief note of introduction with a more detailed communication that reached his niece by the ordinary postal service at an earlier hour than the other. At all events, when Mr Carrados presented himself at the toy villa on the following afternoon he found Elsie Bellmark suspiciously disposed to accept him and his rather gratuitous intervention among her suburban troubles as a matter of course.

When the car drew up at the bright green wooden gate of Fountain Cottage another visitor, apparently a good-class working man, was standing on the path of the trim front garden, lingering over a reluctant departure. Carrados took sufficient time in alighting to allow the man to pass through the gate before he himself entered. The last exchange of sentences reached his ear.

"I'm sure, marm, you won't find anyone to do the work at less."

"I can quite believe that," replied a very fair young lady who stood nearer the house, "but, you see, we do all the gardening ourselves, thank you."

Carrados made himself known and was taken into the daintily pretty drawing-room that opened on to the lawn behind the house.

"I do not need to ask if you are Mrs Bellmark," he had declared.

"I have Uncle Louis's voice?" she divined readily.

"The niece of his voice, so to speak," he admitted. "Voices mean a great deal to me, Mrs Bellmark."

"In recognizing and identifying people?" she suggested.

"Oh, very much more than that. In recognizing and identifying their moods—their thoughts even. There are subtle lines of trouble and the deep rings of anxious care quite as patent to the ear as to the sharpest eye sometimes."

Elsie Bellmark shot a glance of curiously interested speculation to the face that, in spite of its frank, open bearing, revealed so marvellously little itself.

"If I had any dreadful secret, I think that I should be a little afraid to talk to you, Mr Carrados," she said, with a half-nervous laugh.

"Then please do not have any dreadful secret," he replied, with quite youthful gallantry. "I more than suspect that Louis has given you a very transpontine idea of my tastes. I do not spend all my time tracking murderers to their lairs, Mrs Bellmark, and I have never yet engaged in a hand-to-hand encounter with a band of cut-throats."

"He told us," she declared, the recital lifting her voice into a tone that Carrados vowed to himself was wonderfully thrilling, "about this: He said that you were once in a sort of lonely underground cellar near the river with two desperate men whom you could send to penal servitude. The police, who were to have been there at a certain time, had not arrived, and you were alone. The men had heard that you were blind but they could hardly believe it. They were discussing in whispers which could not be overheard what would be the best thing to do, and they had just agreed that if you really were blind they would risk the attempt to murder you. Then, Louis said, at that very moment you took a pair of scissors from your pocket, and coolly asking them why they did not have a lamp down there, you actually snuffed the candle that stood on the table before you. Is that true?"

Carrados's mind leapt vividly back to the most desperate moment of his existence, but his smile was gently deprecating as he replied:

"I seem to recognize the touch of truth in the inclination to do anything rather than fight," he confessed. "But, although he never suspects it, Louis really sees life through rose-coloured opera glasses. Take the case of your quite commonplace neighbour——"

"That is really what you came about?" she interposed shrewdly.

"Frankly, it is," he replied. "I am more attracted by a turn of the odd and grotesque than by the most elaborate tragedy. The fantastic conceit of throwing stewed kidneys over into a neighbour's garden irresistibly appealed to me. Louis, as I was saying, regards the man in the romantic light of a humanitarian monomaniac or a demented food reformer. I take a more subdued view and I think that his action, when rightly understood, will prove to be something quite obviously natural."

"Of course it is very ridiculous, but all the same it has been desperately annoying," she confessed. "Still, it scarcely matters now. I am only sorry that it should have been the cause of wasting your valuable time, Mr Carrados."

"My valuable time," he replied, "only seems valuable to me when I am, as you would say, wasting it. But is the incident closed? Louis told me that he had drafted you a letter of remonstrance. May I ask if it has been effective?"

Instead of replying at once she got up and walked to the long French window and looked out over the garden where the fruit-trees that had been spared from the older cultivation were rejoicing the eye with the promise of their pink and white profusion.

"I did not send it," she said slowly, turning to her visitor again. "There is something that I did not tell Uncle Louis, because it would only have distressed him without doing any good. We may be leaving here very soon."

"Just when you had begun to get it well in hand?" he said, in some surprise.

"It is a pity, is it not, but one cannot foresee these things. There is no reason why you should not know the cause, since you have interested yourself so far, Mr Carrados. In fact," she added, smiling away the seriousness of the manner into which she had fallen, "I am not at all sure that you do not know already."

He shook his head and disclaimed any such prescience.

"At all events you recognized that I was not exactly light-hearted," she insisted. "Oh, you did not say that I had dark rings under my eyes, I know, but the cap fitted excellently.... It has to do with my husband's business. He is with a firm of architects. It was a little venturesome taking this house—we had been in apartments for two years—but Roy was doing so well with his people and I was so enthusiastic for a garden that we did—scarcely two months ago. Everything seemed quite assured. Then came this thunderbolt. The partners—it is only a small firm, Mr Carrados—required a little more capital in the business. Someone whom they know is willing to put in two thousand pounds, but he stipulates for a post with them as well. He, like my husband, is a draughtsman. There is no need for the services of both and so——"

"Is it settled?"

"In effect, it is. They are as nice as can be about it but that does not alter the facts. They declare that they would rather have Roy than the new man and they have definitely offered to retain him if he can bring in even one thousand pounds. I suppose they have some sort of compunction about turning him adrift, for they have asked him to think it over and let them know on Monday. Of course, that is the end of it. It may be—I don't know—I don't like to think, how long before Roy gets another position equally good. We must endeavour to get this house off our hands and creep back to our three rooms. It is ... luck."

Carrados had been listening to her wonderfully musical voice as another man might have been drawn irresistibly to watch the piquant charm of her delicate face.

"Yes," he assented, almost to himself, "it is that strange, inexplicable grouping of men and things that, under one name or another, we all confess ... just luck."

"Of course you will not mention this to Uncle Louis yet, Mr Carrados?"

"If you do not wish it, certainly not."

"I am sure that it would distress him. He is so soft-hearted, so kind, in everything. Do you know, I found out that he had had an invitation to dine somewhere and meet some quite important people on Tuesday. Yet he came here instead, although most other men would have cried off, just because he knew that we small people would have been disappointed."

"Well, you can't expect me to see any self-denial in that," exclaimed Carrados. "Why, I was one of them myself."

Elsie Bellmark laughed outright at the expressive disgust of his tone.

"I had no idea of that," she said. "Then there is another reason. Uncle is not very well off, yet if he knew how Roy was situated he would make an effort to arrange matters. He would, I am sure, even borrow himself in order to lend us the money. That is a thing Roy and I are quite agreed on. We will go back; we will go under, if it is to be; but we will not borrow money, not even from Uncle Louis."

Once, subsequently, Carrados suddenly asked Mr Carlyle whether he had ever heard a woman's voice roll like a celestial kettle-drum. The professional gentleman was vastly amused by the comparison, but he admitted that he had not.

"So that, you see," concluded Mrs Bellmark, "there is really nothing to be done."

"Oh, quite so; I am sure that you are right," assented her visitor readily. "But in the meanwhile I do not see why the annoyance of your next-door neighbour should be permitted to go on."

"Of course: I have not told you that, and I could not explain it to uncle," she said. "I am anxious not to do anything to put him out because I have a hope—rather a faint one, certainly—that the man may be willing to take over this house."

It would be incorrect to say that Carrados pricked up his ears—if that curious phenomenon has any physical manifestation—for the sympathetic expression of his face did not vary a fraction. But into his mind there came a gleam such as might inspire a patient digger who sees the first speck of gold that justifies his faith in an unlikely claim.

"Oh," he said, quite conversationally, "is there a chance of that?"

"He undoubtedly did want it. It is very curious in a way. A few weeks ago, before we were really settled, he came one afternoon, saying he had heard that this house was to be let. Of course I told him that he was too late, that we had already taken it for three years."

"You were the first tenants?"

"Yes. The house was scarcely ready when we signed the agreement. Then this Mr Johns, or Jones—I am not sure which he said—went on in a rather extraordinary way to persuade me to sublet it to him. He said that the house was dear and I could get plenty, more convenient, at less rent, and it was unhealthy, and the drains were bad, and that we should be pestered by tramps and it was just the sort of house that burglars picked on, only he had taken a sort of fancy to it and he would give me a fifty-pound premium for the term."

"Did he explain the motive for this rather eccentric partiality?"

"I don't imagine that he did. He repeated several times that he was a queer old fellow with his whims and fancies and that they often cost him dear."

"I think we all know that sort of old fellow," said Carrados. "It must have been rather entertaining for you, Mrs Bellmark."

"Yes, I suppose it was," she admitted. "The next thing we knew of him was that he had taken the other house as soon as it was finished."

"Then he would scarcely require this?"

"I am afraid not." It was obvious that the situation was not disposed of. "But he seems to have so little furniture there and to live so solitarily," she explained, "that we have even wondered whether he might not be there merely as a sort of caretaker."

"And you have never heard where he came from or who he is?"

"Only what the milkman told my servant—our chief source of local information, Mr Carrados. He declares that the man used to be the butler at a large house that stood here formerly, Fountain Court, and that his name is neither Johns nor Jones. But very likely it is all a mistake."

"If not, he is certainly attached to the soil," was her visitor's rejoinder. "And, apropos of that, will you show me over your garden before I go, Mrs Bellmark?"

"With pleasure," she assented, rising also. "I will ring now and then I can offer you tea when we have been round. That is, if you——?"

"Thank you, I do," he replied. "And would you allow my man to go through into the garden—in case I require him?"

"Oh, certainly. You must tell me just what you want without thinking it necessary to ask permission, Mr Carrados," she said, with a pretty air of protection. "Shall Amy take a message?"

He acquiesced and turned to the servant who had appeared in response to the bell.

"Will you go to the car and tell my man—Parkinson—that I require him here. Say that he can bring his book; he will understand."

"Yes, sir."

They stepped out through the French window and sauntered across the lawn. Before they had reached the other side Parkinson reported himself.

"You had better stay here," said his master, indicating the sward generally. "Mrs Bellmark will allow you to bring out a chair from the drawing-room."

"Thank you, sir; there is a rustic seat already provided," replied Parkinson.

He sat down with his back to the houses and opened the book that he had brought. Let in among its pages was an ingeniously contrived mirror.

When their promenade again brought them near the rustic seat Carrados dropped a few steps behind.

"He is watching you from one of the upper rooms, sir," fell from Parkinson's lips as he sat there without raising his eyes from the page before him.

The blind man caught up to his hostess again.

"You intended this lawn for croquet?" he asked.

"No; not specially. It is too small, isn't it?"

"Not necessarily. I think it is in about the proportion of four by five all right. Given that, size does not really matter for an unsophisticated game."

To settle the point he began to pace the plot of ground, across and then lengthways. Next, apparently dissatisfied with this rough measurement, he applied himself to marking it off more exactly by means of his walking-stick. Elsie Bellmark was by no means dull but the action sprang so naturally from the conversation that it did not occur to her to look for any deeper motive.

"He has got a pair of field-glasses and is now at the window," communicated Parkinson.

"I am going out of sight," was the equally quiet response. "If he becomes more anxious tell me afterwards."

"It is quite all right," he reported, returning to Mrs Bellmark with the satisfaction of bringing agreeable news. "It should make a splendid little ground, but you may have to level up a few dips after the earth has set."

A chance reference to the kitchen garden by the visitor took them to a more distant corner of the enclosure where the rear of Fountain Cottage cut off the view from the next house windows.

"We decided on this part for vegetables because it does not really belong to the garden proper," she explained. "When they build farther on this side we shall have to give it up very soon. And it would be a pity if it was all in flowers."

With the admirable spirit of the ordinary Englishwoman, she spoke of the future as if there was no cloud to obscure its prosperous course. She had frankly declared their position to her uncle's best friend because in the circumstances it had seemed to be the simplest and most straightforward thing to do; beyond that, there was no need to whine about it.

"It is a large garden," remarked Carrados. "And you really do all the work of it yourselves?"

"Yes; I think that is half the fun of a garden. Roy is out here early and late and he does all the hard work. But how did you know? Did uncle tell you?"

"No; you told me yourself."

"I? Really?"

"Indirectly. You were scorning the proffered services of a horticultural mercenary at the moment of my arrival."

"Oh, I remember," she laughed. "It was Irons, of course. He is a great nuisance, he is so stupidly persistent. For some weeks now he has been coming time after time, trying to persuade me to engage him. Once when we were all out he had actually got into the garden and was on the point of beginning work when I returned. He said he saw the milkmen and the grocers leaving samples at the door so he thought that he would too!"

"A practical jester evidently. Is Mr Irons a local character?"

"He said that he knew the ground and the conditions round about here better than anyone else in Groat's Heath," she replied. "Modesty is not among Mr Irons's handicaps. He said that he——How curious!"

"What is, Mrs Bellmark?"

"I never connected the two men before, but he said that he had been gardener at Fountain Court for seven years."

"Another family retainer who is evidently attached to the soil."

"At all events they have not prospered equally, for while Mr Johns seems able to take a nice house, poor Irons is willing to work for half-a-crown a day, and I am told that all the other men charge four shillings."

They had paced the boundaries of the kitchen garden, and as there was nothing more to be shown Elsie Bellmark led the way back to the drawing-room. Parkinson was still engrossed in his book, the only change being that his back was now turned towards the high paling of clinker-built oak that separated the two gardens.

"I will speak to my man," said Carrados, turning aside.

"He hurried down and is looking through the fence, sir," reported the watcher.

"That will do then. You can return to the car."

"I wonder if you would allow me to send you a small hawthorn-tree?" inquired Carrados among his felicitations over the teacups five minutes later. "I think it ought to be in every garden."

"Thank you—but is it worth while?" replied Mrs Bellmark, with a touch of restraint. As far as mere words went she had been willing to ignore the menace of the future, but in the circumstances the offer seemed singularly inept and she began to suspect that outside his peculiar gifts the wonderful Mr Carrados might be a little bit obtuse after all.

"Yes; I think it is," he replied, with quiet assurance.

"In spite of——?"

"I am not forgetting that unless your husband is prepared on Monday next to invest one thousand pounds you contemplate leaving here."

"Then I do not understand it, Mr Carrados."

"And I am unable to explain as yet. But I brought you a note from Louis Carlyle, Mrs Bellmark. You only glanced at it. Will you do me the favour of reading me the last paragraph?"

She picked up the letter from the table where it lay and complied with cheerful good-humour.

"There is some suggestion that you want me to accede to," she guessed cunningly when she had read the last few words.

"There are some three suggestions which I hope you will accede to," he replied. "In the first place I want you to write to Mr Johns next door—let him get the letter to-night—inquiring whether he is still disposed to take this house."

"I had thought of doing that shortly."

"Then that is all right. Besides, he will ultimately decline."

"Oh," she exclaimed—it would be difficult to say whether with relief or disappointment—"do you think so? Then why——"

"To keep him quiet in the meantime. Next I should like you to send a little note to Mr Irons—your maid could deliver it also to-night, I dare say?"

"Irons! Irons the gardener?"

"Yes," apologetically. "Only a line or two, you know. Just saying that, after all, if he cares to come on Monday you can find him a few days' work."

"But in any circumstances I don't want him."

"No; I can quite believe that you could do better. Still, it doesn't matter, as he won't come, Mrs Bellmark; not for half-a-crown a day, believe me. But the thought will tend to make Mr Irons less restive also. Lastly, will you persuade your husband not to decline his firm's offer until Monday?"

"Very well, Mr Carrados," she said, after a moment's consideration. "You are Uncle Louis's friend and therefore our friend. I will do what you ask."

"Thank you," said Carrados. "I shall endeavour not to disappoint you."

"I shall not be disappointed because I have not dared to hope. And I have nothing to expect because I am still completely in the dark."

"I have been there for nearly twenty years, Mrs Bellmark."

"Oh, I am sorry!" she cried impulsively.

"So am I—occasionally," he replied. "Good-bye, Mrs Bellmark. You will hear from me shortly, I hope. About the hawthorn, you know."

It was, indeed, in something less than forty-eight hours that she heard from him again. When Bellmark returned to his toy villa early on Saturday afternoon Elsie met him almost at the gate with a telegram in her hand.

"I really think, Roy, that everyone we have to do with here goes mad," she exclaimed, in tragi-humorous despair. "First it was Mr Johns or Jones—if he is Johns or Jones—and then Irons who wanted to work here for half of what he could get at heaps of places about, and now just look at this wire that came from Mr Carrados half-an-hour ago."

This was the message that he read:

Please procure sardine tin opener mariner's compass and bottle of champagne. Shall arrive 6.45 bringing Crataegus Coccinea.—Carrados.

"Could anything be more absurd?" she demanded.

"Sounds as though it was in code," speculated her husband. "Who's the foreign gentleman he's bringing?"

"Oh, that's a kind of special hawthorn—I looked it up. But a bottle of champagne, and a compass, and a sardine tin opener! What possible connexion is there between them?"

"A very resourceful man might uncork a bottle of champagne with a sardine tin opener," he suggested.

"And find his way home afterwards by means of a mariner's compass?" she retorted. "No, Roy dear, you are not a sleuth-hound. We had better have our lunch."

They lunched, but if the subject of Carrados had been tabooed the meal would have been a silent one.

"I have a compass on an old watch-chain somewhere," volunteered Bellmark.

"And I have a tin opener in the form of a bull's head," contributed Elsie.

"But we have no champagne, I suppose?"

"How could we have, Roy? We never have had any. Shall you mind going down to the shops for a bottle?"

"You really think that we ought?"

"Of course we must, Roy. We don't know what mightn't happen if we didn't. Uncle Louis said that they once failed to stop a jewel robbery because the jeweller neglected to wipe his shoes on the shop doormat, as Mr Carrados had told him to do. Suppose Johns is a desperate anarchist and he succeeded in blowing up Buckingham Palace because we——"

"All right. A small bottle, eh?"

"No. A large one. Quite a large one. Don't you see how exciting it is becoming?"

"If you are excited already you don't need much champagne," argued her husband.

Nevertheless he strolled down to the leading wine-shop after lunch and returned with his purchase modestly draped in the light summer overcoat that he carried on his arm. Elsie Bellmark, who had quite abandoned her previous unconcern, in the conviction that "something was going to happen," spent the longest afternoon that she could remember, and even

Bellmark, in spite of his continual adjurations to her to "look at the matter logically," smoked five cigarettes in place of his usual Saturday afternoon pipe and neglected to do any gardening.

At exactly six-forty-five a motor car was heard approaching. Elsie made a desperate rally to become the self-possessed hostess again. Bellmark was favourably impressed by such marked punctuality. Then a Regent Street delivery van bowled past their window and Elsie almost wept.

The suspense was not long, however. Less than five minutes later another vehicle raised the dust of the quiet suburban road, and this time a private car stopped at their gate.

"Can you see any policemen inside?" whispered Elsie.

Parkinson got down and opening the door took out a small tree which he carried up to the porch and there deposited. Carrados followed.

"At all events there isn't much wrong," said Bellmark. "He's smiling all the time."

"No, it isn't really a smile," explained Elsie; "it's his normal expression."

She went out into the hall just as the front door was opened.

"It is the 'Scarlet-fruited thorn' of North America," Bellmark heard the visitor remarking. "Both the flowers and the berries are wonderfully good. Do you think that you would permit me to choose the spot for it, Mrs Bellmark?"

Bellmark joined them in the hall and was introduced.

"We mustn't waste any time," he suggested. "There is very little light left."

"True," agreed Carrados. "And Coccinea requires deep digging."

They walked through the house, and turning to the right passed into the region of the vegetable garden. Carrados and Elsie led the way, the blind man carrying the tree, while Bellmark went to his outhouse for the required tools.

"We will direct our operations from here," said Carrados, when they were half-way along the walk. "You told me of a thin iron pipe that you had traced to somewhere in the middle of the garden. We must locate the end of it exactly."

"My rosary!" sighed Elsie, with premonition of disaster, when she had determined the spot as exactly as she could. "Oh, Mr Carrados!"

"I am sorry, but it might be worse," said Carrados inflexibly. "We only require to find the elbow-joint. Mr Bellmark will investigate with as little disturbance as possible."

For five minutes Bellmark made trials with a pointed iron. Then he cleared away the soil of a small circle and at about a foot deep exposed a broken inch pipe.

"The fountain," announced Carrados, when he had examined it. "You have the compass, Mr Bellmark?"

"Rather a small one," admitted Bellmark.

"Never mind, you are a mathematician. I want you to strike a line due east."

The reel and cord came into play and an adjustment was finally made from the broken pipe to a position across the vegetable garden.

"Now a point nine yards, nine feet and nine inches along it."

"My onion bed!" cried Elsie tragically.

"Yes; it is really serious this time," agreed Carrados. "I want a hole a yard across, digging here. May we proceed?"

Elsie remembered the words of her uncle's letter—or what she imagined to be his letter—and possibly the preamble of selecting the spot had impressed her.

"Yes, I suppose so. Unless," she added hopefully, "the turnip bed will do instead? They are not sown yet."

"I am afraid that nowhere else in the garden will do," replied Carrados.

Bellmark delineated the space and began to dig. After clearing to about a foot deep he paused.

"About deep enough, Mr Carrados?" he inquired.

"Oh, dear no," replied the blind man.

"I am two feet down," presently reported the digger.

"Deeper!" was the uncompromising response.

Another six inches were added and Bellmark stopped to rest.

"A little more and it won't matter which way up we plant Coccinea," he remarked.

"That is the depth we are aiming for," replied Carrados.

Elsie and her husband exchanged glances. Then Bellmark drove his spade through another layer of earth.

"Three feet," he announced, when he had cleared it.

Carrados advanced to the very edge of the opening.

"I think that if you would loosen another six inches with the fork we might consider the ground prepared," he decided.

Bellmark changed his tools and began to break up the soil. Presently the steel prongs grated on some obstruction.

"Gently," directed the blind watcher. "I think you will find a half-pound cocoa tin at the end of your fork."

"Well, how on earth you spotted that——!" was wrung from Bellmark admiringly, as he cleared away the encrusting earth. "But I believe you are about right." He threw up the object to his wife, who was risking a catastrophe in her eagerness to miss no detail. "Anything in it besides soil, Elsie?"

"She cannot open it yet," remarked Carrados. "It is soldered down."

"Oh, I say," protested Bellmark.

"It is perfectly correct, Roy. The lid is soldered on."

They looked at each other in varying degrees of wonder and speculation. Only Carrados seemed quite untouched.

"Now we may as well replace the earth," he remarked.

"Fill it all up again?" asked Bellmark.

"Yes; we have provided a thoroughly disintegrated subsoil. That is the great thing. A depth of six inches is sufficient merely for the roots."

There was only one remark passed during the operation.

"I think I should plant the tree just over where the tin was," Carrados suggested. "You might like to mark the exact spot." And there the hawthorn was placed.

Bellmark, usually the most careful and methodical of men, left the tools where they were, in spite of a threatening shower. Strangely silent, Elsie led the way back to the house and taking the men into the drawing-room switched on the light.

"I think you have a tin opener, Mrs Bellmark?"

Elsie, who had been waiting for him to speak, almost jumped at the simple inquiry. Then she went into the next room and returned with the bull-headed utensil.

"Here it is," she said, in a voice that would have amused her at any other time.

"Mr Bellmark will perhaps disclose our find."

Bellmark put the soily tin down on Elsie's best table-cover without eliciting a word of reproach, grasped it firmly with his left hand, and worked the opener round the top.

"Only paper!" he exclaimed, and without touching the contents he passed the tin into Carrados's hands.

The blind man dexterously twirled out a little roll that crinkled pleasantly to the ear, and began counting the leaves with a steady finger.

"They're bank-notes!" whispered Elsie in an awestruck voice. She caught sight of a further detail. "Bank-notes for a hundred pounds each. And there are dozens of them!"

"Fifty, there should be," dropped Carrados between his figures. "Twenty-five, twenty-six——"

"Good God," murmured Bellmark; "that's five thousand pounds!"

"Fifty," concluded Carrados, straightening the edges of the sheaf. "It is always satisfactory to find that one's calculations are exact." He detached the upper ten notes and held them out. "Mrs Bellmark, will you accept one thousand pounds as a full legal discharge of any claim that you may have on this property?"

"Me—I?" she stammered. "But I have no right to any in any circumstances. It has nothing to do with us."

"You have an unassailable moral right to a fair proportion, because without you the real owners would never have seen a penny of it. As regards your legal right"—he took out the thin pocket-book and extracting a business-looking paper spread it open on the table before them—"here is a document that concedes it. 'In consideration of the valuable services rendered by Elsie Bellmark, etc., etc., in causing to be discovered and voluntarily surrendering the sum of five thousand pounds deposited and not relinquished by Alexis Metrobe, late of, etc., etc., deceased, Messrs Binstead & Polegate, solicitors, of 77a Bedford Row, acting on behalf of the administrator and next-of-kin of the said etc., etc., do hereby'—well, that's what they do. Signed, witnessed and stamped at Somerset House."

"I suppose I shall wake presently," said Elsie dreamily.

"It was for this moment that I ventured to suggest the third requirement necessary to bring our enterprise to a successful end," said Carrados.

"Oh, how thoughtful of you!" cried Elsie. "Roy, the champagne."

Five minutes later Carrados was explaining to a small but enthralled audience.

"The late Alexis Metrobe was a man of peculiar character. After seeing a good deal of the world and being many things, he finally embraced spiritualism, and in common with some of its most pronounced adherents he thenceforward abandoned what we should call 'the common-sense view.'

"A few years ago, by the collation of the Book of Revelations, a set of Zadkiel's Almanacs, and the complete works of Mrs Mary Baker Eddy, Metrobe discovered that the end of the world would take place on the tenth of October 1910. It therefore became a matter of urgent importance in his mind to ensure pecuniary provision for himself for the time after the catastrophe had taken place."

"I don't understand," interrupted Elsie. "Did he expect to survive it?"

"You cannot understand, Mrs Bellmark, because it is fundamentally incomprehensible. We can only accept the fact by the light of cases which occasionally obtain prominence. Metrobe did not expect to survive, but he was firmly convinced that the currency of this world would be equally useful in the spirit-land into which he expected to pass. This view was encouraged by a lady medium at whose feet he sat. She kindly offered to transmit to his banking account in the Hereafter, without making any charge whatever, any sum that he cared to put into her hands for the purpose. Metrobe accepted the idea but not the offer. His plan was to deposit a considerable amount in a spot of which he alone had knowledge, so that he could come and help himself to it as required."

"But if the world had come to an end——?"

"Only the material world, you must understand, Mrs Bellmark. The spirit world, its exact impalpable counterpart, would continue as before and Metrobe's hoard would be spiritually intact and available. That is the prologue.

"About a month ago there appeared a certain advertisement in a good many papers. I noticed it at the time and three days ago I had only to refer to my files to put my hand on it at once. It reads:

"'Alexis Metrobe. Any servant or personal attendant of the late Alexis Metrobe of Fountain Court, Groat's Heath, possessing special knowledge of his habits and movements may hear of something advantageous on applying to Binstead & Polegate, 77a Bedford Row, W.C.'

"The solicitors had, in fact, discovered that five thousand pounds' worth of securities had been realized early in 1910. They readily ascertained that Metrobe had drawn that amount in gold out of his bank immediately after, and there the trace ended. He died six months later. There was no hoard of gold and not a shred of paper to show where it had gone, yet Metrobe lived very simply within his income. The house had meanwhile been demolished but there was no hint or whisper of any lucky find.

"Two inquirers presented themselves at 77a Bedford Row. They were informed of the circumstances and offered a reward, varying according to the results, for information that would lead to the recovery of the money. They are both described as thoughtful, slow-spoken men. Each heard the story, shook his head, and departed. The first caller proved to be John Foster, the ex-butler. On the following day Mr Irons, formerly gardener at the Court, was the applicant.

"I must now divert your attention into a side track. In the summer of 1910 Metrobe published a curious work entitled 'The Flame beyond the Dome.' In the main it is an eschatological treatise, but at the end he tacked on an epilogue, which he called 'The Fable of the Chameleon.' It is even more curious than the rest and with reason, for under the guise of a speculative essay he gives a cryptic account of the circumstances of the five thousand pounds and, what is more important, details the exact particulars of its disposal. His reason for so doing is characteristic of the man. He was conscious by experience that he possessed an utterly treacherous memory, and having had occasion to move the treasure from one spot to another he feared that when the time came his bemuddled shade would be unable to locate it. For future reference, therefore, he embodied the details in his book, and to make sure that plenty of copies should be in existence he circulated it by the only means in his power—in other words, he gave a volume to everyone he knew and to a good many people whom he didn't.

"So far I have dealt with actualities. The final details are partly speculative but they are essentially correct. Metrobe conveyed his gold to Fountain Court, obtained a stout oak coffer for it, and selected a spot west of the fountain. He chose a favourable occasion for burying it, but by some mischance Irons came on the scene. Metrobe explained the incident by declaring that he was burying a favourite parrot. Irons thought nothing particular about it then, although he related the fact to the butler, and to others, in evidence of the general belief that 'the old cock was quite barmy.' But Metrobe himself was much disturbed by the accident. A few days later he dug up the box. In pursuance of his new plan he carried his gold to the Bank of England and changed it into these notes. Then transferring the venue to one due east of the fountain, he buried them in this tin, satisfied that the small space it occupied would baffle the search of anyone not in possession of the exact location."

"But, I say!" exclaimed Mr Bellmark. "Gold might remain gold, but what imaginable use could be made of bank-notes after the end of the world?"

"That is a point of view, no doubt. But Metrobe, in spite of his foreign name, was a thorough Englishman. The world might come to an end, but he was satisfied that somehow the Bank of England would ride through it all right. I only suggest that. There is much that we can only guess."

"That is all there is to know, Mr Carrados?"

"Yes. Everything comes to an end, Mrs Bellmark. I sent my car away to call for me at eight. Eight has struck. That is Harris announcing his arrival."

He stood up, but embarrassment and indecision marked the looks and movements of the other two.

"How can we possibly take all this money, though?" murmured Elsie, in painful uncertainty. "It is entirely your undertaking, Mr Carrados. It is the merest fiction bringing me into it at all."

"Perhaps in the circumstances," suggested Bellmark nervously—"you remember the circumstances, Elsie?—Mr Carrados would be willing to regard it as a loan——"

"No, no!" cried Elsie impulsively. "There must be no half measures. We know that a thousand pounds would be nothing to Mr Carrados, and he knows that a thousand pounds are everything to us." Her voice reminded the blind man of the candle-snuffing recital. "We will take this great gift, Mr Carrados, quite freely, and we will not spoil the generous satisfaction that you must have in doing a wonderful and a splendid service by trying to hedge our obligation."

"But what can we ever do to thank Mr Carrados?" faltered Bellmark mundanely.

"Nothing," said Elsie simply. "That is it."

"But I think that Mrs Bellmark has quite solved that," interposed Carrados.

The Game Played in the Dark

"It's a funny thing, sir," said Inspector Beedel, regarding Mr Carrados with the pensive respect that he always extended towards the blind amateur, "it's a funny thing, but nothing seems to go on abroad now but what you'll find some trace of it here in London if you take the trouble to look."

"In the right quarter," contributed Carrados.

"Why, yes," agreed the inspector. "But nothing comes of it nine times out of ten, because it's no one's particular business to look here or the thing's been taken up and finished from the other end. I don't mean ordinary murders or single-handed burglaries, of course, but"—a modest ring of professional pride betrayed the quiet enthusiast—"real First-Class Crimes."

"The State Antonio Five per cent. Bond Coupons?" suggested Carrados.

"Ah, you are right, Mr Carrados." Beedel shook his head sadly, as though perhaps on that occasion someone ought to have looked. "A man has a fit in the inquiry office of the Agent-General for British Equatoria, and two hundred and fifty thousand pounds' worth of faked securities is the result in Mexico. Then look at that jade fylfot charm pawned for one-and-three down at the Basin and the use that could have been made of it in the Kharkov 'ritual murder' trial."

"The West Hampstead Lost Memory puzzle and the Baripur bomb conspiracy that might have been smothered if one had known."

"Quite true, sir. And the three children of that Chicago millionaire—Cyrus V. Bunting, wasn't it?—kidnapped in broad daylight outside the New York Lyric and here, three weeks later, the dumb girl who chalked the wall at Charing Cross. I remember reading once in a financial article that every piece of foreign gold had a string from it leading to Threadneedle Street. A figure of speech, sir, of course, but apt enough, I don't doubt. Well, it seems to me that every big crime done abroad leaves a finger-print here in London—if only, as you say, we look in the right quarter."

"And at the right moment," added Carrados. "The time is often the present; the place the spot beneath our very noses. We take a step and the chance has gone for ever."

The inspector nodded and contributed a weighty monosyllable of sympathetic agreement. The most prosaic of men in the pursuit of his ordinary duties, it nevertheless subtly appealed to some half-dormant streak of vanity to have his profession taken romantically when there was no serious work on hand.

"No; perhaps not 'for ever' in one case in a thousand, after all," amended the blind man thoughtfully. "This perpetual duel between the Law and the Criminal has sometimes appeared to me in the terms of a game of cricket, inspector. Law is in the field; the Criminal at the wicket. If Law makes a mistake—sends down a loose ball or drops a catch—the Criminal scores a little or has another lease of life. But if he makes a mistake—if he lets a straight ball pass or spoons towards a steady man—he is done for. His mistakes are fatal; those of the Law are only temporary and retrievable."

"Very good, sir," said Mr Beedel, rising—the conversation had taken place in the study at The Turrets, where Beedel had found occasion to present himself—"very apt indeed. I must remember that. Well, sir, I only hope that this 'Guido the Razor' lot will send a catch in our direction."

The 'this' delicately marked Inspector Beedel's instinctive contempt for Guido. As a craftsman he was compelled, on his reputation, to respect him, and he had accordingly availed himself of Carrados's friendship for a confabulation. As a man—he was a foreigner: worse, an Italian, and if left to his own resources the inspector would have opposed to his sinuous flexibility those rigid, essentially Britannia-metal, methods of the Force that strike the impartial observer as so ponderous, so amateurish and conventional, and, it must be admitted, often so curiously and inexplicably successful.

The offence that had circuitously brought "il Rasojo" and his "lot" within the cognizance of Scotland Yard outlines the kind of story that is discreetly hinted at by the society paragraphist of the day, politely disbelieved by the astute reader, and then at last laid indiscreetly bare in all its details by the inevitable princessly "Recollections" of a generation later. It centred round an impending royal marriage in Vienna, a certain jealous "Countess X." (here you have the discretion of the paragrapher), and a document or two that might be relied upon (the aristocratic biographer will impartially sum up the contingencies) to play the deuce with the approaching nuptials. To procure the evidence of these papers the Countess enlisted the services of Guido, as reliable a scoundrel as she could probably have selected for the commission. To a certain point—to the abstraction of the papers, in fact—he succeeded, but it was with pursuit close upon his heels. There was that disadvantage in employing a rogue to do work that implicated roguery, for whatever moral right the Countess had to the property, her accomplice had no legal right whatever to his liberty. On half-a-dozen charges at least he could be arrested on sight in as many capitals of Europe. He slipped out of Vienna by the Nordbahn with his destination known, resourcefully stopped the express outside Czaslau and got away across to Chrudim. By this time the game and the moves were pretty well understood in more than one keenly interested quarter. Diplomacy supplemented justice and the immediate history of Guido became that of a fox hunted from covert to covert with all the familiar earths stopped against him. From Pardubitz he passed on to Glatz, reached Breslau and went down the Oder to Stettin. Out of the liberality of his employer's advances he had ample funds to keep going, and he dropped and rejoined his accomplices as the occasion ruled. A week's harrying found him in Copenhagen, still with no time to spare, and he missed his purpose there. He crossed to Malmo by ferry, took the connecting night train to Stockholm and the same morning sailed down the Saltsjon, ostensibly bound for Obo, intending to cross to Revel and so get back to central Europe by the less frequented routes. But in this move again luck was against him and receiving warning just in time, and by the mysterious agency that had so far protected him, he contrived to be dropped from the steamer by boat among the islands of the crowded Archipelago, made his way to Helsingfors and within forty-eight hours was back again on the Frihavnen with pursuit for the moment blinked and a breathing-time to the good.

To appreciate the exact significance of these wanderings it is necessary to recall the conditions. Guido was not zigzagging a course about Europe in an aimless search for the picturesque, still less inspired by any love of the melodramatic. To him every step was vital, each tangent or rebound the necessary outcome of his much-badgered plans. In his pocket reposed the papers for which he had run grave risks. The price agreed upon for the service was sufficiently lavish to make the risks worth taking time after time; but in order to consummate the transaction it was necessary that the booty should be put into his employer's hand. Half-way across Europe that employer was waiting with such patience as she could maintain, herself watched and shadowed at every step. The Countess X. was sufficiently exalted to be personally immune from the high-handed methods of her country's secret service, but every approach to her was tapped. The problem was for Guido to earn a long enough respite to enable him to communicate his position to the Countess and for her to go or to reach him by a trusty hand. Then the whole fabric of intrigue could fall to pieces, but so far Guido had been kept successfully on the run and in the meanwhile time was pressing.

"They lost him after the Hutola," Beedel reported, in explaining the circumstances to Max Carrados. "Three days later they found that he'd been back again in Copenhagen but by that time he'd flown. Now they're without a trace except the inference of these 'Orange peach blossom' agonies in The

Times. But the Countess has gone hurriedly to Paris; and Lafayard thinks it all points to London."

"I suppose the Foreign Office is anxious to oblige just now?"

"I expect so, sir," agreed Beedel, "but, of course, my instructions don't come from that quarter. What appeals to us is that it would be a feather in our caps—they're still a little sore up at the Yard about Hans the Piper."

"Naturally," assented Carrados. "Well, I'll see what I can do if there is real occasion. Let me know anything, and, if you see your chance yourself, come round for a talk if you like on—to-day's Wednesday?—I shall be in at any rate on Friday evening."

Without being a precisian, the blind man was usually exact in such matters. There are those who hold that an engagement must be kept at all hazard: men who would miss a death-bed message in order to keep literal faith with a beggar. Carrados took lower, if more substantial, ground. "My word," he sometimes had occasion to remark, "is subject to contingencies, like everything else about me. If I make a promise it is conditional on nothing which seems more important arising to counteract it. That, among men of sense, is understood." And, as it happened, something did occur on this occasion.

He was summoned to the telephone just before dinner on Friday evening to receive a message personally. Greatorex, his secretary, had taken the call, but came in to say that the caller would give him nothing beyond his name—Brebner. The name was unknown to Carrados, but such incidents were not uncommon, and he proceeded to comply.

"Yes," he responded; "I am Max Carrados speaking. What is it?"

"Oh, it is you, sir, is it? Mr Brickwill told me to get to you direct."

"Well, you are all right. Brickwill? Are you the British Museum?"

"Yes. I am Brebner in the Chaldean Art Department. They are in a great stew here. We have just found out that someone has managed to get access to the Second Inner Greek Room and looted some of the cabinets there. It is all a mystery as yet."

"What is missing?" asked Carrados.

"So far we can only definitely speak of about six trays of Greek coins—a hundred to a hundred and twenty, roughly."

"Important?"

The line conveyed a caustic bark of tragic amusement.

"Why, yes, I should say so. The beggar seems to have known his business. All fine specimens of the best period. Syracuse—Messana—Croton—Amphipolis. Eumenes—Evainetos—Kimons. The chief quite wept."

Carrados groaned. There was not a piece among them that he had not handled lovingly.

"What are you doing?" he demanded.

"Mr Brickwill has been to Scotland Yard, and, on advice, we are not making it public as yet. We don't want a hint of it to be dropped anywhere, if you don't mind, sir."

"That will be all right."

"It was for that reason that I was to speak with you personally. We are notifying the chief dealers and likely collectors to whom the coins, or some of them, may be offered at once if it is thought that we haven't found it out yet. Judging from the expertness displayed in the selection, we don't think that there is any danger of the lot being sold to a pawnbroker or a metal-dealer, so that we are running very little real risk in not advertising the loss."

"Yes; probably it is as well," replied Carrados. "Is there anything that Mr Brickwill wishes me to do?"

"Only this, sir; if you are offered a suspicious lot of Greek coins, or hear of them, would you have a look—I mean ascertain whether they are likely to be ours, and if you think they are communicate with us and Scotland Yard at once."

"Certainly," replied the blind man. "Tell Mr Brickwill that he can rely on me if any indication comes my way. Convey my regrets to him and tell him that I feel the loss quite as a personal one.... I don't think that you and I have met as yet, Mr Brebner?"

"No, sir," said the voice diffidently, "but I have looked forward to the pleasure. Perhaps this unfortunate business will bring me an introduction."

"You are very kind," was Carrados's acknowledgment of the compliment. "Any time ... I was going to say that perhaps you don't know my weakness, but I have spent many pleasant hours over your wonderful collection. That ensures the personal element. Good-bye."

Carrados was really disturbed by the loss although his concern was tempered by the reflection that the coins would inevitably in the end find their way back to the Museum. That their restitution might involve ransom to the extent of several thousand pounds was the least poignant detail of the situation. The one harrowing thought was that the booty might, through stress or ignorance, find its way into the melting-pot. That dreadful contingency, remote but insistent, was enough to affect the appetite of the blind enthusiast.

He was expecting Inspector Beedel, who would be full of his own case, but he could not altogether dismiss the aspects of possibility that Brebner's communication opened before his mind. He was still concerned with the chances of destruction and a very indifferent companion for Greatorex, who alone sat with him, when Parkinson presented himself. Dinner was over but Carrados had remained rather longer than his custom, smoking his mild Turkish cigarette in silence.

"A lady wishes to see you, sir. She said you would not know her name, but that her business would interest you."

The form of message was sufficiently unusual to take the attention of both men.

"You don't know her, of course, Parkinson?" inquired his master.

For just a second the immaculate Parkinson seemed tongue-tied. Then he delivered himself in his most ceremonial strain.

"I regret to say that I cannot claim the advantage, sir," he replied.

"Better let me tackle her, sir," suggested Greatorex with easy confidence. "It's probably a sub."

The sportive offer was declined by a smile and a shake of the head. Carrados turned to his attendant.

"I shall be in the study, Parkinson. Show her there in three minutes. You stay and have another cigarette, Greatorex. By that time she will either have gone or have interested me."

In three minutes' time Parkinson threw open the study door.

"The lady, sir," he announced.

Could he have seen, Carrados would have received the impression of a plainly, almost dowdily, dressed young woman of buxom figure. She wore a light veil, but it was ineffective in concealing the unattraction of the face beneath. The features were swart and the upper lip darkened with the more than incipient moustache of the southern brunette. Worse remained, for a disfiguring rash had assailed patches of her skin. As she entered she swept the room and its occupant with a quiet but comprehensive survey.

"Please take a chair, Madame. You wished to see me?"

The ghost of a demure smile flickered about her mouth as she complied, and in that moment her face seemed less uncomely. Her eye lingered for a moment on a cabinet above the desk, and one might have noticed that her eye was very bright. Then she replied.

"You are Signor Carrados, in—in the person?"

Carrados made his smiling admission and changed his position a fraction—possibly to catch her curiously pitched voice the better.

"The great collector of the antiquities?"

"I do collect a little," he admitted guardedly.

"You will forgive me, Signor, if my language is not altogether good. When I live at Naples with my mother we let boardings, chiefly to Inglish and Amerigans. I pick up the words, but since I marry and go to live in

Calabria my Inglish has gone all red—no, no, you say, rusty. Yes, that is it; quite rusty."

"It is excellent," said Carrados. "I am sure that we shall understand one another perfectly."

The lady shot a penetrating glance but the blind man's expression was merely suave and courteous. Then she continued:

"My husband is of name Ferraja—Michele Ferraja. We have a vineyard and a little property near Forenzana." She paused to examine the tips of her gloves for quite an appreciable moment. "Signor," she burst out, with some vehemence, "the laws of my country are not good at all."

"From what I hear on all sides," said Carrados, "I am afraid that your country is not alone."

"There is at Forenzana a poor labourer, Gian Verde of name," continued the visitor, dashing volubly into her narrative. "He is one day digging in the vineyard, the vineyard of my husband, when his spade strikes itself upon an obstruction. 'Aha,' says Gian, 'what have we here?' and he goes down upon his knees to see. It is an oil jar of red earth, Signor, such as was anciently used, and in it is filled with silver money.

"Gian is poor but he is wise. Does he call upon the authorities? No, no; he understands that they are all corrupt. He carries what he has found to my husband for he knows him to be a man of great honour.

"My husband also is of brief decision. His mind is made up. 'Gian,' he says, 'keep your mouth shut. This will be to your ultimate profit.' Gian understands, for he can trust my husband. He makes a sign of mutual implication. Then he goes back to the spade digging.

"My husband understands a little of these things but not enough. We go to the collections of Messina and Naples and even Rome and there we see other pieces of silver money, similar, and learn that they are of great value. They are of different sizes but most would cover a lira and of the thickness of two. On the one side imagine the great head of a pagan deity; on the other—oh, so many things I cannot remember what." A gesture of circumferential despair indicated the hopeless variety of design.

"A biga or quadriga of mules?" suggested Carrados. "An eagle carrying off a hare, a figure flying with a wreath, a trophy of arms? Some of those perhaps?"

"Si, si bene," cried Madame Ferraja. "You understand, I perceive, Signor. We are very cautious, for on every side is extortion and an unjust law. See, it is even forbidden to take these things out of the country, yet if we try to dispose of them at home they will be seized and we punished, for they are tesoro trovato, what you call treasure troven and belonging to the

State—these coins which the industry of Gian discovered and which had lain for so long in the ground of my husband's vineyard."

"So you brought them to England?"

"Si, Signor. It is spoken of as a land of justice and rich nobility who buy these things at the highest prices. Also my speaking a little of the language would serve us here."

"I suppose you have the coins for disposal then? You can show them to me?"

"My husband retains them. I will take you, but you must first give parola d'onore of an English Signor not to betray us, or to speak of the circumstance to another."

Carrados had already foreseen this eventuality and decided to accept it. Whether a promise exacted on the plea of treasure trove would bind him to respect the despoilers of the British Museum was a point for subsequent consideration. Prudence demanded that he should investigate the offer at once and to cavil over Madame Ferraja's conditions would be fatal to that object. If the coins were, as there seemed little reason to doubt, the proceeds of the robbery, a modest ransom might be the safest way of preserving irreplaceable treasures, and in that case Carrados could offer his services as the necessary intermediary.

"I give you the promise you require, Madame," he accordingly declared.

"It is sufficient," assented Madame. "I will now take you to the spot. It is necessary that you alone should accompany me, for my husband is so distraught in this country, where he understands not a word of what is spoken, that his poor spirit would cry 'We are surrounded!' if he saw two strangers approach the house. Oh, he is become most dreadful in his anxiety, my husband. Imagine only, he keeps on the fire a cauldron of molten lead and he would not hesitate to plunge into it this treasure and obliterate its existence if he imagined himself endangered."

"So," speculated Carrados inwardly. "A likely precaution for a simple vine-grower of Calabria! Very well," he assented aloud, "I will go with you alone. Where is the place?"

Madame Ferraja searched in the ancient purse that she discovered in her rusty handbag and produced a scrap of paper.

"People do not understand sometimes my way of saying it," she explained. "Sette, Herringbone——"

"May I——?" said Carrados, stretching out his hand. He took the paper and touched the writing with his finger-tips. "Oh yes, 7 Heronsbourne Place. That is on the edge of Heronsbourne Park, is it not?" He transferred the paper casually to his desk as he spoke and stood up. "How did you come, Madame Ferraja?"

Madame Ferraja followed the careless action with a discreet smile that did not touch her voice.

"By motor bus—first one then another, inquiring at every turning. Oh, but it was interminable," sighed the lady.

"My driver is off for the evening—I did not expect to be going out—but I will 'phone up a taxi and it will be at the gate as soon as we are." He despatched the message and then, turning to the house telephone, switched on to Greatorex.

"I'm just going round to Heronsbourne Park," he explained. "Don't stay, Greatorex, but if anyone calls expecting to see me, they can say that I don't anticipate being away more than an hour."

Parkinson was hovering about the hall. With quite novel officiousness he pressed upon his master a succession of articles that were not required. Over this usually complacent attendant the unattractive features of Madame Ferraja appeared to exercise a stealthy fascination, for a dozen times the lady detected his eyes questioning her face and a dozen times he looked guiltily away again. But his incongruities could not delay for more than a few minutes the opening of the door.

"I do not accompany you, sir?" he inquired, with the suggestion plainly tendered in his voice that it would be much better if he did.

"Not this time, Parkinson."

"Very well, sir. Is there any particular address to which we can telephone in case you are required, sir?"

"Mr Greatorex has instructions."

Parkinson stood aside, his resources exhausted. Madame Ferraja laughed a little mockingly as they walked down the drive.

"Your man-servant thinks I may eat you, Signor Carrados," she declared vivaciously.

Carrados, who held the key of his usually exact attendant's perturbation—for he himself had recognized in Madame Ferraja the angelic Nina Brun, of the Sicilian tetradrachm incident, from the moment she opened her mouth—admitted to himself the humour of her audacity. But it was not until half-an-hour later that enlightenment rewarded Parkinson. Inspector Beedel had just arrived and was speaking with Greatorex when the conscientious valet, who had been winnowing his memory in solitude, broke in upon them, more distressed than either had ever seen him in his life before, and with the breathless introduction: "It was the ears, sir! I have her ears at last!" poured out his tale of suspicion, recognition and his present fears.

In the meanwhile the two objects of his concern had reached the gate as the summoned taxicab drew up.

"Seven Heronsbourne Place," called Carrados to the driver.

"No, no," interposed the lady, with decision, "let him stop at the beginning of the street. It is not far to walk. My husband would be on the verge of distraction if he thought in the dark that it was the arrival of the police;—who knows?"

"Brackedge Road, opposite the end of Heronsbourne Place," amended Carrados.

Heronsbourne Place had the reputation, among those who were curious in such matters, of being the most reclusive residential spot inside the four-mile circle. To earn that distinction it was, needless to say, a cul-de-sac. It bounded one side of Heronsbourne Park but did not at any point of its length give access to that pleasance. It was entirely devoted to unostentatious little houses, something between the villa and the cottage, some detached and some in pairs, but all possessing the endowment of larger, more umbrageous gardens than can generally be secured within the radius. The local house agent described them as "delightfully old-world" or "completely modernized" according to the requirement of the applicant.

The cab was dismissed at the corner and Madame Ferraja guided her companion along the silent and deserted way. She had begun to talk with renewed animation, but her ceaseless chatter only served to emphasize to Carrados the one fact that it was contrived to disguise.

"I am not causing you to miss the house with looking after me—No. 7, Madame Ferraja?" he interposed.

"No, certainly," she replied readily. "It is a little farther. The numbers are from the other end. But we are there. Ecco!"

She stopped at a gate and opened it, still guiding him. They passed into a garden, moist and sweet-scented with the distillate odours of a dewy evening. As she turned to relatch the gate the blind man endeavoured politely to anticipate her. Between them his hat fell to the ground.

"My clumsiness," he apologized, recovering it from the step. "My old impulses and my present helplessness, alas, Madame Ferraja!"

"One learns prudence by experience," said Madame sagely. She was scarcely to know, poor lady, that even as she uttered this trite aphorism, under cover of darkness and his hat, Mr Carrados had just ruined his signet ring by blazoning a golden "7" upon her garden step to establish its identity if need be. A cul-de-sac that numbered from the closed end seemed to demand some investigation.

"Seldom," he replied to her remark. "One goes on taking risks. So we are there?"

Madame Ferraja had opened the front door with a latchkey. She dropped the latch and led Carrados forward along the narrow hall. The room they entered was at the back of the house, and from the position of the road it therefore overlooked the park. Again the door was locked behind them.

"The celebrated Mr Carrados!" announced Madame Ferraja, with a sparkle of triumph in her voice. She waved her hand towards a lean, dark man who had stood beside the door as they entered. "My husband."

"Beneath our poor roof in the most fraternal manner," commented the dark man, in the same derisive spirit. "But it is wonderful."

"The even more celebrated Monsieur Dompierre, unless I am mistaken?" retorted Carrados blandly. "I bow on our first real meeting."

"You knew!" exclaimed the Dompierre of the earlier incident incredulously. "Stoker, you were right and I owe you a hundred lire. Who recognized you, Nina?"

"How should I know?" demanded the real Madame Dompierre crossly. "This blind man himself, by chance."

"You pay a poor compliment to your charming wife's personality to imagine that one could forget her so soon," put in Carrados. "And you a Frenchman, Dompierre!"

"You knew, Monsieur Carrados," reiterated Dompierre, "and yet you ventured here. You are either a fool or a hero."

"An enthusiast—it is the same thing as both," interposed the lady. "What did I tell you? What did it matter if he recognized? You see?"

"Surely you exaggerate, Monsieur Dompierre," contributed Carrados. "I may yet pay tribute to your industry. Perhaps I regret the circumstance and the necessity but I am here to make the best of it. Let me see the things Madame has spoken of, and then we can consider the detail of their price, either for myself or on behalf of others."

There was no immediate reply. From Dompierre came a saturnine chuckle and from Madame Dompierre a titter that accompanied a grimace. For one of the rare occasions in his life Carrados found himself wholly out of touch with the atmosphere of the situation. Instinctively he turned his face towards the other occupant of the room, the man addressed as "Stoker," whom he knew to be standing near the window.

"This unfortunate business has brought me an introduction," said a familiar voice.

For one dreadful moment the universe stood still round Carrados. Then, with the crash and grind of overwhelming mental tumult, the whole strategy revealed itself, like the sections of a gigantic puzzle falling into place before his eyes.

There had been no robbery at the British Museum! That plausible concoction was as fictitious as the intentionally transparent tale of treasure trove. Carrados recognized now how ineffective the one device would have been without the other in drawing him—how convincing the two together—and while smarting at the humiliation of his plight he could not restrain a dash of admiration at the ingenuity—the accurately conjectured line of inference—of the plot. It was again the familiar artifice of the cunning pitfall masked by the clumsily contrived trap just beyond it. And straightway into it he had blundered!

"And this," continued the same voice, "is Carrados, Max Carrados, upon whose perspicuity a government—only the present government, let me in justice say—depends to outwit the undesirable alien! My country; O my country!"

"Is it really Monsieur Carrados?" inquired Dompierre in polite sarcasm. "Are you sure, Nina, that you have not brought a man from Scotland Yard instead?"

"Basta! he is here; what more do you want? Do not mock the poor sightless gentleman," answered Madame Dompierre, in doubtful sympathy.

"That is exactly what I was wondering," ventured Carrados mildly. "I am here—what more do you want? Perhaps you, Mr Stoker——?"

"Excuse me. 'Stoker' is a mere colloquial appellation based on a trifling incident of my career in connection with a disabled liner. The title illustrates the childish weakness of the criminal classes for nicknames, together with their pitiable baldness of invention. My real name is Montmorency, Mr Carrados—Eustace Montmorency."

"Thank you, Mr Montmorency," said Carrados gravely. "We are on opposite sides of the table here to-night, but I should be proud to have been with you in the stokehold of the Benvenuto."

"That was pleasure," muttered the Englishman. "This is business."

"Oh, quite so," agreed Carrados. "So far I am not exactly complaining. But I think it is high time to be told—and I address myself to you—why I have been decoyed here and what your purpose is."

Mr Montmorency turned to his accomplice.

"Dompierre," he remarked, with great clearness, "why the devil is Mr Carrados kept standing?"

"Ah, oh, heaven!" exclaimed Madame Dompierre with tragic resignation, and flung herself down on a couch.

"Scusi," grinned the lean man, and with burlesque grace he placed a chair for their guest's acceptance.

"Your curiosity is natural," continued Mr Montmorency, with a cold eye towards Dompierre's antics, "although I really think that by this time you ought to have guessed the truth. In fact, I don't doubt that you have guessed, Mr Carrados, and that you are only endeavouring to gain time. For that reason—because it will perhaps convince you that we have nothing to fear—I don't mind obliging you."

"Better hasten," murmured Dompierre uneasily.

"Thank you, Bill," said the Englishman, with genial effrontery. "I won't fail to report your intelligence to the Rasojo. Yes, Mr Carrados, as you have already conjectured, it is the affair of the Countess X. to which you owe this inconvenience. You will appreciate the compliment that underlies your temporary seclusion, I am sure. When circumstances favoured our plans and London became the inevitable place of meeting, you and you alone stood in the way. We guessed that you would be consulted and we frankly feared your intervention. You were consulted. We know that Inspector Beedel visited you two days ago and he has no other case in hand. Your quiescence for just three days had to be obtained at any cost. So here you are."

"I see," assented Carrados. "And having got me here, how do you propose to keep me?"

"Of course that detail has received consideration. In fact we secured this furnished house solely with that in view. There are three courses before us. The first, quite pleasant, hangs on your acquiescence. The second, more drastic, comes into operation if you decline. The third—but really, Mr Carrados, I hope you won't oblige me even to discuss the third. You will understand that it is rather objectionable for me to contemplate the necessity of two able-bodied men having to use even the smallest amount of physical compulsion towards one who is blind and helpless. I hope you will be reasonable and accept the inevitable."

"The inevitable is the one thing that I invariably accept," replied Carrados. "What does it involve?"

"You will write a note to your secretary explaining that what you have learned at 7 Heronsbourne Place makes it necessary for you to go immediately abroad for a few days. By the way, Mr Carrados, although this is Heronsbourne Place it is not No. 7."

"Dear, dear me," sighed the prisoner. "You seem to have had me at every turn, Mr Montmorency."

"An obvious precaution. The wider course of giving you a different street altogether we rejected as being too risky in getting you here. To continue: To give conviction to the message you will direct your man Parkinson to follow by the first boat-train to-morrow, with all the requirements for a short stay, and put up at Mascot's, as usual, awaiting your arrival there."

"Very convincing," agreed Carrados. "Where shall I be in reality?"

"In a charming though rather isolated bungalow on the south coast. Your wants will be attended to. There is a boat. You can row or fish. You will be run down by motor car and brought back to your own gate. It's really very pleasant for a few days. I've often stayed there myself."

"Your recommendation carries weight. Suppose, for the sake of curiosity, that I decline?"

"You will still go there but your treatment will be commensurate with your behaviour. The car to take you is at this moment waiting in a convenient spot on the other side of the park. We shall go down the garden at the back, cross the park, and put you into the car—anyway."

"And if I resist?"

The man whose pleasantry it had been to call himself Eustace Montmorency shrugged his shoulders.

"Don't be a fool," he said tolerantly. "You know who you are dealing with and the kind of risks we run. If you call out or endanger us at a critical point we shall not hesitate to silence you effectively."

The blind man knew that it was no idle threat. In spite of the cloak of humour and fantasy thrown over the proceedings, he was in the power of coolly desperate men. The window was curtained and shuttered against sight and sound, the door behind him locked. Possibly at that moment a revolver threatened him; certainly weapons lay within reach of both his keepers.

"Tell me what to write," he asked, with capitulation in his voice.

Dompierre twirled his mustachios in relieved approval. Madame laughed from her place on the couch and picked up a book, watching Montmorency over the cover of its pages. As for that gentleman, he masked his satisfaction by the practical business of placing on the table before Carrados the accessories of the letter.

"Put into your own words the message that I outlined just now."

"Perhaps to make it altogether natural I had better write on a page of the notebook that I always use," suggested Carrados.

"Do you wish to make it natural?" demanded Montmorency, with latent suspicion.

"If the miscarriage of your plan is to result in my head being knocked—yes, I do," was the reply.

"Good!" chuckled Dompierre, and sought to avoid Mr Montmorency's cold glance by turning on the electric table-lamp for the blind man's benefit. Madame Dompierre laughed shrilly.

"Thank you, Monsieur," said Carrados, "you have done quite right. What is light to you is warmth to me—heat, energy, inspiration. Now to business."

He took out the pocket-book he had spoken of and leisurely proceeded to flatten it down upon the table before him. As his tranquil, pleasant eyes ranged the room meanwhile it was hard to believe that the shutters of an impenetrable darkness lay between them and the world. They rested for a moment on the two accomplices who stood beyond the table, picked out Madame Dompierre lolling on the sofa on his right, and measured the proportions of the long, narrow room. They seemed to note the positions of the window at the one end and the door almost at the other, and even to take into account the single pendent electric light which up till then had been the sole illuminant.

"You prefer pencil?" asked Montmorency.

"I generally use it for casual purposes. But not," he added, touching the point critically, "like this."

Alert for any sign of retaliation, they watched him take an insignificant penknife from his pocket and begin to trim the pencil. Was there in his mind any mad impulse to force conclusions with that puny weapon? Dompierre worked his face into a fiercer expression and touched reassuringly the handle of his knife. Montmorency looked on for a moment, then, whistling softly to himself, turned his back on the table and strolled towards the window, avoiding Madame Nina's pursuant eye.

Then, with overwhelming suddenness, it came, and in its form altogether unexpected.

Carrados had been putting the last strokes to the pencil, whittling it down upon the table. There had been no hasty movement, no violent act to give them warning; only the little blade had pushed itself nearer and nearer to the electric light cord lying there ... and suddenly and instantly the room was plunged into absolute darkness.

"To the door, Dom!" shouted Montmorency in a flash. "I am at the window. Don't let him pass and we are all right."

"I am here," responded Dompierre from the door.

"He will not attempt to pass," came the quiet voice of Carrados from across the room. "You are now all exactly where I want you. You are both covered. If either moves an inch, I fire—and remember that I shoot by sound, not sight."

"But—but what does it mean?" stammered Montmorency, above the despairing wail of Madame Dompierre.

"It means that we are now on equal terms—three blind men in a dark room. The numerical advantage that you possess is counterbalanced by the fact that you are out of your element—I am in mine."

"Dom," whispered Montmorency across the dark space, "strike a match. I have none."

"I would not, Dompierre, if I were you," advised Carrados, with a short laugh. "It might be dangerous." At once his voice seemed to leap into a passion. "Drop that matchbox," he cried. "You are standing on the brink of your grave, you fool! Drop it, I say; let me hear it fall."

A breath of thought—almost too short to call a pause—then a little thud of surrender sounded from the carpet by the door. The two conspirators seemed to hold their breath.

"That is right." The placid voice once more resumed its sway. "Why cannot things be agreeable? I hate to have to shout, but you seem far from grasping the situation yet. Remember that I do not take the slightest risk. Also please remember, Mr Montmorency, that the action even of a hair-trigger automatic scrapes slightly as it comes up. I remind you of that for your own good, because if you are so ill-advised as to think of trying to pot me in the dark, that noise gives me a fifth of a second start of you. Do you by any chance know Zinghi's in Mercer Street?"

"The shooting gallery?" asked Mr Montmorency a little sulkily.

"The same. If you happen to come through this alive and are interested you might ask Zinghi to show you a target of mine that he keeps. Seven shots at twenty yards, the target indicated by four watches, none of them so loud as the one you are wearing. He keeps it as a curiosity."

"I wear no watch," muttered Dompierre, expressing his thought aloud.

"No, Monsieur Dompierre, but you wear a heart, and that not on your sleeve," said Carrados. "Just now it is quite as loud as Mr Montmorency's watch. It is more central too—I shall not have to allow any margin. That is right; breathe naturally"—for the unhappy Dompierre had given a gasp of apprehension. "It does not make any difference to me, and after a time holding one's breath becomes really painful."

"Monsieur," declared Dompierre earnestly, "there was no intention of submitting you to injury, I swear. This Englishman did but speak within his hat. At the most extreme you would have been but bound and gagged. Take care: killing is a dangerous game."

"For you—not for me," was the bland rejoinder. "If you kill me you will be hanged for it. If I kill you I shall be honourably acquitted. You can imagine the scene—the sympathetic court—the recital of your villainies—the story of my indignities. Then with stumbling feet and groping hands the helpless blind man is led forward to give evidence. Sensation! No, no, it isn't really fair but I can kill you both with absolute certainty and Providence will be saddled with all the responsibility. Please don't fidget with your feet, Monsieur Dompierre. I know that you aren't moving but one is liable to make mistakes."

"Before I die," said Montmorency—and for some reason laughed unconvincingly in the dark—"before I die, Mr Carrados, I should really like to know what has happened to the light. That, surely, isn't Providence?"

"Would it be ungenerous to suggest that you are trying to gain time? You ought to know what has happened. But as it may satisfy you that I have nothing to fear from delay, I don't mind telling you. In my hand was a sharp knife—contemptible, you were satisfied, as a weapon; beneath my nose the 'flex' of the electric lamp. It was only necessary for me to draw the one across the other and the system was short-circuited. Every lamp on that fuse is cut off and in the distributing-box in the hall you will find a burned-out wire. You, perhaps—but Monsieur Dompierre's experience in plating ought to have put him up to simple electricity."

"How did you know that there is a distributing-box in the hall?" asked Dompierre, with dull resentment.

"My dear Dompierre, why beat the air with futile questions?" replied Max Carrados. "What does it matter? Have it in the cellar if you like."

"True," interposed Montmorency. "The only thing that need concern us now——"

"But it is in the hall—nine feet high," muttered Dompierre in bitterness. "Yet he, this blind man——"

"The only thing that need concern us," repeated the Englishman, severely ignoring the interruption, "is what you intend doing in the end, Mr Carrados?"

"The end is a little difficult to foresee," was the admission. "So far, I am all for maintaining the status quo. Will the first grey light of morning find us still in this impasse? No, for between us we have condemned the room to eternal darkness. Probably about daybreak Dompierre will drop off to sleep and roll against the door. I, unfortunately mistaking his intention, will send a bullet through——Pardon, Madame, I should have remembered—but pray don't move."

"I protest, Monsieur——"

"Don't protest; just sit still. Very likely it will be Mr Montmorency who will fall off to sleep the first after all."

"Then we will anticipate that difficulty," said the one in question, speaking with renewed decision. "We will play the last hand with our cards upon the table if you like. Nina, Mr Carrados will not injure you whatever happens—be sure of that. When the moment comes you will rise——"

"One word," put in Carrados with determination. "My position is precarious and I take no risks. As you say, I cannot injure Madame Dompierre, and you two men are therefore my hostages for her good behaviour. If she rises from the couch you, Dompierre, fall. If she advances another step Mr Montmorency follows you."

"Do nothing rash, carissima," urged her husband, with passionate solicitude. "You might get hit in place of me. We will yet find a better way."

"You dare not, Mr Carrados!" flung out Montmorency, for the first time beginning to show signs of wear in this duel of the temper. "He dare not, Dompierre. In cold blood and unprovoked! No jury would acquit you!"

"Another who fails to do you justice, Madame Nina," said the blind man, with ironic gallantry. "The action might be a little high-handed, one admits, but when you, appropriately clothed and in your right complexion, stepped into the witness-box and I said: 'Gentlemen of the jury, what is my crime? That I made Madame Dompierre a widow!' can you doubt their gratitude and my acquittal? Truly my countrymen are not all bats or monks, Madame." Dompierre was breathing with perfect freedom now, while from the couch came the sounds of stifled emotion, but whether the lady was involved in a paroxysm of sobs or of laughter it might be difficult to swear.

It was perhaps an hour after the flourish of the introduction with which Madame Dompierre had closed the door of the trap upon the blind man's entrance.

The minutes had passed but the situation remained unchanged, though the ingenuity of certainly two of the occupants of the room had been tormented into shreds to discover a means of turning it to their advantage. So far the terrible omniscience of the blind man in the dark and the respect for his markmanship with which his coolness had inspired them, dominated the group. But one strong card yet remained to be played, and at last the moment came upon which the conspirators had pinned their despairing hopes.

There was the sound of movement in the hall outside, not the first about the house, but towards the new complication Carrados had been strangely unobservant. True, Montmorency had talked rather loudly, to carry over the dangerous moments. But now there came an unmistakable step and to the accomplices it could only mean one thing. Montmorency was ready on the instant.

"Down, Dom!" he cried, "throw yourself down! Break in, Guido. Break in the door. We are held up!"

There was an immediate response. The door, under the pressure of a human battering-ram, burst open with a crash. On the threshold the intruders—four or five in number—stopped starkly for a moment, held in astonishment by the extraordinary scene that the light from the hall, and of their own bull's-eyes, revealed.

Flat on their faces, to present the least possible surface to Carrados's aim, Dompierre and Montmorency lay extended beside the window and behind the door. On the couch, with her head buried beneath the cushions, Madame Dompierre sought to shut out the sight and sound of violence. Carrados—Carrados had not moved, but with arms resting on the table and fingers placidly locked together he smiled benignly on the new arrivals. His attitude, compared with the extravagance of those around him, gave the impression of a complacent modern deity presiding over some grotesque ceremonial of pagan worship.

"So, Inspector, you could not wait for me, after all?" was his greeting.

THE END

CPSIA information can be obtained
at www.ICGtesting.com
Printed in the USA
LVOW13s1449101116
512465LV00009B/809/P